MADHATTAN
MYSTERY

MADHATTAN MYSTERY

John J. Bonk

Walker & Company

New York

First published in the United States of America in May 2012
by Walker Publishing Company, Inc., a division of Bloomsbury Publishing, Inc.
www.bloomsburykids.com

For information about permission to reproduce selections from this book, write to
Permissions, Walker BFYR, 175 Fifth Avenue, New York, New York 10010

Library of Congress Cataloging-in-Publication Data
Bonk, John J.
Madhattan mystery / by John J. Bonk.
p.   cm.
Summary: On her first day in New York City with her younger brother, Kevin,
twelve-year-old Lexi overhears thieves discussing where to hide stolen jewels,
and the siblings, along with their aunt's neighbor, Kim Ling, skip day camp to
investigate "the crime of the century."
ISBN 978-0-8027-2349-9 (hardback)
[1. Mystery and detective stories.   2. New York (N.Y.)—New York—Fiction.
3. Brothers and sisters—Fiction.   4. Robbers and outlaws—Fiction.
5. Aunts—Fiction.   6. Camps—Fiction.]   I. Title.
PZ7.B6417Mad 2012   [Fic]—dc23   2011034590

Book design by Donna Mark
Typeset by Westchester Book Composition
Printed in the U.S.A. by Quad/Graphics, Fairfield, Pennsylvania
2   4   6   8   10   9   7   5   3   1

All papers used by Bloomsbury Publishing, Inc., are natural, recyclable products
made from wood grown in well-managed forests. The manufacturing processes
conform to the environmental regulations of the country of origin.

For Mama Rose

Be not forgetful to entertain strangers,
for thereby some have entertained angels unawares.

—HEBREWS 13:2

MADHATTAN MYSTERY

WHISPERING GALLERY

"Woo-hoo, we're finally here. You excited?" Lexi McGill turned to her little brother, who was slumped in the train seat next to her. She yanked the earbuds from his ears but he still didn't budge. This was weird—he was usually as jumpy as a hummingbird on sugar. "C'mon, Kevin, wake up!" she said, rattling him.

His eyes sprang wide open. Then clamped shut.

"Okay, that is *so* not funny. You scared me half to—" *Death* got stuck in her throat.

"Not trying to be funny. Just doing one of Dr. Lucy's calming exercises. Picturing yellow tulips. Butterflies. A smiling cow." Kevin opened his big green eyes again and innocently blinked up at Lexi. "So even though we're going to Murderville, my brain thinks we're, like, in some sunny meadow somewhere munching on egg salad sandwiches."

"That explains the drool. Wait—you don't even like egg salad."

At least he had made it through the tunnel okay. Lexi knew for a fact that Kevin was especially terrified of tunnels. And he always clenched up in trains, cars, buses, boats, bumper cars, recreational vehicles, and airplanes. For him, it seemed traveling to a place was much scarier than the place itself. But she wasn't exactly sure what would happen in—

"NEEEW *YAWK* CITY! *GRRR*-RAND CENTRAL STATION. FINAL STOP!"

The announcement rang through the train car and everyone gathered their belongings. Lexi felt the weight of Kevin's blinkless stare the whole time she was grabbing their duffel bags from the overhead shelf and squishing through the doors onto the crowded platform. But what did she expect? Coming from the sleepy village of Cold Spring, New York, the big city was like another planet.

"Aunt Roz is supposed to meet us right here at eleven." Lexi checked her watch. "It's two minutes after and I don't see her, do you, Kev?"

"No, and she's hard to miss."

"You think maybe she's waiting at the other end of the platform?" She strained to see through a thicket of people. It was impossible. "Okay, listen. I'm not going to make you hold my hand or anything, but stick close to my side at all times."

Lexi winced at her own words as they hoisted their

duffels and melted into a blur of business suits and brief-cases. Twelve going on thirteen was way too young to be a mother, but that was how she felt—and she had to admit she was good at it. Too darn good. *I might as well start learning how to scrapbook and get grass stains out of corduroy.* There was less than three years' difference between Lexi and Kevin, but ever since their mother died almost two years ago, Lexi automatically morphed into the parent and Kevin became the toddler whenever the situation called for it. Like right now!

"Watchit!" She tugged Kevin to her side. Two police-men and a sniffing German shepherd sliced right by and he was off in la-la land. "Stay alert and don't dawdle." *Dawdle? Total mom word—from, like, the fifties.*

"Who do you think they're tracking, Lex? Serial killer? Drug lord? Jewel thief?"

"You watch too much TV. Just picture yourself back in that sunny meadow."

Kevin's eyelids fluttered shut. "It's not working anymore. Somebody mugged the cow."

After saying she wouldn't, Lexi grabbed his sweaty hand and led him to the platform entrance, where they dropped their duffels and planted themselves. The sight of the gigantic main concourse in Grand Central Terminal alone was almost too much to take in all at once. Hundreds of people were rushing in different directions, their muffled murmurs sounding like a whole summer's worth of bees trapped in a jar.

"Wow," Kevin said, summing it up in a word.

"They don't call it 'Grand' for nothing. This place has everything."

"Except Aunt Roz. Where the heck is she?"

"Stores, restaurants, banks—"

"A psycho guy dressed in a giant milk carton costume, handing out free samples."

"Don't point." Lexi lowered his arm and they both scanned the terminal, looking this way and that like two bobblehead dolls. "Think about it, Kev. You could probably live your whole life in the train station and never have to leave."

He pondered it for a second. "Where would you sleep?" Then his head fell back and his jaw dropped open. "*Oooh, check out the ceiling!*"

It was a rich greenish blue, stretching farther than a football field. A ram, a scorpion, a crab, and the rest of the zodiac symbols were outlined in yellow, and tiny white lights dotted the constellations. Kevin, who loved all things celestial, reached into his backpack and removed his digital camera, a gift from their new stepmother, Clare—or as Lexi called it, "another desperate attempt to buy our affection."

Lexi checked her cell phone for any messages from Aunt Roz. Nothing. "Well, we might as well wait for her here," she told Kevin. "You don't need to use the bathroom or anything, do you? Any emergencies? Speak now or forever hold your . . . pee."

He was going snap-happy taking pictures of the ceiling from every angle and mumbled something about not being a baby.

"I'll take that as a no," Lexi said. She dropped her phone into her backpack, slid out an NYC guidebook, and cracked it open. A brochure fell to the ground.

Kevin stopped snapping and fell to his knees to snatch it up. "Hey, is this the new one?" The cover had a picture of three smiling kids in a swimming pool with a city skyline in the background. " 'Camp NYC, offering the best of both worlds,' " he read.

Lexi groaned. Not just because of the summer camp, but the reason they were enrolled. Their dad was leaving that same day for an extended honeymoon in France and Greece with his new, very rich wife. The trip was on her dollar and summer camp was too. A double whammy. When Aunt Roz was asked if she wanted roommates for a few weeks, she said she was only too happy to have the company—but what else could she say, really?

" 'A fun-packed three-week program,' " Kevin read out loud, " 'offering everything from row boating and rock climbing in magnificent Central Park to world—uh, world-renowned museums and thrilling theatrical productions, Camp NYC provides a broad experience unlike any other.' Just FYI: that rock-climbing thing—not gonna happen. 'Now entering its sixth year, this extraordinary program . . .' "

That was the problem—it didn't sound that extraordinary. Not to Lexi anyway. Kevin's voice became a distant buzz as she stared into the endless parade of commuters. *It's like they all have fantastically important things to do and can't wait to go do them*, she thought, fanning herself with her guidebook. She was wishing something extraordinary would happen to her this summer when a raggedy man wearing a cardboard sign caught her eye. GIVE TO THE NEW YORK WILDLIFE PIZZA FUND. A street person with a sense of humor—Lexi couldn't resist. She tore into her backpack for her wallet, slipped out a dollar, and dropped it into the Easter basket the man was carrying.

"Thank you kindly, young lady. You have a delicious day now!"

"You're wel—I mean, you too."

That was when someone rammed into her. *"Ugh!"* Hard.

"Sorry," was all the rushing girl said before disappearing behind an archway.

"Uh, no prob!" Lexi called out. She didn't mean it, though. It felt as if she had been hit by a wrecking ball, and sorry, but that klutz did not sound *sorry* at all!

"You all right?" Kevin asked, looking stunned.

Lexi pushed up her sleeve to check out the damage. "Shoot, I'll bet that leaves a mark." She rubbed her arm, riding a wave of dizziness, but assured Kevin she was okay, that accidents happen. With a sudden gasp, her hand shot up to the pendant of her necklace. It was still there, thank goodness. Her mom had given it to her for her tenth birthday and it was her favorite possession. Genuine opal.

She tucked the necklace safely under her shirt and over her wildly beating heart, believing disaster would strike if it ever left her neck. Of course, that bit of strangeness she kept strictly to herself.

"Alexandra! Kevin!"

Speaking of strange, Aunt Roz was tearing through the crowd at a mad clip, wearing giant sunglasses and a floppy, wide-brim straw hat with a polka-dot bow. Finally! She looked like something out of old Hollywood.

"I'm *so* sorry I'm late!" Aunt Roz said, fighting for breath as if she had just run the New York City Marathon in her slingbacks. "My lord, you must be panicking. Traffic was atrocious. Some bigwig politician's in town or something and they blocked off Sixth Avenue . . . or Avenue of the Americas . . . whatever they're calling it these days." She clasped her hand to her chest. "Oh, just look at the two of you! I can't believe how much you've grown. Hugs!"

Aunt Roz scooped them into an embarrassing group hug, rocking them back and forth like some strange stationary ballroom dance. "I hope you kids are hungry," she said as she eventually let them go. She whipped off her sunglasses and dropped them into her giant straw tote with a wink. "I made reservations downstairs at the Oyster Bar and Restaurant. We should vamoose."

"That was nice of you," Lexi said, smiling. "Thanks, Aunt Roz."

"Oh, you can thank the New York Lottery."

"Awesome!" Kevin gushed. "You won the lottery?"

"From your lips to God's ears. No, I did a commercial for them last year." She grabbed one handle strap of Kevin's duffel, he grabbed the other, and Lexi followed them into the endless swirl of commuters. "I'm about to blow my last residual check on our fancy-shmancy lunch, so I hope you guys can survive on mac and cheese for the next few weeks."

Aunt Roz tittered as if that were a joke, but Lexi wondered if she was serious. Kevin probably was wondering too, judging from his twisted face.

"So, kids, how was your train ride in? It's such a lovely trip along the Hudson."

"Fine," Kevin told her. "Until somebody bashed into Lexi, like, a minute ago."

Aunt Roz came to a worried standstill. "Oh, sweetheart! Are you all right?"

"Yeah," Lexi said, shooting Kevin a why'd-you-have-to-open-your-big-mouth glare. "It was no big deal."

"Well, I wouldn't be too concerned, dear." And Aunt Roz took off again. "With eight million–plus people running around this city like chickens with their heads cut off, rumps will be bumped and toes will be stepped on. Right? Right. So why I'm wearing open-toed pumps—well, you tell me."

The conversation skipped from pumps to bunions to the big gold clock that sprouted from the center of the information kiosk in Grand Central. Aunt Roz said it was supposed to be some rare, priceless treasure but passersby were hardly giving it a second glance except maybe to double-check the time. Lexi quickly looked it up in her guidebook. It said the gilded clock was literally priceless, that all four faces were made of precious opal. *Opal?* But they were a drab, blah white compared to the iridescent luster of her opal pendant.

"Funny," Lexi said, still gazing at the clock, "how you could be staring right at a priceless treasure and never know it."

"Oh, honey, you just said a mouthful."

Aunt Roz started rattling off a whole list of obscure New York treasures—theaters, monuments, sculptures, herself—as they picked up speed, heading for the split marble staircase that led down to the dining concourse. When they reached the lower level, a burst of delicious aromas greeted them full force, and so did the walking, talking milk carton man.

"C'mon, folks," he said, "gimme a break. I'm dressed like milk and you won't even take my free samples?"

"I think that guy is stalking us." Kevin jackknifed his duffel in an effort to steer clear. "No. Really."

Aunt Roz practically twisted an ankle reaching for a packet of the man's Dairy-Eze Chewables. She probably didn't want to hurt his feelings. Lexi took two samples as well, just to show her brother he was being paranoid, if nothing else. They all took a second to regroup, then journeyed on through an open seating area, which was a symphony of chatting diners, clashing silverware, and smacking lips. When they rounded a corner where the Oyster Bar was in full view, Aunt Roz dropped her end of the duffel and did a kind of trancelike twirl.

"Oh, kids," she puffed. "Do you know where we're standing right now?"

"Um, in front of the restaurant?" Kevin answered.

"No, wisenheimer. Well, yes, but that's not what I mean. We're in the Whispering Gallery."

"The what?" Lexi looked around for signs—or paintings? There were none. Other than the entrance to the restaurant, it was just a darkish bare hallway with a series of large marble archways.

"Savvy New Yorkers know that if someone whispers something facing one of these four corners—say, this one," Aunt Roz said, gesturing to it like a model from *The Price Is Right*, "another person can hear them in the opposite corner way over there."

"Photo op!" Kevin blurted and took a snapshot of Aunt Roz in her silly pose.

"Fair warning next time," Aunt Roz said, blinking. "Now I'll be seeing spots all through lunch. Anyway, it has something to do with the acoustics—how the sound travels. They say this is where sweethearts used to whisper their fond farewells when the young men were leaving their beloveds to serve in World War Two."

"I don't get it." Kevin scuttled to one of the corners, gazing up at the herringbone pattern of shiny bricks covering the low, rounded ceiling. "So, what do I do? Just talk?"

"No." Lexi dropped her bag in the opposite corner. "*Whisper.*"

"You'll get the hang of it," Aunt Roz said, and breezed toward the door of the Oyster Bar, leaving a perfume trail. "You two have fun while I check on our reservations."

Lexi swept her sweaty curls up the back of her neck and leaned into her corner to give the Whispering Gallery a try. "Hel*looo*," she sang like a bashful ghost. "How are *yooou?*"

Kevin squealed. "I heard that!" he cried out over his shoulder, then turned back to the wall. "Testing, testing. Do you read me?"

"Totally!" She heard him as clearly as if he were standing right in front of her. "How amazing is this?"

"Okay, listen," Kevin said, dropping his voice an octave, "I have top-secret information for agent Alexandra McGill. But first you must prove that you're really you—*her*. Over."

"Huh? Oh. I am p*rrr*epared to answer any and all q*v*estions," Lexi replied in her best Russian accent, holding in her laugh. "Please to p*rrr*oceed."

"Roger. Only the *real* Alexandra McGill would know her home address. Over."

"Wait, that's not true, but—okay, it's tree-tventy-tree Barrett Pond R*rrr*oad. Cold Spring, New York, von-o-five-von-six."

"Roger that. Only the *real* Alexandra McGill would know—her favorite color. Over."

"Pink. Pale, not hot."

"Only the *real*—"

"Just get on with it already, bonehead!"

"I'm thinking." Kevin cleared his throat. "Your mission, Miss McGill, should-a you choose-a to accept," he said in an even goofier accent than Lexi's, "is to carry out the original plan—you know, as planned, but—oh, never mind, there's Aunt Roz! Abort. Abort."

Lexi spun around to see their aunt waving from the doorway of the Oyster Bar. She turned to grab her bag and heard another weird voice. British this time?

"Wait, let's settle this first. Where're we hiding the bloody jewels?"

She smirked. "How about next to the body we buried?" was waiting on her lips, but a quick glance over her shoulder told her to hush. Kevin and Aunt Roz were already entering the restaurant, and two men dressed in black were huddled together in the very same spot where Kevin had stood. Lexi's heart skipped a beat. She hooked her hair behind one ear and leaned into the corner as casually as possible to eavesdrop on their conversation.

"There's an abandoned train station here in Grand Central," the other man said, sounding American, "several levels below the East Terminal. Track Sixty-one."

"So, what're you suggesting, burying them down there? Don't be absurd."

"Until things die down and they can be stripped and shipped to Cartagena."

"Are you winding me up, mate? It's too—crazy."

"Or is it genius?"

Omigod! Now Lexi's heart was pounding so hard, her entire body was vibrating. In the smoothest of moves she peeked over the top of her guidebook to spy on the possible criminals—just in case she had to pick them out of a lineup. *Please don't make me have to do that!* She should at least get a good description. *Okay, focus.* They were facing each other—tough to see clearly but definitely dressed in black, sipping from steamy cups. Average height and weight. *What's average?* The one with the British accent was bald with orangish glasses and a funky little goatee. The American was wearing a Yankees cap that shadowed his face.

"Listen, man, there's zero time to plot this out!"

"I know . . . bloody brilliant alternative . . . right under their noses . . . never suspect."

What? A rush of people were passing by and Lexi was losing every other word. *What alternative they'll never suspect?* She grabbed a pen from her backpack to scrawl random words across her guidebook as she heard them. *Shoot. Needle. Oval disk? Park!* Lexi dotted the exclamation mark with such gusto, the book went flying. She lunged for it and froze in a heap on the ground. They might have seen her face!

"—under Grand Central is the best bet," the American said. "Of course, we'll have those *mole* people to deal with."

"You mean, the homeless living in the tunnels? I thought that was just an urban myth."

"About as mythical as rats and taxicabs."

"Alexandra!" Aunt Roz called out, gesturing wildly from the restaurant doorway. "Come on, dear, we have our table!"

2

SEVENTY-THIRD AND WEST END AVENUE

Even though she loved them, Lexi couldn't stomach her crab cakes at first. Overhearing a possible crime in the making was definitely an appetite buster. She thought about mentioning it to Aunt Roz during lunch, but could barely get a word in. Plus, Kevin was right there. New York City was overwhelming enough and she didn't want to push him over the edge with what she had heard. By the time their leftovers were being wrapped in aluminum-foil swans, Lexi had decided that the men in black were probably just having an innocent conversation that she had blown way out of proportion. Caught up in the moment. Wild imagination. That type of thing. And so while she, Kevin, and Aunt Roz were piling into a taxi, Lexi added the entire experience to her mental list of things that never happened.

The windows in the back of the cab were filthy and would only go down halfway. Still, Lexi and Kevin stared pie-eyed through the layer of muck at the sights of the city whizzing by. So much concrete and glass. So many weirdos. And to add to the mix, Aunt Roz decided to join Frank Sinatra for a duet when his voice came on the radio singing "New York, New York."

"My dah-dah-dah blues," she sang in a sturdy soprano, "are melting away—"

"So's my butt," Kevin muttered. "Isn't there air-conditioning?"

Everyone laughed. Even Akbar, the driver. Aunt Roz had made it a point to get his name after giving him very specific directions on how to get to her apartment, which he said he really didn't need. Typical Aunt Roz.

Her singing faded to a hum, thank goodness, which eventually petered out altogether. "Okay, I'll shut up. I know I'm embarrassing you guys already." She fanned the kids with her giant hat—her sleek, silvery bob cut blowing in the breeze. "Better?"

Lexi had almost forgotten what a character her aunt was, but it all came flooding back. She was an actress. Mostly commercials and voice-over work these days, which were difficult jobs to land, Lexi had learned during lunch—especially for a woman of a certain age. Fifty-five? Forty-nine? Thirty-seven? No one knew for sure. According to Aunt Roz, age was just a number—and hers was unlisted. The *Putnam County News and Recorder* did a little piece on her awhile back when she grew the largest Sweet Surrender rose at the county fair, and Lexi had the article pinned to her bulletin board.

ROSALIND MCGILL began her career back at the age of twenty as a high-kicking Rockette at the famous Radio City Music Hall in New York. She had barely gotten her feet off the ground, so to speak, when she met her husband-to-be, Ed Lantry, who swept her back to Cold Spring. And according to Ms. McGill (yes, she still goes by her maiden name), she's never looked back since. Aside from raising her two sons, Brian and Henry, she enjoys baking pies, organizing potlucks, and tending her award-winning roses.

As it turned out, Aunt Roz had looked back all right. When Brian and Henry grew up and made their moves to the West Coast, Uncle Ed made his moves on the new cashier at the local Walmart. And so Aunt Roz hightailed it back to New York City to pick up where she had left off. That was three years ago. Everyone in the McGill family said she had completely lost her mind, except for Lexi's mom, who had called her "plucky" and "heroic." Lexi agreed.

The first ten minutes in the cab were like *Mr. Toad's Wild Ride*, and Kevin was red-faced and white-knuckled, clinging to the armrest. Lexi playfully pecked at him with the aluminum-foil swan to get him to loosen up. Didn't happen. He decapitated the poor thing.

"Oh, my goodness gracious, this is it!" Aunt Roz cried out. "I wasn't paying attention. On your right, Akbar."

The cab screeched to a crooked stop on the corner of West End Avenue and Seventy-Third Street. Akbar unloaded the luggage from the trunk and Aunt Roz gave him a generous tip and an inappropriate hug before he hopped back into the cab and sped off.

"You know, Alexandra, in this light you're the spitting image of your mother."

Well, *that* came out of nowhere. "Huh. Really? The same hair, I guess, kinda-sorta, but . . ." She hoisted her bag up the curb and headed toward the brownstone, and when Aunt Roz caught up with her to help, Lexi changed the subject. "So, any new acting jobs on the horizon?"

"Well, I do have a few callbacks coming up. A faded Southern belle in an off-Broadway musical and another commercial—a national." The glint in Aunt Roz's eye disappeared when they reached the landing and she dropped her end of the bag. "For adult diapers," she said out of the side of her mouth as if they were illegal. "Hi-ho, the glamorous life."

Lexi managed to keep a straight face reaching for the doorknob. Someone kicked the double doors from the other side and she jumped. A blob of pig-nosed flesh was pressed against the murky glass.

"Go in, go in," Aunt Roz said, waving them onward. "That's just Kimmy, my little neighbor."

She turned out to be pretty, this Kimmy, but Weird with a capital *W*. An Asian-American girl around Lexi's age, wearing a SpongeBob T-shirt knotted above her belly button, a pair of men's striped boxer shorts, and bright-orange three-inch platform flip-flops. There were streaks of turquoise in her otherwise ink-black hair, which was gathered into bristly pigtails jetting out of her head like sheaves of wheat. *Is the circus in town?* Kevin appeared to be studying her as if she were some fascinating abstract painting, but it was dislike at first sight for Lexi.

"Hi, Kimmy." Aunt Roz removed her hat and gracefully smoothed down her hair. "Meet Kevin and Lexi, my niece and nephew—or nephew and niece. Well, let's hope you can figure out which one is which."

"Kim Ling Levine," she said without so much as a glance. Then in a fit of rage, she ripped off the small NO MENUS, PLEASE sign that was taped to the door and crumpled it into a wad. "Look at this pile! Un-freakin'-believable. Westside Wok, Tex-Mex Express, Giovanni's. How rude!"

While she collected the menus that were carpeting the hallway by the fistful and stuffed them into a trash bag, Aunt Roz explained what was going on to Lexi and Kevin—how food deliverymen left stacks of menus in their wake every time they made a delivery. And with thousands of restaurants in Manhattan, these things could add up.

Kim Ling was down on her knees now with a smelly red marker, squeaking a message onto half a piece of poster board. She held the sign up for approval. "How's this grab you?"

> Absolutely NO MENUS are to be left on the premises! Violators will be reported to the NYPD, hunted down, and punished to the full extent of the law! THIS MEANS YOU!!!

"Subtle," Aunt Roz said with a smile dancing on her lips. "But I think it just might do the trick."

"Provided these morons can read."

Lexi managed a weak "Nice meeting you" as they started up the stairs, but Kim Ling was too busy ripping a piece of masking tape off the roll with her teeth to even notice. How bizarre that this nut job was ranting about people being rude, when she was just about the rudest girl Lexi had ever met. "Uh, nice girl," she said when they got to the second landing, meaning the exact opposite of course.

"She *really* is," Aunt Roz whispered. "Her mother's Chinese and her father's Jewish. They bought the building last January and didn't even raise my rent—which they could have, lord knows. They're wonderful people."

The whispering jolted Lexi's thoughts from Kim Ling back to Grand Central as they climbed the creaky stairway, and the entire Whispering Gallery scenario replayed in her head—dark and creepy like some old slasher flick. The mysterious men in black. The talk of jewels being stripped and shipped. Mole people. Why did she have to go and eavesdrop? A single droplet of sweat ran down Lexi's neck, sending an icy shiver up her spine, even on the hottest of days.

"Your building needs an elevator," Kevin puffed, and the stairs kept on coming.

"Nonsense, this is fabulous exercise." Without warning, Aunt Roz hiked her skirt over one knee and beveled her foot in a chorus-girl pose. "Just get a load of these pins!"

"I'll pass," Kevin said, gliding by without even glancing at her legs.

"Oh, you!"

Lexi laughed and sucked in a lungful of cabbage soup stench, or whatever was stinking up the entire third and fourth floors. Finally reaching Apartment 5F, she dropped her bag and shook life back into her cramped fingers. "Aunt Roz, have you ever heard of mole people?"

"Well, let's see." She was catching her breath, struggling with a clump of keys worthy of San Quentin Prison. "There's that ex-supermodel—what's her name? Cindy Crawford, that's it. She's famous for her mole. More like a beauty mark, actually." She handed Lexi her hat. "And don't forget John-Boy from *The Waltons*. What a whopper he had! Oh, but you kids are too young to remember—"

"There's Whack-a-Mole," Kevin offered, and mimed clobbering a plastic mole with a club. *"Poom! Poom!"*

"No, no, wrong moles. I think they're supposed to be these people who live under Grand Central Station. I forget where I read that."

"Sounds like a bunch of hooey to me, Alexandra."

That's when all the lights went out and Lexi's heart lurched.

"Uh-oh." She clutched her opal. "Kevin, what did you touch?"

"Nothing!"

They stood in complete darkness, listening to each other breathe. Aunt Roz started saying something about "These things happen . . . ," but Lexi was concentrating on twisting her opal pendant nine times—nine being her lucky number. It was quirky and weird, but oh well. So what if she had convinced her dad to move the trip from yesterday to today because it was June ninth? And the fact that she had packed nine lucky pennies, a rabbit's foot, and a laminated four-leaf clover in case of emergencies was nobody's business but her own.

Lexi flinched at the *slappity-slappity-slap* of climbing flip-flops.

"Mrs. Krauss must've blown a freakin' fuse again!" Kim Ling yelled up the stairwell. "Looks like the electricity in the entire building's out this time—and it's gonna be awhile. Snaggit!"

There was the sound of keys unlocking locks. A thump. A sigh from Aunt Roz as the door squeaked open.

"Well, kids, what can I say? Never a dull moment in the Big Apple! Right?"

She should only know.

3

SCOOPS

The Big Apple was more like the Baked Apple without power in the building. No electricity obviously meant no air-conditioning, lights, television, computer—basically no comfort at all. Lexi and Kevin spent the rest of the day playing Pictionary by flashlight while Aunt Roz hunted for candles, matches, and her blood pressure medicine. The good news came the next morning in four simple words: ice cream for breakfast. Aunt Roz had stocked the freezer with the stuff and it was rapidly turning into slush, so she insisted Lexi and Kevin eat it down on the front stoop where they might at least catch a breeze.

" 'Member how Mom wouldn't let us eat ice cream right out of the carton?" Kevin rolled his container of rocky road across his forehead as he and Lexi stepped into the thick summer air. " 'Cause she said we weren't barbarians and that's why bowls were invented?" He snickered.

"Like barbarians really ate ice cream. Oh, remember when Mom—"

"Yeah, yeah, I remember." Lexi's stomach still turned into a bag full of stones every time someone even mentioned her mother. Sometimes she missed her so much, she could hardly breathe, but that didn't mean they had to talk about it every second. "Remind me to remind you to get your stuff ready for City Camp orientation tonight so we won't have to rush tomorrow morning."

"What time do we have to get up?"

"I dunno. Eightish? Wait, don't sit! There's pigeon poop all over the steps."

Lexi set down her carton of French vanilla and dashed into the foyer to get the *New York Times* she'd seen lying on a stack of phone books. She pulled it apart on the way back and shoved half under her brother.

"Eight o'clock is totally unfair," Kevin said, and plopped down on the sports section. "It's summer vacation. We should be able to sleep till noon at least."

"Well, it'll be noon somewhere in the world." Lexi spread her half of the newspaper onto the step and shooed an army of gnats away from her face. Just as she was about to sit, the headline screamed off the front page.

CLEOPATRA'S JEWELS VANISH!

"Whoa." It was in bold block letters above a photo of two stunned-looking security guards. Lexi ripped the paper out from under herself and checked the date. "It's today's, June tenth!" The images of the two mystery men in Grand Central invaded her brain and her heart was racing all over again. *Could there be a connection? It would make total—* Without finishing her thought, she began reading the article aloud.

> WHAT SOME HAD CALLED "the find of the century" has quickly turned into "the crime of the century." An exquisitely well-preserved assortment of necklaces, rings, bangles, and headdresses, possibly dating back to Queen Cleopatra herself, went missing in Manhattan late Monday night after arriving from the Cairo Museum. This astonishing collection, discovered outside of Alexandria, Egypt, by archaeologist Josef Grunberg last April, disappeared en route to the Metropolitan Museum of Art on 82nd Street and Fifth Avenue, where it was to have been the centerpiece of the highly anticipated "Queen of the Nile" exhibit, scheduled to premiere on June 17th.

Lexi collapsed onto a smattering of pigeon droppings and sped through the rest of the article in silence. *"The* Cleopatra? Omigod."

"So who cares?" Kevin said, picking nuts and

marshmallow chunks out of his mushy ice cream. "Rocky road? More like rocky river."

"No, you don't understand. Remember the Whispering Gallery?" Lexi stopped herself. She didn't want to turn him into a basket case on the very first day of their visit. Then again, if she didn't tell someone she might burst. "Listen, Kev, I don't want you to get all weirded out or anything, okay? Promise?"

Those words alone brought a look of horror to his face. Luckily, the front door of the brownstone squeaked open just then and Kim Ling appeared with two large garbage bags in tow. She clomped down the stairs between Kevin and Lexi, practically bopping them in the head, unloaded the trash, then took the same obnoxious route back up.

Lexi waited for the sound of the closing door behind her and turned to see why it never came.

"Problem?" a smirking Kim Ling asked. She was leaning against the door with her arms folded, staring down at them like she owned the place—which she kind of did.

"Nuh-uh." Lexi turned back around and grabbed her carton of French vanilla. The girl was megarude, that was for sure. Still, Lexi was glad for the interruption. Spilling the beans to Kevin would have been a total mistake.

"That Lincoln's been parked across the street ever since you guys got here," Kim Ling said, stroking her chin. "Look, someone's in there. See—there's cigarette smoke coming from the window. Strange."

Lexi and Kevin scrambled to their feet to get a better look.

"Sit down!" Kim Ling hissed.

Lexi crumpled back onto the step like a humiliated puppy, pulling Kevin with her. "You just said—"

"Well, don't be so obvious about it." She rolled her eyes in disgust. "You guys won't last a week in this town."

Lexi's shoulders tightened into a rigid two-by-four plank. *Oh, great. Now there's a suspicious black car with tinted windows to worry about too. The exact kind jewel thieves would drive.* Maybe they had seen her eavesdropping at Grand Central and followed her here. Stalking. Plotting.

"Don't be stupid," Kim Ling said, as if she were reading Lexi's mind. "I mean, while you're in New York. It'll get you into trouble." Her dark, questioning eyes darted between the McGills like they were two mutant life forms that dropped out of the sky and landed on her steps. "Our super's on vacation, and my dad's still at my *bubbe's* house on Long Island, and I can't reach him on his cell phone 'cause he probably forgot to turn it on, as usual, and Grandma Levine's not answering either, so I'm just here with my mom and neither one of us knows squat about changing fuses." She sighed like a deflating tire and adjusted one of her pigtail bands with a *snap*. "You guys don't by any chance—?"

"No," Lexi said flatly.

"I didn't think so. What a conundrum."

Lexi focused back on her ice cream—stabbing at it, stirring it into a lumpy milkshake. She purposely let her shoulder-length curls conceal her face from the mysterious Lincoln. Just in case.

"Hey, uh, Madison, was it?" Kim Ling said.

"Lexi."

"Oh yeah, like Lexington Avenue—I knew it was some street name. Sorry about the no-electricity thing. But you guys must be used to it, right? Living out there on Little House on the Prairie." She snorted and slapped her thigh like it was actually funny. "No, seriously, though, you're probably roasting your butts off in your aunt's apartment."

"That's why we're sitting out here," Kevin answered. "Waiting for a breeze to come along."

"Uh-huh. I see. Well, don't hold your breath."

And with those final words of wisdom Kim Ling disappeared into the foyer, slamming the door behind her.

Lexi was about to explode with "What is the deal with that girl?" but the door sprang open again.

"I know a better spot," Kim Ling said, waggling her finger. "Follow me, but keep quiet. I've been avoiding the tenants like the plague ever since the blackout."

The girl was a major pain, that was for sure, but with criminals parked across the street possibly sizing Lexi up for who knows what, she didn't think twice. She quickly ripped the article out of the *Times* and shoved it into her back pocket, grabbed her ice cream and her brother, and followed Kim Ling into the brownstone. A lizardy-looking guy slithered out of Apartment 1R and right past them carrying too many shopping bags. *Does anyone ever say hello in this town? Do people even know their own neighbors?* There was a pasty-faced man peeking out of the same apartment, but when he saw the kids approaching, he quickly shut his door.

"Ew, what smells?" Kevin asked.

"Blanca, Eddie-Spaghetti, Mao-Mao, Simba, the Colonel, and Mrs. Wigglesworth," Kim Ling said, leading them up the stairs. "Cats. They belong to Mr. Carney. That was him just now. He's certifiable. Oh, and Gingersnap."

"Kim! *Dios mio!*" came ringing from above before Lexi could ask Kim Ling about the shopping-bag-man. The silhouette of a woman with an armful of screaming baby was pacing on the second floor. "I miss all *mis programas* on the *televisión.*"

"*Sí, sí,* I know, Mrs. Rivera, please be patient. *Sea paciente, por favor.*"

They ran into a whole hodgepodge of fuming tenants on their way up, most of them just shadows in the dark. Except for Miss Carelli, who appeared in a greenish toga and wielded a flashlight.

"What was that?" Kevin puffed. "The Statue of Liberty?"

"Miss Carelli, an opera singer," Kim Ling said over her shoulder. "She always wears costume pieces from her shows. I'm guessing today's ensemble is from *Antony and Cleopatra.*"

Lexi swallowed hard. It was eerie how the name Cleopatra came out of Kim Ling's mouth just seconds after Lexi had found that newspaper article. And as they reached the top landing, something else was bugging her. In the time it took to climb six flights, Kim Ling had exhibited a freaky ability for remembering cat names, a semi-knowledge of opera, plus conversational foreign language skills. Lexi wondered if she was one of those scary-smart kids with a brain the size of Utah.

"Okay, listen up—I'm gonna need you guys to keep low to the ground," Kim Ling said with the authority of a police academy field-training officer. "We're exiting onto the roof past a burglar alarm with extremely sensitive sensors."

"But there's no electricity," Kevin reminded her.

"Battery backup. And we *do not* want to set it off under any circumstances. Got it? Good. Now just do what I do."

She ducked down and carefully scooted across the floor sideways like a Dungeness crab, then slowly slid flat-backed up the heavy metal door with her face in sharp profile.

Is she kidding with this? Lexi wondered if a breeze was worth such a crazy maneuver. She took a deep breath and an even deeper plié and, thanks to having two years of ballet under her belt, wound up safely next to Kim Ling—in fifth position. She turned to see how Kevin was doing when—*RIIIIIIIIIING*—the bone-rattling alarm went off. Kevin and rocky road were flying through the air.

"Great!" Kim Ling barked. "I said, 'do not under any circumstances set off the alarm,' and he freakin' sets off the alarm."

"Sorry."

"It was an accident." Lexi grabbed her brother and led him onto the roof deck away from the deafening noise— and Kim Ling.

A few seconds later, the alarm stopped screaming and Kim Ling tore out of the building and hurled the rocky road into a trash can where Kevin was standing. "Snaggit! You are such a little klutz."

Lexi's face went hot. "Listen, he said he was sorry, didn't he? No need for name-calling. And why do you keep saying 'snaggit' anyway? That's not even a word."

Kim Ling looked at her with the eyes of a girl who had surprisingly met her match. "Blame my parents," she said in a normal conversational tone. "They charge me fifty cents every time they hear me swear. I had to start making up my own PG-rated curse words—either that or take out a loan."

Lexi willed what could have been a smile into a scowl and sauntered over to the edge of the roof. "Kev, come here. You can totally see the river and clear into—I don't know where."

"New Jersey," Kim Ling offered. "The armpit state."

Eventually all three wound up leaning on the low wall that trimmed the rooftop, staring in silence at the pinkish submarine-shaped clouds floating in neat rows across the sky. Lexi could feel her tension melting away along with the French vanilla as she handed the pint to Kevin. Finally, that cool breeze they had been looking for wafted up from the Hudson River and kissed their faces.

"It's nice on the roof, isn't it?" Kim Ling said dreamily. "Pots of hydrangeas, patio furniture . . . since we installed the alarm, hardly anyone ventures up here anymore. Well, except three-R. She likes to sunbathe without a top."

"Really?" Kevin asked.

"Stick your tongue back in your mouth. She's, like, seventy."

Everyone laughed out loud—even Lexi. But she quickly snuffed out any glint of joy with tightly folded arms. "You sure seem to have your nose in everyone's business."

"I'm going to be an investigative journalist. Nosy will come in handy," was Kim Ling's oddball response. "Sorry I tore your head off, Kevin. I get like that sometimes."

"That's okay. Want some ice cream?" he asked her as his face turned three shades of blotchy red. "Before it's total soup?"

"Nah, I don't do dairy. Lactose intolerant."

Lexi froze. *She did* not *just say that!* Almost against her will, Lexi's hand slipped into her pocket and pulled out the sample of Dairy-Eze Chewables she had taken from the human milk carton in Grand Central. On the back it read, *Fast-acting dietary supplements for lactose intolerance. Enjoy the dairy foods you love without stomach upset.* Was this some sort of weird fate? Lexi, not wanting to mess with the power of the universe, begrudgingly handed Kim Ling the free sample. "Here, knock yourself out."

"What?" Kim Ling looked down and her eyes widened. "*Gracias*, Lexington Avenue! Man, I hope you're around if I ever need a kidney."

Lexi had to admit that Kim was kind of funny—for a psychopath. But it hardly made up for her quick temper, made-up curse words, and the way she tromped around like she was queen of the universe. Lexi could never imagine being friends with this girl. Witty, city, brainy, zany. She seemed totally in control and Lexi was anything but. Together they were like a left-to-right-hand handshake— they just didn't fit.

Lexi quickly polished her spoon on her shirttail and was handing it to Kim Ling as a final goodwill gesture when the burglar alarm went off again and Aunt Roz came barreling through the door.

"There you are!" she cried, her hands covering her ears. "Oh, that wretched, wretched sound! I thought you kids were on the front stoop but Miss Carelli told me she saw you heading up—oh, Kimmy, make it stop!"

"What is it?" Lexi shouted with a pang of concern. "What's happened?"

Aunt Roz waited for Kim Ling to rush into the building and turn off the alarm. "It's your father," she said, panting. "Nothing's wrong. He phoned from Paris and wants you to call him right back—before he and Clare leave the hotel."

Kevin bolted through the door and thundered down the steps followed by Aunt Roz, but Lexi stayed put.

"Lemme guess," Kim Ling said, inching toward her. "Not getting along with the new stepmom, eh, Cinderella?"

"Why would you think that?"

"Don't kid a kidder, kiddo. It's written all over your face."

Lexi closed her eyes, wishing Kim Ling would disappear. *Why is there never a fairy godmother around when you need one?*

The ringing in her ears must still be from the burglar alarm, she was thinking, but when her eyes popped open she realized the noise was coming from the street. Kim Ling was back at the roof's edge, and when Lexi joined her, the sound of at least fifty screaming sirens was piercing the air.

"A fleet of squad cars," Kim Ling reported at the top of her lungs, "parading around town! It usually happens when the city's on high alert, like, if there's a bomb threat or a major crime—to warn criminals they'd better watch out."

"So many flashing lights!"

"It must be because of that Cleopatra jewel heist. You've heard about it, right?"

Lexi stiffened. "No electricity, remember? I—don't have a clue what you're talking about."

As the motorcade disappeared down West End Avenue, Kim Ling turned and headed for the door, but with the smuggest look on her face. "Uh, that newspaper headline sticking out of your back pocket begs to differ."

"Oh, yeah," Lexi muttered. "Right."

And she was left alone, biting her bottom lip and staring into New Jersey.

4

DISORIENTATION

It was just after midnight when the electricity returned to the brownstone and the AC kicked on with a loud rattle. "Hallelujah," Lexi mumbled to herself. "Maybe I'll finally get some sleep." The guilt, however, from not talking to her father on the return phone call kept her up long into the night—that and images of creepy jewel thieves and flashing patrol cars. If only the police would hurry up and solve that crime, it would be one less annoying thing to deal with.

Why Aunt Roz woke everyone up at seven thirty a.m. to get to a ten o'clock orientation was yet another unsolved crime. They had arrived way too early, and Lexi and Kevin were sitting on hard folding chairs next to Aunt Roz, doing nothing but stifling yawns and sizing up the other campers trickling into the gymnasium.

"I'll wait just a few more minutes till everyone gets here before I begin," Mr. Glick, the jittery head counselor, finally announced into an old-fashioned microphone. He wore a toothy smile and plaid shorts with droopy black socks, putting the *eek* in geek. "In the meantime, folks, let's keep it down to a dull roar, shall we?"

The YMCA, which happened to be only a few blocks away from Grand Central—way too close to where Lexi had encountered the thieves for her comfort—was filling up with kids and parents of every age, shape, size, and ethnicity. In the middle of counting Hello Kitty backpacks, Lexi happened to spot a TV mounted on the wall of an adjacent office with the door half open. She couldn't hear the sound, but a close-up of a gaudy green necklace flashed on the screen. *Home Shopping Network?* Then a chunky gold arm cuff—a jewel-encrusted, ancient Egyptian-looking arm cuff? It wasn't HSN, it was CNN. *Cleopatra's jewels? They found them?* Her heart did a backflip. *Wait. Maybe not.* "Photos courtesy of Cairo Museum" was in teeny print. Now the gray-haired anchorman was onscreen yapping silently. Lexi strained to read the tiny text in the crawler at the bottom of the screen.

WHILE TALKS RESUME ON CAPITOL HILL . . . *CNN* . . . NYPD SLOW IN GATHERING CLUES RE: CLEOPATRA JEWEL HEIST. THIEVES STILL AT LARGE AND POSSIBLY ARMED AND DANGEROUS . . .

Don't freak out! Just put it out of your mind. Think calm camp thoughts. Woodpeckers, canoes, mosquito bites . . .

"Okay, people, listen up!" Mr. Glick clapped his hands.

"I need seven- to eleven-year-olds to form a line at the table to my right." He pointed to a foldout table with neat stacks of papers on it manned by a pimply-faced beanpole of a girl. "And twelve- to sixteen-year-olds at my table, please."

"Why are they putting us in different lines?" Kevin asked as they all stood up, gathering their things. "Nobody said we'd have to be in different lines."

"It's probably just for registration," Lexi told him, her eyes still glued to the TV.

"Well, I'd better scoot if I'm going to make it to my callback on time," Aunt Roz said over the sound of swelling chatter. "Or—oh, Alexandra, maybe I'd better not go. I really shouldn't leave you kids alone."

"We'll be fine, Aunt Roz."

"Are you sure? How do I look?" She sprang up and did a little turn, showing off her flowery dress.

"Not a day over twenty-nine."

"Well, that's not right. I'm up for the role of the mother in the musical version of *The Glass Menagerie*. I was going for over-the-hill and dowdy."

Lexi was about to backpedal when someone goosed her from behind. *"Ow!"*

"You could never pull off dowdy, Ms. McGill."

"Kim Ling!" Lexi's jaw actually dropped. "What're you doing here?"

"Stalking you," she said with a deadpan stare.

"Orientation, whaddya think? Now close your mouth—you're attracting flies."

"Hey," Kevin said to Kim Ling, "you never told us you were going to City Camp."

"You never asked."

"She's the one who told me about it in the first place," Aunt Roz said. "I happened to mention it to your dad and the next thing I know—bibbidi-bobbidi-boo, you and Kevin are enrolled!" She grabbed Kim Ling and gave her one of her trademark rocking hugs. "Oh, this makes me feel so much better about dashing off."

"With all due respect, Ms. M., you're smothering the life out of me."

"Well, I *am* trying out for the role of a smothering mother." Aunt Roz released her with a chuckle and began rifling through her tote. "Is your mom here, Kimmy?"

"No. I'm fourteen."

"Well, I suppose you'll be retiring to Boca Raton pretty soon."

"A New York City fourteen-year-old is equivalent to, like, a seventeen-year-old anywhere else. It's a proven—" Her attention switched to a group of giggly girls and she cringed. "Oh, no, it looks like Jen Peterson got Invisibraces and they're hideously obvious. I'll be right back." And she was off.

Aunt Roz muttered something about Kim Ling being "a pistol" and motioned for Lexi and Kevin to come closer.

She slipped a crisp twenty-dollar bill into Lexi's hand, then sealed it in her fist. "For emergencies," she whispered. "Now, I have to put in a few hours selling ballet subscriptions after my audition, but I'll see you right back here at a quarter to six. Wait in the vestibule, okay? I don't want you kids wandering around the city." She gave Lexi and Kevin identical pecks on the cheek and swept toward the double doors, waving behind her. "Stick close to Kimmy— and have fun!"

It was one or the other. Both was asking the impossible.

"Attention, people!" Mr. Glick's voice echoed through the sound system. "Please button your lips and listen up 'cause I'm only going to say this—" He dropped the mic with an explosive *boom!* Screechy feedback and laughter filled the gymnasium. "All right, ha-ha, very funny. Can everyone please line up at your assigned tables so we can get this show on the road?"

Lexi rushed Kevin to his lineup, then flew over to her designated line without waiting for Kim Ling. Who needed the extra aggravation? She quickly signed in, picked up her registration form, emergency information card, *Safety First* printout, and camp uniform: a puke-green T-shirt with a picture of a tree sprouting musical instruments instead of leaves and CITY CAMP, WHERE NATURE MEETS CULTURE printed on the back. She checked to make sure Kevin and Kim Ling were still in line, and made a mad dash back to the empty office where the television set was still on. She hovered near the doorway. This time she could hear.

"The mayor made a statement earlier," the gray-haired anchorman said straight to the camera. "Do we—have we got the footage? No? Okay, I'll just read the quote."

Lexi's ears perked up, wondering if they were still on the jewel heist story.

" 'New Yorkers are being strongly urged to come forward immediately with any information they may have pertaining to this case. Our foremost concern, of course, lies in the safety of our citizens and the apprehension of these dangerous suspects—but, in addition, relations between the United States and the Arab Republic of Egypt could be dramatically affected if this scandalous crime remains unsolved. Once again, I implore anyone with information about the Cleopatra jewel theft to please contact the NYPD.' "

Oh, great. No pressure.

"Can I help you?"

Lexi jumped. There was a tiny woman behind a large desk at the other end of the room. Lexi hadn't even noticed her before.

"Fascinating case, isn't it?" the lady chirped. "I can't seem to tear myself away."

Lexi shot her a jittery smile and quickly tore *herself* away. *At least things couldn't possibly get worse.* When she met up with Kevin and Kim Ling at the water fountain, she realized she was still strangling the sweaty twenty in her fist. She dug into the pouch on her backpack where her wallet always lived, to put it away, but had to keep digging.

"Shoot! Where is it?" Lexi shoved her papers and balled-up T-shirt over to Kevin so she could search more thoroughly. "My pink wallet. It's missing!"

Kevin gasped. "Pickpockets?"

Kim Ling gasped too. "*Pink*? Well, I doubt any of these campers would've ripped you off in front of all these doting parents. When'd you last see it?"

"Oh, man, I'm not sure. In the train station, I think." Lexi handed her a hairbrush and a stash of peanut-butter crackers from her backpack. *Could the jewel thieves have stolen it somehow? No, they were never that close. But it could've fallen out of my bag when I rushed into the restaurant and they might've picked it up. Why is this happening?*

"Anything important in it?" Kim Ling said.

"Just, like, my life. My library card and my student—oh no!" Lexi turned to Kevin. "My favorite picture of Mom was in there. You know the one—on the boardwalk in Atlantic City. Oh, great, and the lipstick blot too!"

"You carry around a blot?" Kim Ling raised a crooked eyebrow. "I won't ask."

"And a Post-it with Aunt Roz's address," Lexi said, half to herself. *Maybe the thieves really were in that black Lincoln, armed and dangerous and following me to my exact location!*

"Pipe down and listen up!" Mr. Glick's amplified voice

rose above the chatter. "We're splitting you kids into two groups again like we always do—older and younger. If you have a green registration card, you're in Group A. Blue, you're in Group B. So if you only remember one thing today, remember your color."

"I'm green," Kevin said, actually turning a pale shade of green. "You guys are blue and I'm green. And you said it was just for registration!"

"Of course, we *will* be joining both groups together for specific activities from time to time," Mr. Glick added, but that wasn't enough to calm Kevin down.

"This is *so* wrong!"

"You'll be fine," Lexi told him. She was too busy freaking out herself at the moment to deal with him freaking out.

She searched desperately for her wallet while Mr. Glick blabbered on about all the exciting activities the staff had planned for the next three weeks and how everyone would undoubtedly meet their best friend for life. *Yeah, right.* She kept searching while they sat through a lame slide show of highlights from previous City Camp summers—while Mr. Glick read through the entire *Safety First* printout—while his pimply beanpole assistant collected the emergency information cards.

By the time Mr. Glick announced, "That's it for today, ladies and gentlemen. See you all tomorrow morning, bright eyed and bushy tailed," Lexi was all searched out and completely deflated. But she refused to cry—she would *not* cry even if the roof came crashing down on her, which just may happen the way things had been going so far.

"But it's only eleven forty-five!" Kevin squawked. He compared the time on his orbiting planets wristwatch with the clock on the wall. "Aunt Roz isn't coming back till six. What're we supposed to do all day?"

"Well, if you goobers had read the schedule, you would've known that orientation day only goes till noon." Kim Ling pulled Kevin's cap down over his face and led the way out the double doors.

"Hey!"

"No worries, McGills. The sun is shining and we're in the greatest city in the world, which I happen to know like the back of my hand."

"So, what're you saying?" Lexi asked.

"Welcome to Camp Kim Ling!"

Ugh. Lexi definitely was not up for whatever that meant.

"You kids wanna hit the usual tourist hotspots? Times Square, Statue of—?"

"Been there, done that," Lexi snapped. "This isn't our first time here. Besides, we're not allowed."

"Well, don't bite my head off. Just being the friendly native." Kim Ling did a strange neck-cracking maneuver that looked and sounded like it hurt. "So, anyway, how insipidly boring was that orientation? A total boondoggle, right?"

"Is that another one of your crazy made-up words?" Lexi had to ask.

"No, it's legit. It means an unnecessary, wasteful activity. Uh, no offense, but you guys might want to start carrying around a pocket dictionary if you're going to be hanging with me."

Lexi added smug and pseudo-intellectual to her mental list of reasons for disliking Kim Ling, although she wasn't sure what pseudo-intellectual meant exactly.

"We can do Macy's," Kim Ling suggested.

"Hello? Missing wallet, remember?" Lexi collapsed onto the smoldering top step of the Y and pulled Kevin down with her. "We only have emergency money, so we plan on spending the day without—spending. But don't let us stop you."

Kim Ling didn't bolt like Lexi thought she would, but plopped down next to her, scratching her head like it was infested with fleas. "Well, Grand Central's right over there. A hop, skip, and jump. We could check out their lost and found—you know, see if your wallet's turned up there."

From the look Lexi gave her, you would have thought she had suggested they jump off the top of the Empire State Building. "Aah-uh-oh," she replied to the tune of "I don't know." She knew it was unlikely she would run into the jewel thieves again at Grand Central, but even that slim possibility made her knees sweat. "I promised my aunt we wouldn't wander."

Two colorful horse-drawn carriages came clopping around the corner and Kevin practically elbowed Lexi's eye out grabbing for his camera. "Photo op! So cool," he gushed. *Snap.* "Are those buggy rides expensive, Kim?" *Snap. Snap.*

"They're called hansom cabs, and this is New York— everything's expensive."

Lexi perked up at the sight of the decked-out horses, too, and the cute drivers in top hats—until the second carriage almost got rammed by a double-decker tour bus. The dapple-gray shook his head with a frustrated whinny, adding to the clamor of horns, sirens, and deafening street drills. "Omigod, did you see that? Poor horse." She let out a groan. "I am so over this place already. All that crime in the news; then my wallet gets lost or stolen, or whatever. I'm sick of breathing in exhaust fumes. And urine. I miss the smell of—I don't know, fresh-cut grass and—"

"Stop dissing my city!" Kim Ling scolded. "If all you're gonna do is kvetch and complain, then keep the lips zipped."

Lexi didn't lash back since she knew Kim was right. *If you haven't got anything good to say . . .* So with chin propped on hands, she watched the hansom cabs disappear into a blinding splotch of sunlight and yellow taxicabs. The other two followed suit. They sat silent and motionless in a grumpy clump, staring at the endless parade of passersby and picking up snippets of their cell-phone conversations.

"He had the nerve to go over my head, straight to the manager of East Coast Operations. What a—"

"—jerk chicken. And these amazing buffalo wings that are super spicy and—"

"—hot under the collar. So, I tell him, I go, 'Dave, give the new guy a shot. I mean, one less commission ain't gonna kill ya.'"

Shot? Kill? Lexi found herself gritting her teeth. She had had more than her fill of eavesdropping, thank you very much! Her heartbeat was giving the street noise a run for its money as she stared down at the cracked sidewalk, thinking what a bummer New York had been so far.

That was when she saw it lying there next to her left sneaker—a pure white feather like the ones her mother used to collect. A tingle wriggled up the back of Lexi's neck. Her mom had called them angel-wing feathers. "They're good luck!" she would always say, and snatch them right up.

"Kev, call Aunt Roz. Tell her she doesn't have to meet us back here, that we'll see her back at the apartment. Say—I don't know, that they have a special bus or something to bring us home. Otherwise she'll drop everything to come get us and we don't want to screw up her whole day."

"You mean lie?"

"No—it's just so she won't worry. Lies don't really count if they're told to make someone feel better," which was yet another lie to make someone feel better. What kind of example was she setting for her little brother? "Ugh, never mind, I'd better do it."

"No, I will!"

"You know," Kim Ling said, "there actually is a City Camp bus with Eastside-Westside drop-off points. It doesn't start till tomorrow, though, and you have to sign up in advance . . ."

While Kim Ling was droning on and Kevin was making the call, Lexi reached down and discreetly grabbed the white feather. In an instant she was six years old again, tugging on her mother's skirt.

"Ew, Mommy, drop it!"

"It's pretty, don't you think?" her mom had said through one of her heart-melting smiles.

"Nooo! It's just a yelchy pigeon feather. Miss Schroeder says that pigeons are rats with wings and that they carry a disease."

"Well, cookie, teachers have to say things like that." Lexi's mom carefully wrapped the feather in a tissue and slipped it into her purse. "How do we know this feather didn't fall from an angel's wings—just like the one Daddy puts on top of our Christmas tree, only real? She could be sitting up on a fluffy cloud right now staring down on us. Look! See?" And she pointed up past the striped awning of the Silver Spoon Cafe. "There she is, *waaay* up there!"

"Where?"

"Oops, you missed her! She just flew up to heaven."

"Nuh-uh." Lexi giggled. "You made that up."

"Now, why would I do a thing like that, silly?" She kissed Lexi's forehead with a giant "Mwah!" and they took off down Main Street again, hand-in-swinging-hand. "Some people think finding a shiny penny is lucky," she had told her, "or four-leaf clovers. But we don't have to believe what everyone else does, right, cookie? Mommy believes in—"

"Angel feathers." Lexi finished the sentence out loud, catching herself back in the present. She was squinting into the sun over the jagged city skyline, and had to quickly look away.

"Huh?" Kevin asked.

"Nothing. What'd Aunt Roz say?"

"No answer. I left a message."

Lexi slid the feather into her shorts pocket. She only half believed these feathers were signs from her mom appearing at just the right time—comforting her, encouraging her to suck it up and move forward. But half believing was more than enough for her.

All of a sudden Kim Ling sprang up like a jack-in-the-box on caffeine. "Guys! You want horses and grass? Follow me." She flew off the steps and plunged into a thick cloud of manhole steam without even turning to see if Kevin and Lexi were behind her.

But they were—watching her curse out a speeding cab.

"The light is still red, moron! Drive much?"

"Okay, tell me, why're we following her again?" Lexi asked Kevin.

"You got me. But she does crack me up."

Lexi shook her head in wonder. "She's like the Pied Piper of Manhattan—with road rage."

5

A HORSE OF A DIFFERENT COLOR

As it turned out, destination Central Park was beyond spectacular! A humongous oasis right in the middle of the city, with more grass and trees than all of Cold Spring. Maybe not, but a full 843 acres, according to Kim Ling. And since the park was blocked off to afternoon traffic, there wasn't a car in sight. Bikers, joggers, and Rollerbladers shared the roadway instead, along with those hansom cabs. And it was cool. At least ten degrees cooler than the rest of the city, Lexi guessed, and seemingly miles away from Grand Central Station with its lurking jewel thieves and mole people. Finally she could breathe.

"Oh, look, you can see 'em from here," Kim Ling said, picking up speed. "A bargain at two bucks a ride."

"You said nothing in New York was cheap," Lexi reminded her.

"Wrong. I said everything in New York was *expensive*."

See, it was answers like that that made Lexi want to

scream. But she didn't. She took a calming, cleansing breath and scoped the area instead. Sure enough, the bobbing helmets of horseback riders were visible just beyond a thick row of trees. Kevin must have noticed them too. He was suddenly clinging onto Lexi's dangling backpack strap.

"Where're we going?" he asked Kim Ling. "I mean, just 'cause I took a picture of a couple of horses—"

"—doesn't mean we know how to ride," Lexi finished. "Don't we need, like, special boots—and an insurance policy?"

"You guys don't ride at home out there in Amish country?" Kim Ling asked, her neon flip-flops kicking up dirt.

"It's not Amish!" Lexi said. "And no."

"Doesn't matter."

"How could it not—?"

"Because I'm not talking about those horses, Patty Paranoia." Kim Ling pointed across the road to a clump of vendors in front of some round brick structure. "I'm talking about *those* horses. Let's go. My treat!" Once again, she took off with no group consensus. And once again, Lexi and Kevin followed her. To the Central Park Carousel?

What a relief! For Lexi anyway. But she wasn't exactly sure how Kevin would react.

"This goes a lot faster than your average carousel," Kim Ling had to go and say when they met up with her at the ticket booth. "A *lot* faster. And no brass ring. That's 'cause they don't want kids reaching for it and busting chins."

"What?" Kevin turned that greenish shade again. "I don't know about this."

"C'mon, Kev, it'll be fun."

"Geez, man up!" Kim Ling said to him, handing three tickets to the ticket-taker. "It's not like it's a mechanical bull—it's a baby ride."

That remark got Kevin unstuck somehow and he followed the girls onto the carousel platform with the enthusiasm of someone boarding the *Titanic*.

"That's what they said about the Haunted Mansion ride at Kingsley Park," Lexi whispered to Kim Ling. She helped Kevin onto the smiliest horse with the shiniest gold mane and just as she was about to mount the one next to it, a boy in a plastic fireman hat beat her to it. "Shoot. Are you going to be okay by yourself, Kev, or should I—?"

"Just go already," he said, wrapping his arms around the shiny pole.

"I'll be on this one right in front of you. Hold on tight."

A rinky-dink rendition of "Do You Know the Way to San Jose" began playing loudly and Lexi quickly hopped onto the horse Kim Ling was saving for her. As soon as the carousel came to life, Kim Ling leaned over to her and shouted, "So, what's the scoop?"

"Shhh! Kevin fell off a ride. He was around five. Split his head open."

"No way."

"Way. They had to shut it down and everything. Me

and my parents and a few park people went back into the tunnel . . ." Reliving it made Lexi's mouth go dry. She forced a swallow. "He was wedged between some giant pulleys and cables but I could see the Day-Glo number nine on his football jersey. I was the only one small enough to fit in there—you know, to yank him out."

"Wow. So you're his *yīng xióng*."

"What?" Lexi could barely hear over the music.

"His hero! No wonder he worships you."

"He does?"

"And let me guess—nine has been your lucky number ever since."

Yes! Lexi had never made that connection before. *The girl really does have a brain the size of Utah.* She brushed a clump of curls off her astonished face and leaned closer to Kim Ling, girl genius. "I mean, he tries to hide it but he's still afraid of, like, absolutely everything. Things got worse when Mom died, but Dr. Lucy says he's making steady progress."

"Dr. Lucy?"

"Our therapist. Lucille Dixon."

"Huh. Well, that explains a lot."

Lexi wasn't sure how to take that remark. "Like what?"

"Like, why your brother is over by the cotton-candy stand right now."

Lexi whipped her head around and saw an abandoned horse grinning back at her. A blur of reds, blues, and yellows spun around the girls as they rose up and down, up and down, waiting for the carousel to stop. It made three more revolutions along with Lexi's stomach before the thing finally slowed down. She flew off her horse before it came to a full stop and rushed over to Kevin, who was sitting cross-legged on the ground. Texting?

"What happened?"

"I'm not riding that death machine."

Kim Ling showed up a second later. "You okay?"

"He'll live," Lexi said. "Who're you texting? It'd better not be Dad."

"Billy Campbell. At space camp." He looked up at Kim Ling with a dim glint in his eyes. "We're both gonna be professional astronauts."

"Oh, interesting," Kim Ling said, nodding. "Lemme get this straight. You can't even survive a carousel ride and you wanna be—?"

A sharp look from Lexi shut her right up. "C'mon." Lexi gently pulled Kevin to his feet by both hands and brushed off his bottom. She was being a parent again big time, but oh well. "We should probably get going." But the park was a gigantic green maze. "Hey, Kim, point us toward the street so we can catch a taxi back to the brownstone."

"Yeah, right—by yourselves? Just follow me."

Kim Ling took charge again, which was no big surprise, and led them past a huge fenced-in spread of grass she said was the Sheep Meadow, but it was peppered with sunbathers, not sheep. They kept trudging along the roadway with Kim Ling pointing out every single statue and endless "flora and fauna" until she took a sharp left, shouting, "Behold, Bethesda Terrace!"

"I thought we were going home," Lexi said.

"We're taking the scenic route. *Trés* European, no?"

Not a big selling point, what with her dad trekking through Europe with her evil stepmother, but when Lexi peered down at the courtyard, she was awestruck by the lovely view. The statue of a glorious angel rose from the center of a circular fountain and there was a small river gleaming in the background alive with ducks and rowboats. The sky couldn't have been more crystal blue— and suddenly there was a billow of white.

"Oh, look, a bride. That's good luck!" Lexi pointed to a wedding party posing on the cement staircase leading down to the courtyard. "Who'd get married on a Wednesday?"

"Well, it does have the word *wed* in it," Kim Ling said to no response. "Oh, wait, that's not real. It's a photo shoot. See? The bride's wearing sneakers and there are clothespins cinching the back of the groom's tux. Nothing escapes the well-trained eye of an investigative journalist."

"How exciting!" Now this was the New York City Lexi had in mind. She did a quick check on Kevin, who was back to quasi-normal, doing his own photo shoot of breakdancers behind them, and returned her gaze to the model bride. "Wouldn't you love to get married in a beautiful dress like that?"

"Who said I want to get married at all?"

A loud blast of music turned the girls' heads. There was a scraggly man on a beat-up bicycle pulling up next to them. He was rapidly changing channels on an old-fashioned radio duct-taped between two whirling pin-wheels on the handlebars. Kim Ling gave Lexi a distorted look of horror.

"Seriously?" Lexi said, trying to keep a straight face and get back to the subject at hand. "You never dream of getting married?"

"I guess we're pretty much antipodes, you and me. Total opposites."

The music was too loud for Lexi to think of anything else to say. She looked down at the photo shoot again just as a wind was lifting the fake bride's veil into a gauzy, white swirl. A picture immediately flashed in Lexi's mind. Her parents' wedding photo. It always used to sit proudly on top of their antique dresser in a sterling silver frame but disappeared when the dreaded day had arrived: the day her father had married Clare.

That wasn't a real wedding, either, as far as Lexi was concerned. A quick, blah ceremony at the Putnam County Courthouse. Clare had carried a bunch of pigmy orchids and worn an icy-blue skintight dress that made her look like a Popsicle. In a moment of panic, she had asked Lexi to lend her the rhinestone hair clip she was wearing. So she did. Reluctantly. "That takes care of something borrowed," Clare had told her. "And my dress is brand new and it's blue—so that's like killing two birds with one stone. Okay, all I need is something old." *Well, you're pretty old,* Lexi had thought. *Now as far as killing things with stones . . .*

Classical music blasted to a static-filled finale on the strange man's bike-radio and a newscaster's voice came on. "This is Marcia Whitaker in for Lloyd Marsh. The FBI remains baffled . . ."

With a watchful eye on Kevin, Lexi was pondering how her new life would be with Clare as her stepmother. *Just like Cinderella's. Before the magic and the prince.* "Kevin Andrew McGill!" she called out. "Don't wander off!"

"Shhh!" Kim Ling hissed. "I wanna hear this."

Lexi turned back and quickly honed in on the newscaster's voice.

"—disappeared without a trace. On loan from Egypt's Cairo Museum, the astonishingly rare jewelry that experts believe can be traced back to Cleopatra herself was to be featured in the Queen of the Nile exhibit at the Metropolitan Museum of Art this summer, now postponed indefinitely. Early this morning, Cairo authorities announced a reward of one million Egyptian pounds—roughly, one hundred and eighty thousand U.S. dollars, to anyone with information leading to the recovery of the irreplaceable artifacts."

Adrenaline rushed through Lexi so swiftly, she thought she would launch clear out of Central Park.

6

NOBODY HAS TO KNOW

That weird man appearing out of nowhere with a radio blasting *that* particular news story at *that* particular time—it was a definite sign that it was time for Lexi to face facts. She had to spill her guts to someone about what she had overheard in the Whispering Gallery before she burst. It couldn't be Kevin, for obvious reasons. And it couldn't be Kim Ling—could it? No, it just couldn't! Then again, she had already told her about Kevin and Kingsley Park. And the girl was megasmart. Maybe she'd know what to do.

"Kim," she said, dragging her behind a nearby ice-cream cart, "swear on your life that you won't repeat what I'm about to tell you to a single, solitary soul."

"Have you lost it? Let go of—"

"Swear!"

With one hand on her heart and the other on a stack of invisible bibles, Kim Ling swore to secrecy and Lexi quickly filled her in on the Whispering Gallery, the mysterious men in black, their plot to bury the stolen jewels in Grand Central Station. Every single detail. *Such a relief!* Then again, watching Kim Ling's face light up the way it did, maybe it was a big mistake. The would-be journalist's mind was obviously already spinning—probably wondering where to score a few pickaxes and night-vision goggles double-quick.

"But how could you not report it?" was the first thing out of Kim Ling's mouth. Not a hint of concern for Lexi's safety or well-being. "Don't you see the exigency of the situation? Urgency?"

Another ten-dollar word. And the definition thrown in afterward felt like an insult. "I know what exigency means." *Now* she did.

"You have to call the cops. Immediately! Never mind the reward money, it's your civic duty. Where's your cell?"

Lexi started clawing through her backpack. "Uh, it's back at the apartment, I think. I could use Kevin's."

"Here, use mine." Kim Ling instantly produced her phone, jabbed the power button, and shoved it over to Lexi. "Dial four-one-one. Ask for the number of the NYPD."

"I know that." She stared at the phone. "But then what do I tell them?"

"Your shoe size," Kim Ling spurted, cocking her head. "Just tell them what you told me. You want me to do it? Here, gimme back my phone."

"No, I can do it."

Lexi kept zipping and unzipping her backpack,

rehearsing what she'd say in her head while she waited for the operator to put her through.

"Fifth Precinct, Sergeant Capaletti," a gruff voice said through the phone. "And tell 'em not to drown it in mayo dis time, Paulie. Hello?"

Lexi went completely rigid except for her heart galloping up into her throat.

"Hi—uh, hello? Yes, I'm calling about the Queen of—"

"Dis is Manhattan. I'll patch ya tru to a precinct in Queens."

"No, officer, the Queen of the Nile exhibit. You know, Cleopatra—her stolen jewelry—it's in all the news. I think I might have some, uh, information on where it could be. Possibly."

"Yeah, you and everybody else in da five boroughs. The phones've been ringin' off da hook ever since dey announced dat hefty reward." There was a sigh of disgust and a rustling of papers. "Name?"

"Lexi. Alexandra, actually, Alexandra McGill. M-C-G-I-double L."

Kim Ling's elbow stabbed her side. "Never give them your name!"

"Now you tell me!"

"Go 'head, Miss McGill."

"Okay. Well, let's see." She took a shaky breath and conjured up the scene in her mind. "When my brother and I arrived in Grand Central on Monday, I accidentally overheard these guys talking about burying jewels there—down in some abandoned train station. It sounded crazy but they said something about having them stripped and shipped somewhere. I forget where. Oh, man— Venezuela, Carbonara, something like that."

"Carbonara is a pasta sauce," Kim Ling said, rolling her eyes.

"How many men? Can ya describe 'em?" The sergeant's voice changed. He sounded genuinely interested.

"Two. I couldn't see them very well, though, 'cause too many people were passing by. But they were dressed all in black—uh, the criminals, not the people. Average height and weight, I guess." She sensed her voice getting higher and higher and willed herself to relax. "Oh! One guy was British and bald with, like, one of those little chin-beard thingies."

"Soul patch?" Kim Ling offered. She pressed her sweaty cheek against Lexi's, listening in.

"A soul patch—oh, and orange glasses, I think. And the other was wearing a Yankees cap. They were both drinking coffee—well, I guess it was coffee. There was steam."

"Bald . . . British . . . Why didn't ya report dis to duh police immediately?"

"Uh, I didn't know I was supposed to. So—like—I can't get in trouble, can I?"

There was a pause. "How old are ya, Miss McGill? Ya sound really young."

Lexi grimaced and covered the phone with her free hand. "He wants to know how old I am," she whispered to Kim Ling.

"He can't ask you that!"

"Well, he just did. Don't I have the right to remain silent?"

A Frisbee scraped to the ground a few feet away from Lexi and two giggly girls on Rollerblades came chasing after it, crashing into each other.

Lexi put the phone back to her ear and heard Sergeant Capaletti squawking, "Hello? Hello?"

"Yes, uh, sergeant, I'm still here." She summoned up what she thought was a mature, confident voice. "I'm twenty. One."

Just then the man on the souped-up bike with the radio pedaled off past the Rollerbladers and they squealed with laughter.

"And I'm the pope!" Sergeant Capaletti growled. "Listen, kid, dare's a lotta crime in dis city and we don't have time for crank calls! And to answer your question, yeah, you could get in *very* serious trouble for—"

"Oops, tunnel. You're breaking up." Lexi did her best imitation of static and tossed the phone back to Kim Ling like a hot potato. "Oh, I can hardly breathe! He thought that was a crank call—I am such a bad liar. So, now what?"

Kim Ling's face tightened. "I'd better not get busted for this, red." She threw her phone into her backpack. "It's *my* info that just showed up on their caller ID. Snaggit!"

Just as she had predicted, Lexi regretted blurting out her story to Kim Ling in the first place. What was she thinking? Barely five minutes had passed and they were already possibly in trouble with the NYPD. Very serious trouble, according to Sergeant Capaletti.

"Well, Kim, if the cops ever follow up on this, which they won't, just give them my name and number and I'll take the rap, okay?"

Kevin appeared out of nowhere, sizing them up through his camera lens. "Rap for what?"

"Making a crank call to the cops," Kim Ling said matter-of-factly. She stuck out a flexed hand. "And do not take my picture or you die."

"You made a crank call to the cops, Lex?" Kevin lowered his camera while his eyebrows shot up behind his bangs. "Why'd you do that?"

"No, it was legit," Kim Ling answered before Lexi could, "but apparently they thought it was a crank. Your sister was just being a standup citizen—reporting those jewel thieves in Grand Central."

"You saw jewel thieves in Grand Central?"

Lexi's mouth fell open. *Shut up, shut up, shut up!* The words had come spewing out of Kim Ling so easily and after taking an oath of secrecy. Talk about untrustworthy! Talk about insensitive! Hadn't she just spilled her guts to her about Kevin's fear of absolutely everything? Hadn't she even mentioned Dr. Lucy? Didn't Miss Know-It-All think before she opened her trap?

"It's no biggie, Kev." Lexi tried looking easy-breezy—as easy-breezy as she possibly could with her left eye twitching. "I overheard two guys in the Whispering Gallery talking about some missing jewelry or something. It was probably nothing."

"Are your curls wound too tight?" Kim Ling said. "That's not what you said two seconds ago."

"That's it. We're outta here." Lexi grabbed Kevin by the hand and hurried away through a flurry of pigeons.

"Hey," Kim Ling called out after them. "Where're you going?"

"Away from you!" Lexi shot back.

"But—what just happened here? Did I miss something?"

Lexi turned abruptly. "Think about it, genius." She looked pointedly to Kevin, then back at Kim Ling, who stood with arms crossed, tapping her heel. "I guess you just don't get the *contingency* of the situation, huh?"

"Exigency," Kim Ling said. "And that's east, dude. You want west if you're going to your aunt's."

Lexi did an awkward about-face, whipping Kevin around like a confused puppy on a leash. She flew past Kim Ling and headed toward the jagged skyline jetting up over the treetops. *How could someone be so smart and stupid at the same time?*

Kevin immediately bombarded Lexi with questions and she considering flat-out lying for his sake. But no— she would fill him in on what she had witnessed in the Whispering Gallery as truthfully as possible without making his head explode.

"Okay, it's true, Kev. I did overhear two men talking

about jewels or something in Grand Central. I tried reporting the details to the police just now but they weren't buying it. That's it. End of story."

It was her second recount that day, third if you considered her conversation with Sergeant Capaletti, and her story had changed slightly with each retelling. Was it really as frightening as the version she had told Kim Ling or as tame as the version she had painted for her brother?

"These robbers—did they see you see them?"

Lexi shook her head no and shrugged, which was meant to be as murky an answer as it seemed.

Kevin was eerily silent after that, all the way from Central Park West to West End Avenue. Lexi guessed he was either doing Dr. Lucy's self-calming exercises or quietly coming unglued like she was. When they arrived at the brownstone and Lexi was digging in her backpack for the extra set of keys her aunt had given her that morning, she had a sudden thought. "Whatever you do," she told Kevin, "don't tell Aunt Roz about any of this when she gets home, okay? She'd totally wig out. That goes for my stolen wallet too. And don't be blabbing to Dad either, 'cause you know you'll want to. Or his wife."

"Clare. She has a name."

"Whatever. Nobody has to know."

She had a funny feeling her last four words were going to be the mantra for the summer.

7

DANGER OR OPPORTUNITY

"I got the part!" Aunt Roz announced, bursting through the door. "Can you believe it? Oh, you kids must've brought me good luck."

It was as if everything went from gloom-and-doom to party central the instant she crossed the threshold of Apartment 5F. At least someone would be in a good mood.

"It's another scorcher out there. The statue of Whoopi Goldberg on display outside of Madame Tussauds wax museum was actually starting to melt." She dropped her shopping bags on the coffee table, then trotted over to the air conditioner, cranked it up, and let the air blow down the top of her dress. "You know, guys, when I got your message to meet you back here, I kept calling and calling—no answer. What happened?"

"That's 'cause I left my phone on your bathroom sink," Lexi said, which was true.

Kevin dug his out of his pocket and checked it. "No juice. No wonder."

"Well, let's not have that happen again, okay? Thank goodness you had Kimmy—and that City Camp bus."

Lexi turned to Kevin and subtly mimed locking her lips and tossing away the key—just as a quick reminder. He gave her a look like she had completely lost her mind and together they followed their aunt into the kitchen.

"Apparently rehearsals started a few weeks ago, but the woman they'd originally cast as Amanda Wingfield landed a soap and dropped out. Boom! Just like that." Aunt Roz grabbed dishes from the cabinet and began debagging the food cartons. Their heavy, spicy smells were instantly unlocked. "So, they needed a quick replacement. Enter *moi*. They said I was perfect for the part! I am over the moon."

"Congrats, Aunt Roz," Kevin said with the enthusiasm of a squashed bug.

"I thought we'd have a little celebration. I hope you kids like Thai food, 'cause I certainly do—even though it always ends up on my thighs. Get it? Oh, and I picked up a scrumptious cheesecake from the Stage Deli for dessert— strawberry—to die for. I can't wait to tell you everything that happened but I want to hear every single detail of your first day of camp, too."

Camp? That was the last thing on Lexi's mind. Food was next to last. But she knew if she didn't eat, neither would Kevin, so she forced herself to nibble off a bite of something called beef satay. "Mmm. This is pretty good."

"Pretty good?" Aunt Roz echoed. "It's heaven on a stick! Here. Try," she said, scooping food from the various cartons and sloshing it onto plates as if she were attempting to beat the clock in the speed round of some cooking show challenge. "The shrimp pad Thai is shrimpalicious. And the yum woon sen chicken—more like yum *swoon* sen chicken!"

She was right. Lexi and Kevin gobbled up the exotic food like it was their last meal on earth, and it wasn't long before they were busting at the seams but still fighting over the last curry puff. You couldn't get that stuff in Cold Spring.

Thankfully, with Aunt Roz's nonstop monologue about her day, Lexi and Kevin hardly got a chance to talk about theirs, and Lexi's haunting thoughts of thieves, police, and civic duty were finally petering out. That is, until they ended up in front of the TV watching one of Aunt Roz's favorite shows, *The Streets of New York*. Murder, mystery, mayhem. No matter. Kevin had conked out on the couch almost immediately and Lexi wasn't too far behind, fading fast from a serious cheesecake overdose.

"I'm glad he passed out, 'cause this isn't really appropriate for young children. Your father would not approve," Aunt Roz whispered. She was painting her toenails now, curled up in her mammoth massage chair: the one piece of non-country furniture that stood out like a black faux-leather thumb. "It's such a smart show, though. Topics ripped from today's headlines. That's their gimmick."

"Huh."

"Sometimes they come up with some pretty convoluted endings, but anyway . . . Did I tell you I'm doing extra-work for them in a few days? You know, that's when TV shows or movies have actors milling around in the background to make the scene look realistic. They needed a bunch of female middle-aged joggers. So that should be interesting, right? Kinda fun?"

"Mm-hmm."

"It helps pay the bills. I just hope I'm not going to be a complete basket case, what with *Streets of New York*, my part-time job at the New York Ballet, and rehearsals for the musical. I mean, honestly, it's absolute madness. Feast or famine, as they say."

"Yup."

"Oh, but Amanda Wingfield is such a lovely role. And it means the world to me that you and Kevin will be there on opening night. You did pack a nice outfit, didn't you, Alexandra? Alex . . . ?"

❦

Apparently, Aunt Roz was too "over the moon" to remember to set the alarm clock and everyone woke up the next morning a half hour late—and a little queasy. Lexi and Kevin skipped showers, threw on their identical puke-green City Camp T-shirts, grabbed their backpacks, and ran out the door with Aunt Roz at their heels, forcing granola bars on them.

"I don't care if you're not hungry, you have to eat something. Take it! Take it!"

They were almost run over by a cardboard-box carrying man on the first floor who came flying out of Mr. Carney's smelly apartment—and without so much as a "pardon me." Then he had the nerve to race them down the front steps of the brownstone so he could catch his precious cab. Lexi thought it was the same guy they had seen two days ago, but it was definitely a different weirdo. This one was covered in tattoos.

"Well, excuse *you!*" Aunt Roz called out after him. "Lord," she said, turning to Lexi and Kevin, "that cat-man sure has a lot of strange people coming and going at all hours. Kimmy says they're his relatives but I don't know." She looked back at the brownstone. "Where is she anyway? Is she meeting us at the City Camp bus?"

"Oh, that's long gone," Lexi said, checking her watch. It turned out to be the perfect excuse—this waking-up-late thing. "It's already nine twenty. The bus leaves at—"

"A quarter to," Kevin finished, lying through his teeth. "Kim Ling probably left."

"Well, we can cab it." Aunt Roz sucked her teeth, looking toward the intersection. "We'll be able to get one quicker if we spread out," she said, which led her into a mini-lesson in Taxicab Hailing 101. "C'mon, you kids have to learn *some*-time. Arms nice 'n' high like you mean it. Good! Okay, I'll man the corner and we'll see who can flag down a cab first. Ready? Go!"

Aunt Roz's high heels went scraping down the sidewalk and Lexi and Kevin were left on the curb, looking like Tweedledum and Tweedledumber waiting to be called on in class. No cabs in sight, but a shiny black Lincoln Town Car, like the one they had seen on Sunday, turned off West End and circled the block like a hungry shark. *Spooky.*

"Geez, you're such a girl." It was Kim Ling on the front stoop, mimicking Lexi and snorting. "It's not like you're working the Miss America runway or anything. No self-respecting cabby's gonna pick you up with that wimpy wave."

Lexi's cheeks were instantly on fire, trying to think of a quick comeback. *Oh, yeah? Well, at least I don't boss people around like a drill sergeant. At least I think before I open my mouth. At least I don't dress like a nearsighted clown* . . . Nothing came to her that was acid enough, and the window of opportunity for a comeback had quickly passed.

"Truce, okay?" Kim Ling said to the back of Lexi's head. "I get it now. But yesterday when you swore me to secrecy, I thought certain parties already knew about the Grand Central thing—namely, your B-R-O-T-H-E-R."

"I'm ten," Kevin said. "I can spell 'brother'!"

"I mean, I assumed he was right there with you at the time." Kim Ling paused to slather her mouth in lip balm.

"My bad. But next time be specific. The devil's in the details."

"Maybe in a perfect world." Lexi had no idea what that meant but at least it was something.

A shrill whistle came from the corner. From Aunt Roz? She was motioning to them wildly with one hand and opening the door of a crookedly parked cab with the other. Lexi, Kevin, and Kim Ling ran up the block and scrambled into the backseat. "Well, look who showed up after all. Good morning, Kimmy."

"Morning."

"Forty-Fourth and Park, please," Aunt Roz instructed the driver. She would be riding shotgun on the other side of the Plexiglas partition—probably talking the guy's ear off.

"Sweet," Kim Ling said and slammed the cab door. "I can fill you guys in on my latest stroke of genius."

"Oh, *plgggh!*"

Lexi's raspberry showered over poor Kevin, who was wincing as if he had just been doused by a fire hose. She reached over him to fasten his seat belt, which he insisted on doing himself, so she focused on fastening her own.

"Listen, we're all in this together now," Kim Ling said in a hushed voice, "like it or not. And I was thinking— there's this major paper I'm doing for a citywide journalism contest in the fall and I need a killer topic. It's, like, all I'm living for these days. Anyway, can you imagine the piece I could deliver if we actually *found* Cleopatra's

stolen jewels buried in Grand Central Station by ourselves? We're talking Pulitzer."

"Don't pay attention to her, Kev. She's obviously lost
her mind."

He was already absorbed in the LCD screen of his
digital camera anyway, reviewing the zillions of New
York photos he had taken so far.

"We can at least give it a shot," Kim Ling went on. "A
secret mission. I mean, how insane would that be?"

"Totally insane. But not in a good way."

Kevin elbowed Lexi. "Hey, look." He held up his camera,
showing her a picture of Aunt Roz in a silly pose on the
LCD screen. "I took this in the Whispering Gallery the day
we arrived," he said, lowering his voice to a whisper.
"There's a man's hand in the background holding a cardboard cup. See? Is that one of the perps you saw?"

Lexi bit her bottom lip, leaning in closer. "Mmm.
Possibly. Yeah, they were definitely drinking coffee or
something."

"So, watch what happens when I zoom in." He worked
a round button on the top of the camera until the photo
grew three times its original size. *"Inky fingers!* That might
be a clue. Let's think. What kind of person would have
inky fingers?"

"An octopus wrangler," Kim Ling said, zeroing in on the
picture.

"I guess anyone can have inky fingers, huh?" Kevin
thought about it for a second. "Teacher . . . writer . . ."

"Leaky pen salesman," Kim Ling finished, finally buckling her seat belt. "We'll keep it in mind moving forward—but for now, put that thing away and let's get back to my genius plan—"

"No," Lexi said simply, and turned her head to stare out the window.

A screaming ambulance paused the conversation and Kim Ling waited for the sirens to die down to regain Lexi's attention. "Excuse me?"

"If *you* have a death wish, Kim, that's your problem, but, shucks, just leave us poor little ol' Amish folk from Little House on the Prairie out of it, okay?" She had attempted a Southern accent—it sounded more Swedish.

Kim Ling's head fell against the seatback with a noisy sigh. "In Chinese, the character for danger is the same as the one for opportunity," she said matter-of-factly. "That's all I have to say."

If only. The girl still wouldn't let up, and by the time they were de-cabbing in front of the YMCA, Lexi had had enough. She mentally agreed that they couldn't just pretend the whole thing never happened, but that didn't mean they had to risk their lives. After all, this was the real world— not some crime novel.

"Have fun today, kids, but be careful!" Aunt Roz said, rolling down the window. "Okay, Leonard, next stop, Greenwich Village."

Kevin waved good-bye as the cab took off, and his cheery smile withered into a thin line of concern. "Maybe we should try calling the cops again. We can tell them about the inky fingers."

"Um, but from a pay phone this time," Lexi reluctantly agreed. "And, Kim, you can do the talking since you sound more mature."

"C-W-O-T. Colossal Waste of Time. If they didn't buy your story yesterday, they're not going to buy it today—with or without inky fingers. We have to take things into our own hands."

"Or not," Lexi shot back. She latched onto Kevin's arm and led him toward the steps of the Y, avoiding the hordes of weary-eyed people trudging along Fifth Avenue. To Lexi's surprise, Kim Ling stayed put, leaning against a mailbox, undoing her ponytail and reconstructing it at the top of her head to form a black-and-turquoise hair fountain. Eventually, she zigzagged through the crowd and stood right in Lexi's face, flashing her fiery eyes. "Think. Of. The. Reward."

"What reward?" Kevin asked. His eyebrows jumped. "There's a *reward*?"

"A hundred and eighty thousand," Lexi told him, as if it were half a cheese sandwich and a pat on the back. She must have left that part out when she filled him in on their way home from Central Park. "But only if we end up tracking the jewels—or the criminals."

"Which we will!" Kim Ling said.

"You don't know. This is just all too crazy."

"It *is* kind of out there," Kevin agreed.

"Look, you guys can have most of the reward money if it comes to that. Sixty-forty. I'm in this strictly for the story. That journalism contest? The winner gets a personal tour of CBS News. I would totally *plotz.*"

"What's *plotz?*" Kevin asked.

"It's Yiddish. It means to faint dead away."

Lexi shook her head. "That's exactly what I'm trying to avoid."

"In Chinese, the character for danger is the same as the one for oppor—"

"Stop saying that!"

Kim Ling growled in frustration and pretended to bang her head against the YMCA door. Repeatedly. "All right, forget it, you win," she finally said, after getting no reaction whatsoever; then she cautiously opened the door a crack and peeked inside. "Hey, no one's even here! They probably already left for the park." She let the door close and leaned into the doorframe, staring at the McGills and cracking her knuckles one by one. "So, here we are again with time to kill—déjà vu. Grand Central's still right over there, you know, red." *Crack.* "We can check for your wallet. Wanna, huh?" *Crack-crack.* "C'mon, you know you wanna."

Lexi really did want to—and really didn't, both at the same time. Without intending it, she found herself cross-armed and crazy-eyed in an unofficial staring contest with Kim Ling—one that might have lasted for days if a giant pigeon hadn't zoomed out of nowhere and skimmed Kevin's head.

"Incoming!" he yelled, shielding his face. "Man, that thing flew right at me!"

"Pigeons and bike messengers stop at nothing," Kim Ling warned.

That was when Lexi saw it. Another long feather whirling down from the sky like a tiny ballerina. Spinning, spinning, spinning, until it landed gracefully at her feet. Luminously white. Pointing directly toward Grand Central Terminal.

8

LOST AND DUMBFOUNDED

Lexi would have probably stayed put at the Y, waiting till doomsday for the campers to return, if it hadn't been for that white feather, which was now pressed gently against her ankle, safely hidden beneath her sock. Her brain told her this didn't make any sense at all—this weird belief that her mom was somehow guiding her along with feathers, but her gut told her that possible signs from the great beyond should never be ignored. Her gut always won out.

"Spare some change to feed my babies?"

A raggedy black woman was slumped on the sidewalk near the entrance of Grand Central shaking a paper cup. Lexi's heart sank. Even though it was over ninety degrees outside, the woman was wrapped in a blanket and wearing a thick nubby ski cap.

What babies? Lexi wondered. The woman looked way too old to have babies. There was a stroller next to her but it was loaded with giant plastic bags of what looked like empty soda cans. Lexi took a few steps closer and spied a striped paw. *Awww.* A pair of cats was on the blanket, snuggled tightly as two puzzle pieces.

"C'mon, hang tough," Kim Ling said. "You can't let these panhandlers get to you or they'll suck you dry. And we're walking—and we're walking . . ."

"Just this once." Lexi figured with the run of bad luck she was having, a random act of kindness couldn't hurt. So, in spite of Kim Ling tugging her arm halfway out of its socket, she dropped a quarter into the cup—and a pack of sugarless gum.

The old woman smiled up at her with the kindest expression. "Pretty hair."

"What? Oh. Thank you so much."

The momentary high Lexi got from the unexpected compliment plummeted the second she stepped foot into the train terminal. And by the time she, Kevin, and Kim Ling had reached the service window of the Lost and Found Department, a dreary room lined with endless metal shelves of gray plastic bins, her head was spinning. It happened to be on the same lower level as the deep-fried-smelling dining concourse and the Whispering Gallery—a recipe for nausea. Lexi twisted her opal nine times for luck while she peered through the window, watching a portly man search through a rainbow of wallets strewn across a table. According to his nametag, he was Burl T. Gibbs.

"Don't see no pink ones right off, but we've got a ton. Over half a million people pass through the terminal on any given day and that's a fact. Oh, hold on now." He held up a sparkly dolphin-shaped coin purse with jiggly eyes, looking hopeful. "This it?"

"Uh, no," Lexi said, embarrassed he could think such a thing.

"I'll bet you get all kinds of bizarre stuff in here, huh?" Kim Ling was craning her neck to see inside the room. "Ever get, like, a glass eye—or a live ferret?"

"Or ancient Egyptian jewelry?" Lexi asked with a curious glance.

Kim Ling swatted her.

"Can't say that I have. But one lady left her dead husband's ashes in a pickle jar on a train once." He looked up, scratching his bristly chin. His bushy white eyebrows danced over his half-glasses like two white caterpillars. "And just last week we found a pair of dentures in the terminal."

"Gross!" Kevin said. "For real?"

"You can't make this stuff up."

Lexi blocked out the conversation. The last thing she wanted to hear was stories about trains—and death. *And why do they have to call it a terminal anyway? Such a depressing word.* She kept checking over her shoulder for any signs of the jewel thieves, even though it was a little farfetched to think they would still be hanging out in the station, especially if they had already carried out their plot. Still, her brain kept replaying their whispered conversation over and over again, like a Disney DVD.

"A real human ear?" Kevin's voice cut through. "No way!"

"Some plastic surgeon from Westchester left it on a Metro North. We never did find out if it wound up on the patient's head or shriveled up like an old potato chip."

"Ew!" Lexi blurted. "Okay, I think we're done here. I hate to say it, but I think my wallet's gone for good."

"I hate to say it," Kim Ling echoed, "but I think you're right."

"Well, you kids keep on your toes, you hear? Lots of sticky fingers in this town." Mr. Gibbs knocked all of the wallets back into their plastic bin with a single arm swipe. "Feel free to come back and check anytime, 'cause we get new ones in on a daily—"

"Excuse us. Mr. Burl T. Gibbs?"

Two men in black were suddenly standing right next to Lexi at the window. They seemed to have appeared out of nowhere. She almost *plotzed.*

"I'm Burl Gibbs. How can I help you gentlemen?"

Holding her breath, Lexi could see the guy nearest her quickly flash an ID card at Mr. Gibbs, then slip it back into his suit jacket—just like they did on *The Streets of New York.*

"FBI," the man said flatly. "We have a few questions for you, if you have a minute."

And Lexi could breathe again. Sort of. At least they were on the right side of the law.

"Certainly. Come in, come in." Mr. Gibbs opened the door next to the service window and let the two men into the room. "We were just finishing up, right, kids?"

"Uh, right," Kim Ling said when nothing came out of Lexi or Kevin. "Thanks."

The door closed but the service window was still open. As usual, Lexi and Kevin followed Kim Ling's lead and as nonchalantly as possible plastered themselves against the wall, hanging on every word coming from inside the Lost and Found Department.

FBI: We understand you were friends with a former Grand Central employee. Benjamin Deets? That name ring a bell?

GIBBS: A number of years ago. Not friends exactly—more like workplace buddies. We'd share a cup of coffee every now and again. Nice enough guy. Used to work in security, if memory serves, but we never stayed in touch. Why? Has he been accused of something?

FBI: We're just doing a routine background check, sir. We have reason to believe he may be connected with the Cleopatra jewel heist that's in all the news.

GIBBS: Oh, sure, I'm familiar! My, my, ain't that something? So, are you saying Ben is a suspect?

FBI: That's not what we're saying exactly . . .

The shutters of the window closed with a bang and Lexi, Kevin, and Kim Ling bolted. They scurried through the marble halls, faster than if they were running on hot coals. The bustling dining concourse with gobs of people standing in tangled lines slowed them down and somehow they got trapped in a mass of hotdog-munching tourists.

"Benjamin Deets," Kim Ling mumbled to herself, scribbling away on a small spiral notebook she had fished out of her backpack. "Suspicious Grand Central employee!"

"*Former* employee," Kevin said with a raised finger.

"Ah, right. In security, no less, which makes total sense. I mean, if anyone's gonna know the ins and outs of an abandoned train station—"

"It'd be him," Kevin finished. "I wonder if the jewels are already buried under the tracks."

"There's only one way to find out—"

"Wait for the story on the news like everyone else," Lexi said, giving Kim Ling one of those *looks that kill* that people talk about. Didn't she realize Kevin was already getting way too involved for his own good? Lexi grabbed his arm and broke free from the tourist trap and Kim Ling. "Now, let's return to the real world and get our butts back to camp."

"Speaking of which—" Kim Ling was instantly in her face, rapidly clicking the top of her pen with her thumb. "What do you say we skip it entirely for today and do a little private investigating ourselves instead? I mean, missing one day at Camp Loser is no big deal—and we're already here, so . . ."

"Ugh," Lexi groaned, "I knew you'd try and pull something."

"Nobody has to know."

And I knew those four words would come back to haunt me!

"Listen, Lexi, we don't know how much the FBI knows at this point, but this much I know—if they *do* know something, security's only gonna get ten times worse, ten times sooner."

"What?"

"All I'm saying is, we have to act fast, so come on."

"No," Lexi said. "No bullying. This is serious stuff. All three of us have to agree on everything from now on or forget it. Right, Kev?"

"Yeah, we definitely should vote." His cheeks were already a splotchy red and getting redder by the second. "And I—seriously, I'm thinking camp. I mean, even if the kids already left for the park, we could probably still catch up, right? It might be fun."

"Dude," Kim Ling said with a disgusted sigh. "They do the same mind-numbingly boring stuff every year." She squatted down, hands to thighs, and looked him straight in the eye. "Day one is always this moronic nature hunt looking for hummingbirds and chipmunks. I've done it three years in a row and never saw one freakin' chipmunk. A couple of rats, one vicious badger, but not a single chipmunk. Then they separate the groups. The blues go row boating— that's the older kids."

"And the greens?" Kevin asked, blinking up at her.

"Carousel. So what's your final answer, short stuff? Tick tock."

Kevin's eyes were jetting back and forth like a ping-pong game on fast-forward. "Uh, I can't think—I have to go to the bathroom. Number one. Wait—yeah, number one."

"Now?" Lexi squawked. "Who knows where the bathrooms even are in this place? I'm a potential eyewitness to a crime plot—what if someone sees me—"

"Calm down, I'll bring him. Just sit over there and breathe." Kim Ling pointed to an empty spot at the end of a crowded wooden bench right behind them. "You can decide what you want to do today, okay?"

"Fine." Lexi parked herself on what looked like a long, giant church pew and removed her backpack. "Just make it fast."

"And don't look so worried, red. I'm not gonna kidnap your brother and sell him for spare parts. Or. Am. I?" Kim Ling laughed like Count Dracula and swept Kevin away in her invisible cape.

Not remotely funny. "Wait!" Lexi called out, motioning them back. "My hair stands out like a flare in the dark—I need coverage." And she snatched Kevin's baseball cap, piled her hair on top of her head, and screwed on the cap as best she could. "Okay, go, go, go." They barely took off a second time when Lexi called them back again. "Kim, do you by any chance have any lip gloss? What if people think I'm a boy?"

"Whoa." Kim Ling slowly led Kevin away, shaking her head. "You really *are* a Miss America."

Lexi watched them disappear around a giant pillar, still jamming telltale curls into the swollen cap. *Miss America. Hmph. Like I'd be caught dead wearing a bikini with high heels.* She noticed her reflection in a glass-covered poster on the opposite wall and used it as a makeshift mirror. TAKE A TRAIN AND TRANSCEND TIME, the vintage poster read, and had a picture of a smiling woman in a white suit—from the forties maybe—holding a suitcase and boarding the train. Even though Lexi was surrounded by gobs of people, she suddenly felt very alone. She hugged her backpack to her chest, gazing down at the endless parade of shoes passing by—sneakers . . . stilettos . . . sandals . . . Oxfords—until they became a liquid blur.

"I'm so glad you came to Atlantic City with me!"

She heard her mother's voice in her head with such clarity it made her heart quake.

"Just in time for the Show Me Your Shoes Parade," her mother had said, pulling nine-year-old Lexi along the crowded boardwalk. "I've never even heard of it before, have you, cookie?"

"Nuh-uh. We lucked out!"

All the Miss America contestants had been perched on the trunks of shiny convertibles rolling along the boardwalk real slow. Spotlights on the hoods were aimed at them. Onlookers shouting, "Show us your shoes!" The beauty queens hiked up their glittery gowns to reveal a little leg.

So corny. Lexi was on tiptoes, straining to see over heads, when she felt a sudden jerk.

"Agh! What was—oh, Lex, my heel. It's stuck between the darn slats!"

It was happening all around them, too—ladies getting their high heels caught in the boardwalk, squealing like alligators were nipping at their ankles. A minefield. Finally, Lexi's mom yanked her pump free with a grunt.

"Hey, Mom." Lexi readied her digital camera. "Show us your shoe!"

Her mother dangled her gnarled high heel between two fingers like it was a smelly dead fish and stuck out her tongue. Lexi roared and snapped a picture. It was definitely a keeper.

Even after taking forty-eight killer shots of the Miss America pageant itself, this photo was still her absolute favorite. That was what she had decided during the first half of their long train ride home.

"Saltwater taffy?" her mom asked, digging through her Fralinger's souvenir tin as the train chugged along. "There're some chocolate ones left, hon, but they're going fast."

Lexi shook her head. Barely. She had gone from rating her photos to studying the contestant bios in her giant souvenir program.

"All these girls have the same crazy-white teeth, Mom—and talent. Look! Classical piano, tap dance, vocal performance . . ." She flipped through the pages. "Plus, they all know ways to save the world. End world hunger, stop global warming—"

"Don't tell me you want to try out for Miss America someday."

"No way." She thought for a second. "But, Mom—shouldn't I start learning how to do *something* soon?"

"Oh, come on. You do cheerleading." She gave Lexi's knee a little jiggle. "And weren't you even voted Best Personality at cheer camp last summer?"

"Everyone got a prize. They just couldn't come up with anything—better."

"I give up." Her mom snapped the lid on the tin of saltwater taffy and shoved it into her tote with a throaty sigh. "You're nine, for heaven's sake. You have plenty of time to discover your hidden talents."

Lexi's shoulders had stiffened against the vinyl seatback. *But what if I don't—what if I wind up being ordinary?* It was true that some people were late bloomers. But if something special was growing inside Lexi other than maybe a perky personality, wouldn't she at least have seen some buds by now?

A squealing baby snapped Lexi back into reality. *Or now?* she thought, folding her arms across her chest. Suddenly Grand Central Terminal was alive as ever and buzzing all around her.

"So, what's it gonna be?" Kim Ling asked, jutting out her hip. "Hello? Earth to Lex! The kid's vein has been drained and I've convinced him to stay. So, that's two votes yea, which leaves it all up to you."

"Huh. Really, Kev?"

"Yeah. She twisted my arm."

"Not literally," Kim Ling said. "Well? Are we heading back to the dork convention, aka City Camp, or are you up for doing something extraordinary?"

What was it about that word? Lexi, who had one time in her life spent a full twelve minutes deciding between chunky and smooth peanut butter, rose to her feet and answered unblinkingly, "Extraordinary."

"You mean it?" Kim Ling asked. "So you're in?"

"I'm in."

And they sealed the deal with a firm handshake.

DOOR NUMBER THREE

"Okay, red, get me up to speed." Kim Ling unshouldered her backpack and began digging through it. "All you told me in the park was that you heard two guys plotting to bury jewels under an abandoned train track until they can have them stripped and shipped. We need specifics. Here, take my notebook and jot down anything that pops into your mind—no matter how trivial."

As soon as Kim Ling handed Lexi the small spiral notebook and pen, her mind was mud. "Well, let's see. The, uh, guy with the accent said 'bloody' a lot."

"So? Brits say bloody for everything—bloody rain, bloody fog, bloody queen—"

"You said no matter how trivial!"

"Anything specific about the location? Concentrate."

Lexi closed her eyes and tried to relive the mystery men's conversation in her mind. "Track Fifty-one—or Sixty-one. East, I think. Yeah, the East Terminal."

"Write it down."

"I remember they said a few levels below—right." A surge of sour acid shot up Lexi's throat and she swallowed it with a squint. "So, we should probably—I don't know, start by going down as far as we can and head east."

"Okay, nice work. Let's jet! And if anyone asks, you guys are two innocent kids from Cold Spring."

Kevin dug his finger in his ear. "We *are* two innocent kids from Cold Spring."

"See how that works?"

There were no elevators in sight, but Lexi remembered seeing one next to the Oyster Bar and Restaurant. So they flew down the hall past the Whispering Gallery and boarded the first elevator to arrive. It only went down one level, so that was where they got off. With the help of Kevin's official NASA space compass replica, the three-some scuttled eastward down an empty hallway and rounded a shadowy corner, scouring every inch for who knew what. They stopped at an unmarked door. Kim Ling was the only one brave enough to open it and peek inside.

"Ugh! Gross!"

It turned out to be a smelly employee bathroom. But there were two bigger doors right next to it. One of them had a sign that read: DO NOT ENTER. AUTHORIZED PERSONNEL ONLY.

"Hmm, that looks promising," Kim Ling said. She twisted the doorknob, but the door was locked so she moved on to Door Number Three.

Of all things, *Alice in Wonderland* popped into Lexi's head. That part where Alice is faced with a hallway of doors. If only she knew they would be stumbling into a painted rose garden or a wacky tea party on the other side, maybe her hands wouldn't have been trembling quite so much.

The third door was also locked.

"Oh, well," Kevin said, turning to go, "can't say we didn't try."

"Not so fast." Kim Ling started searching through her backpack again. "Make yourself useful, short stuff, and keep a sharp lookout—lemme know if anyone's coming around that corner. And you, Lex Luthor, stand here to block me from view, just in case. And try to unclench a little."

"What're you gonna do?"

"Don't do it!" Kevin cried, as if she were about to shoot someone.

"Geez. Chill." Kim Ling calmly unsnapped her wallet and removed her plastic library card. "This always works in the movies."

"Oh, great," Kevin said. "*Flying* always works in the movies too, ya know!"

Lexi moved in closer to camouflage Kim Ling, fanning herself with the small notebook until Kim Ling swiped it away and dropped it into her backpack, mumbling something about drawing too much attention. "Sorry," Lexi whispered. She watched closely as Kim Ling carefully slipped the library card between the door and the door-frame. Once. Twice. Three times. This seemed as goofy as trying to pick a lock with a hairpin, but after the fourth try there was a definite *click*.

Kim Ling tried the doorknob and this one turned. With a smug grin, she leaned into the door and opened it just a crack.

"Someone's coming!" Kevin hissed.

"Hustle!" Lexi said, hearing the heavy footsteps.

In the span of a heartbeat, all three slithered through the doorway into the thick blackness. The door closed behind them quietly but surely. Lexi felt something sweaty clinging to her arm. Hopefully her brother.

"Just for the record," he said in the faintest whisper, "if we wind up dead, I'm totally telling Dad."

10

"I 💔 NY"

The air felt ten degrees cooler on the other side of the door. Lexi, Kevin, and Kim Ling took a deep collective breath, staring into the dark unknown. There was the strangest smell—you could practically taste it. Stale. Metallic. Like sipping spoiled milk through a steel straw.

They stood motionless at first, listening to the electrical hum and waiting for their eyes to adjust. Lexi tried to loosen Kevin's life-or-death grip on her arm, and when she did, she immediately grabbed his clammy hand. Little by little, they all inched forward until the cavernous room slowly bled into view.

"Whoa," Kevin muttered, looking straight up.

The room was a mile tall at least. Grated staircases zigzagged from ceiling to floor, and long steel catwalks outlined the walls at every level. There were rows and rows of pipes, and thick black wires were snaking everywhere.

It was like being inside a gigantic computer. The mother of all motherboards.

"Don't touch anything," Lexi warned, thinking they might get electrocuted.

"This doesn't look like an abandoned train station to me," Kevin said in a shaky whisper. "Happy now? Have we had enough?"

"Suck it up, tadpole," Kim Ling said, "we're not turning back now."

"Famous last words."

They were taking bigger, bolder steps when Lexi noticed a wedge of light in the far corner, spilling onto what looked like a burlap sack or something. Probably not the jewels—it could never be that easy—plus, they were supposed to have been buried under some tracks. Still, it was worth checking out.

"Come on," Lexi whispered, riding a wave of bravery.

"Do you see something?" Kim Ling asked.

Lexi's quickening pace was her answer. She kept a steady gaze on her target and cautiously led the others along the endless wall, counting her steps—one for every heartbeat so she could easily find her way back to the door. *Thirty-eight, thirty-nine footsteps exactly.* They came to an accordion stop.

Now the electrical hum was competing with a strange rumbling that seemed to come from the bowels of the earth as they sized up the brownish lump. It was woolly. Dirty. Looked more like a rumpled blanket up close than

a sack. And there was definitely something under it. After a
few uncertain seconds, Kim Ling gave the edge of the
blanket a little kick and quickly backed off. Nothing
happened.

Not a dead body, Lexi prayed, her bravery shriveling
instantly like aluminum foil in a microwave. *Anything but
that.*

Kim Ling kicked it a little harder and this time it
moved. Everyone flinched.

"Oh, God, please don't let it be rats, either," Lexi said.

In a very bizarre move, Kim Ling wriggled a foot under
the dusty blanket and, with one mighty kick, it flew
into the air.

"No!" Kevin cried as a girl jolted upright.

"Okay, I'm leaving right now," the girl said through
a drape of greasy blond hair that hung from her purple
bandanna like wet spaghetti. "Just be cool, be cool." She
scrambled to her knees, swiftly gathering the things
around her—Chinese food cartons, half a box of doughnuts. When she happened to glance up at the three gawking faces, she stopped cold. "What the—whadda you rug
rats want?" she snarled, collapsing onto her heels. "Take a
wrong turn on the Yellow Brick Road?"

"Mixed metaphor," Kim Ling said.

"I thought you were the cops!"

Her voice was gravelly with a New York twang. From
the Bronx, Lexi guessed, or Brooklyn maybe. The girl shook
her head and crammed half a doughnut into her mouth,

raining crumbs down her grungy I ❤ NY T-shirt. It was
like the ones sold all over the city except the heart was broken with a zigzag crack. When the splotch of light caught
the girl's face, Lexi guessed she couldn't have been much
older than fifteen maybe. Sixteen tops.

"I hate it when visitors show up unannounced," the
girl said with her mouth full, retrieving her ratty blanket.

Now Lexi was clinging to *Kevin's* arm like a tree frog.
Kim Ling grabbed her free hand, and the threesome stood
gawking down at the rumpled teenager in total disbelief.
At her makeshift bed made out of flattened cardboard
boxes; at the rolled-up jeans she used for a pillow; at the
filth upon filth.

"So, how'd you guys end up in the boiler room?" the
girl asked through a crooked yawn. "You lost or somethin'?"

Lexi scanned the place again. "Boiler room?"

"We wandered in by mistake," Kim Ling answered.
"So, what's your excuse?"

The girl gave her armpit a ferocious scratch. "I live
here, if you must know. Ain't much sunlight but I love
the high ceilings and it's definitely affordable." She adjusted
her purple bandanna, brushed crumbs off her jeans-pillow,
and collapsed back down. "Well, show's over, kiddies. You'll
have to see yourselves out." And yanking the disgusting
blanket over herself, that was the end of that.

Lexi, Kim Ling, and Kevin did an awkward about-face,
coughing a little from the dust. They started toward the

door, but after a few steps, Lexi had a thought and rushed back to the girl.

"Knock-knock," she said softly. "Sorry, but you don't by any chance know where the abandoned section of the train terminal is, do you? Track Sixty-one? We were actually—"

"GET OUUUT!" a voice roared out of nowhere.

Lexi bolted for the exit, her heart beating wildly. Kim Ling and Kevin were in full throttle ahead of her with Kevin screeching like a boiling teakettle.

"I wouldn't be hangin' at Grand Central no more if I was you!" the girl called out. "The cops'll cart your butts off to juvie!"

"Thanks for the heads-up," Lexi yelled back. "Sorry we interru— Bye!"

A burst of wicked laughter erupted from the rafters and Lexi flew into a full gallop. Ghostly images were emerging from everywhere. A leg dangling from a platform— then an arm—two heads poking through a steel stairway. It was as if she was escaping from some eerie catacomb where all the dead bodies were rising from their graves. Like the Haunted Mansion at Kingsley Park, only real.

She couldn't get to the triangle of light fast enough, where Kim Ling was holding the door open, frantically waving her on. Laughter ricocheted off the walls as Lexi finally flew out the door and closed it behind her with a slam.

"Thanks-sorry-bye?" Kim Ling spouted. "Are you for real?"

"There's, like, a whole bunch of mole people in there—hiding in the shadows!" Lexi clung to the doorknob, catching her breath. "Where's Kevin? Is he all right?"

"I'm okay." He was behind Kim Ling with his hands on his thighs, panting and wheezing.

Lexi rushed over and smothered him in a desperate hug, surprised he wasn't bawling. "That was so not cool," she said to Kim Ling. She could feel Kevin's heart about to explode from his chest. "*So* not cool."

Kim Ling's eyeballs shifted from left to right. "Or was it, like, the coolest thing ever?"

Lexi pretended she didn't hear that. She took Kevin by the hand and led him to the elevators with Kim Ling right beside them. She couldn't help wondering if any further damage had been done to Kevin's internal panic button. And as far as the treasure hunt, well, that was a harebrained idea and they were definitely calling it quits.

The elevator *ding* came like a wrong answer in a spelling bee. Lexi was first on and jabbed MAIN FLOOR with a shaky sense of relief. Game over.

No sooner had the elevator doors snapped shut when Kim Ling turned to Lexi with dancing eyes. "We have to go back!"

"*What?* In your dreams."

"Think about it. That homeless chick could be a freakin' gold mine of information. She must know the uncharted tunnels and passageways of this place like the back of her hand. And she gave us a legitimate warning about the cops so there must be a heart in there somewhere under all that grunge. This is too good. We can't let her get away—we have to drill her. *You* have to drill her."

"Back off, Nancy Drew," Lexi warned.

"If anyone's gonna win her trust, it's you. You've got that pie-eyed, naive, small-town thing going on."

The elevator doors opened and they exited into the buzzing main concourse. "So wait," Lexi said, "let me get this straight. You want to just use that girl—correction— you want *me* to use that poor girl just so we can find the jewels and you can have your stupid story?"

"Mm-hmm—and the problem with that is?"

"Tell me again how you're able to sleep at night."

"Listen to me. We've got a very small window of opportunity here. We have to go back right now, before she disappears forever!"

"I'm afraid *we* might disappear forever!"

"Don't be such a sissy."

Lexi's eyes snapped shut like two deflective shields, shutting out Kim Ling's words. She blinked them open again, reached out and grabbed Kim Ling's hand with both of hers, and gave it a civilized shake. "I believe this is where we part company," she said with the warmth of a prison guard dismissing an inmate. "Thanks for your time; thanks for almost getting us killed—and have a nice day."

Kim Ling ripped her hand away. "Aww, don't bail on me now, dude."

"I am not bailing. Freak-face!"

So much for civilized. Lexi grabbed Kevin and stormed off through the concourse. She was beginning to see a pattern—hadn't she done this before in the park? This would be the last time.

"I could really use a Snapple now," Kevin said. "Mango Madness."

Lexi was moving faster than her brain could think. Sweating. Fuming. The annoying sound of Kim-Ling's slapping flip-flops following her and Kevin through the crowd, around the corner, and up the ramp toward the Forty-Second Street exit.

"Take it all, okay?" Kim Ling called out. "Every last cent."

"Go away," Lexi snapped.

"I reiterate, I'm in this strictly for the story, so you can have *all* of the reward money. Besides, my dad's a successful attorney so I'm pretty much set. C'mon, think about it—one hundred and eighty thousand dollars is a life-changing amount of money."

It really was. Lexi had always believed that her father, not being able to work much after Mom's death, had married Clare strictly for her money—a quick answer to a desperate situation. A windfall like this could change everything. But it was way too far-fetched.

"Can't you call one of your stupid friends and drag them along instead?" Lexi said.

"No time! Besides, I don't have any stupid friends, okay? Or smart ones. I mean, no *real* friend-friends exactly."

Lexi's sneakers came to a squeaky stop. Okay, this had to be a trick—some kind of twisted strategy. She turned to Kim Ling and searched her eyes for sincerity. Either she was the greatest wool-puller-over-the-eyes in the world or the girl wasn't kidding. What kind of kid doesn't have any friends and admits it? Kim Ling, that's who. How awful. And totally embarrassing.

"I'm sorry," she said, her thoughts in a jumble, "but I can't drag Kevin back to that horrible place again."

"Uh, I don't think you're gonna have to," Kevin said, staring into the distance. "Purple bandanna at nine o'clock. Isn't that the girl over there? Digging through the garbage can?"

11

PIZZA BURN

Without discussion, Lexi, Kim Ling, and Kevin zoomed toward the figure in the purple bandanna like paper clips to a magnet. But was it the teenage girl from the boiler room? It had to be. Another dead giveaway: the I ♥ NY T-shirt. She was sniffing something she had fished out of the garbage can—a gnarled pizza crust?—and was about to take a bite.

"Don't!" Lexi cried, running up to her.

The girl almost bolted, until she saw who it was. "Oh, man," she said, her shoulders slumping. "What do you three pains in the butt want now?"

"Wouldn't you like a slice of fresh hot pizza instead? On me?"

She cocked her head and sized up Lexi through cautious eye slits. "Well, I hate to see perfectly good food go to waste," she said, "but what the hey?" and tossed the crust over her shoulder, just missing the trash can. "You're on."

Lexi picked up the crust and disposed of it properly, wondering what she had just gotten herself into. "So, what do you like on your pizza? Pepperoni? Mushrooms? The works?"

"We can't afford that," Kevin said in too loud of a whisper.

"Whatever won't break the bank," the girl answered.

"The works it is." Lexi brushed off her hands and leaned into Kim Ling. "You might have to lend me some cash, okay?"

"I guess. But if I'm pitching in, then I deserve the credit." She turned to the homeless girl. "Uh, yoo-hoo—I don't know your name, but the pizza is going to be *our* treat, not *her* treat. Just to be clear."

The girl shrugged like she couldn't give a rat's behind and all four took off, strolling along the perimeter of the busy grand concourse, heading toward the marble staircase that led to the dining concourse.

"So, what *is* your name anyway? I'm Kim Ling Levine, Manhattan native. This is Lexi McGill and her little brother, Kevin. They're just visiting. I'd shake your hand but—under the circumstances . . ."

The girl was staring off into the distance as if she had already left the conversation. "Huh—what?"

"Your *name*?"

"Oh, sorry, I'm spacing out. That would be Melrose—Merritt. With two r's and two t's."

"Melrose? Cool." Kevin's twisted face looked up at her. "That your real name?"

"Real enough. No, I'm just kidding. It's, uh, short—for Melanie Rose. When I become an actress, I'm thinkin' of losin' the Merritt altogether and just goin' by Melrose."

"I love it!" Lexi gushed. "My name's really Alexandra, but Alex and Al are way too boyish so people call me Lexi or Lex for short, which is cool—even though Lex is still kinda masculine, but I don't mind that as much."

"Geez, come up for air why don't ya?" Kevin teased.

"I'm just saying."

The stroll of awkwardness took them down to the Two Boots Pizzeria in the food court area, where the aroma was thick and delicious. Melrose told the others that she'd grab a table while they were ordering at the counter—but when the girls and Kevin turned around with food and drinks, there was no sign of her. Lexi thought Melrose had ditched them for sure, until she heard a "Yo!" from the darkest corner table.

"Hey. I got a medium pie with just cheese so we can all indulge," Lexi reported, approaching the table. She slid the sizzling pizza down in front of Melrose and took a seat opposite her. "Sorry, but with drinks, it's all I could afford."

"All *we* could afford," Kim Ling said, setting down the tray of sodas, paper plates, napkins, and plastic utensils. She collapsed into the chair next to Lexi, distributed the plates like a card dealer, and helped herself to a slice, which she very carefully slid from the pan onto her plate.

Melrose tore off a bubbling slice and shoved it directly into her mouth. "Haah!" she garbled, fanning her tongue. "Izza-burr!"

"Hot. Pizza burn," Lexi translated. "The worst, right?"

"Well, what'd you expect?" Kim Ling said, barely looking up from her plate. She was methodically laying napkins onto her slice and patting them down with her fingertips.

"I'm not real used to hot meals, okay?" Melrose said.

"Right." Kim Ling peeled the greasy napkins off her slice and held them up like two soiled mud flaps. "Look at this oil slick. It's enough to clog a major artery. Disgusting."

"Delicious!" Melrose countered, and chewed off a big bite of pizza, scorching or not, as if to stick it to Kim Ling.

Lexi maneuvered a goopy slice onto Kevin's plate and accidentally knocked over the salt shaker, which she immediately grabbed and shook over her left shoulder to prevent bad luck. A loud "ahem" came from the woman sitting behind her. "Sorry," Lexi muttered, and helped herself to the smallest slice of pizza left in the pan. She glared at it, waiting for a hint of appetite to appear—but the thought of someone snacking on garbage to survive stuck in her gut like a cinder block. So she sat plucking strings of cheese off her pizza and watching Melrose chow down like a vulture to fresh kill. You would've thought it was her first meal in weeks. Maybe it was. Her first real meal, anyway. Lexi, who had always complained about being served leftovers, even lasagna, wondered what it would be like to survive on scraps from the trash. Partially eaten doughnuts. Rancid old chicken parts.

And that wasn't the half of it. What she could see of Melrose's blond hair looked greasier than Kim Ling's napkins. Plus, she had an undeniably ripe odor, which was probably why the group of older ladies sitting next to them just got up and moved to another table. How horrible, knowing you smell like raw sewage. And to never be able to take a long bubble bath whenever you liked. Or a plain bath. A hot shower even.

"What, do I reek? Is that why those blue-hairs left?" Melrose sniffed an armpit. "After a while you get used to it and you can't tell anymore. I just ain't had the chance to wash my shirts out lately."

"Where do you—?" Kevin began, but Lexi gave him a swat.

"In the john when no one's around," Melrose answered anyway. "Bryant Park's got a decent one too. Sometimes I hit the park fountains late at night if I'm really stankified."

Lexi, Kevin, and Kim Ling just stared in amazement.

"What?" Melrose said with a mouthful. "You have to suffer to become a great actress! So it's all good."

"Oh, right, you wanna be an actress," Lexi said, remembering their earlier conversation. "Cool. Yeah, our aunt's an actress, so . . ."

"An independent girl with big dreams," Kim Ling chirped, sounding very un-Kim-like. "Good for you." She was smiling too wide—obviously sucking up. "So, you must know this train terminal inside and out, huh, Mel? I'll bet you can find your way into some really obscure spots."

"I get around. What's it to you?"

And her suck-up approach wasn't working. "She's writing a paper," Lexi said, carefully choosing her words, "on the secret underground world of Manhattan or something." It wasn't exactly a lie—just almost.

"I want to delve into the underbelly of the city—maybe even interview some other mole people like yourself," Kim Ling said, going along with the bending of the truth. "Oh, no offense!"

"It's June." Melrose paused and sucked her teeth. "This for summer school? What, did you flunk English or somethin'?"

"As if!" Kim Ling grumbled. "I've been in the National Honor Society since preschool. Just getting an early start for fall. It's called being conscientious."

Lexi rolled her eyes. "It's called being an obnoxious overachiever," she said in one of her aunt's stage whispers.

Kim Ling kicked Lexi under the table with a bare foot; Lexi, in turn, flung a handful of plasticware at her head.

"Hey! You could've put my eye out with that fork!"

"It's not a fork—it's a spork—half spoon, half fork."

"And you're a sputz—half spaz, half nuts."

"Yeah? Well, *you're* a hundred percent nuts," Lexi shot back. "Your toenails are lethal. You should issue an official warning when you unsheathe those things."

"Unsheathe." Kevin snorted and slapped his thigh. "You guys crack me up. You should have, like, your own sitcom."

"So, is that what I am then—a mole person?" Melrose went in for slice number two, then blew across it, right into Kim Ling's face. "Ya know, if you really want some gritty stories, you should talk to Sophie. D'ya ever see her sittin' outside the main entrance?"

"No. Oh, yeah, with the stroller?" Lexi said, remembering the woman who had told her she had pretty hair. "And the cats?"

"Been hangin' out there for years. The cops're always chasin' her away but she keeps comin' back, like a bad rash." Her heavily outlined eyes went dim. "It's sad, though. Yesterday she told me she didn't think she'd last another winter."

"You mean on the streets?" Lexi asked.

"I mean on the planet. And would I please look after her babies for her—those mangy cats. Yeah, right, like that's gonna happen." Melrose tore the crust off her slice, flung it aside, and took a big, crooked bite. "The older ones can't get around so good," she said with a mouthful. "The homeless, I mean. Ya know, squeezin' through tight places, dodgin' security guards and stuff. So, they usually end up stayin' outside, gettin' heatstroke in the summer or frostbite in the winter. Eventually they just—you know . . ."

Lexi swallowed hard. She knew.

A burst of laughter came from a table of teenagers, which only emphasized the depressing topic of conversation at their table. There was a prickly quiet after that— except for the muffled conversations swirling around them—and Lexi could only guess that Melrose, Kevin, and Kim Ling were deep in thought. *She* was, at least. Greasy hair and living off food scraps suddenly seemed pretty mild compared to dying on the streets.

"Why're you always starin'?" Melrose asked, sucking sauce off her chipped, black-painted fingernails.

"Me? I didn't know I was." Lexi forced a smile. "How's the pizza?"

"*Pree goo.*"

"Pretty good," Lexi translated. "That last slice has your name on it."

"So, Melrose Merritt, what do you think?" Kim Ling was sounding fake-friendly again, drumming her fingers on the table—the sound of an army of ants marching into battle. "There's an abandoned train station under Grand Central that I'm dying to get to but it's probably off-limits to the general public. And with the security—well, forget it. But I'll bet you can show us a secret way in. Am I right?"

"Prob'ly. What's in it for me?"

"I dunno." Kim Ling thought about it for a second. "A sumptuous gastronomic feast?"

"How 'bout another hot meal instead?"

Lexi kicked Kim Ling under the table this time—to get her to hold back the wisecrack she knew was on her lips.

"That'd work too," Kim Ling answered with the faintest smile on her face.

"Something homemade, if you can swing it," Melrose said, fishing a clawful of drippy ice cubes from her cup and dropping them into her mouth. "No nuts, though." *Crunch-crunch.* "I'm allergic."

"Sure, no prob," Lexi said. "I'll put together something really yummy for you."

It looked as if Melrose was picturing her dream meal while she chomped mercilessly on the ice, fingering the metal studs that outlined her entire right ear. "So, meet me tomorrow morning at the lobby clock with the chow—around ten-ish—and I'll see if I can hook you up."

Lexi nodded in agreement, and before she could give Kim Ling a victory look, Kevin was whispering in Lexi's ear. Something about having to cut City Camp for the second day in a row if they followed through with that stupid plan; plus, lying to Aunt Roz and breaking the rules again. "We'll work it out," she whispered back, but all the plotting and dishonesty was already gnawing at her gut.

"No secrets," Melrose warned, still chomping.

"Family stuff," Kevin said.

Kim Ling licked a splotch of tomato sauce off the corner

of her mouth and turned to Melrose. "So, why'd you run away from home in the first place?" she asked, broaching the touchy subject with the delicacy of a Mack truck. "Details."

"Mind your business."

Kim Ling's eyes narrowed. "Just asking an innocent question."

"Well, knock it off."

"Okay. I take it back."

"Good."

With an impatient exhale, Kim Ling innocently plucked the straw from her cup and shook off the droplets. She flattened it on the table with her thumbnail, then slowly and methodically began folding it into sharp, even zigzags, eyeing Melrose the whole time as if the runaway was a deadly cobra about to strike. "Deadbeat dad?"

"Drop it. Stop grillin' me."

"Alcoholic mom?"

"I said, *shut your face!*"

Melrose shot up in an instant rage, almost toppling the table. Drinks spilling. Kevin squawking. Ice flying everywhere.

Lexi quickly scooped the icy slush into her cup, acting as if that was the problem. "Don't worry, I've got it." This was a peacemaking technique she had seen her mom use a thousand times—pretending things were perfectly normal right when the stuff was hitting the fan. "Kim, uh, why don't you and Kevin go wait upstairs—by the main entrance. I'll meet you guys in, like, five minutes."

Surprisingly, Kim Ling immediately got up from her chair and shouldered her backpack. "C'mon, Kev," she said, trudging away, "before I say something I'll really regret."

"Too late." Kevin grabbed his backpack too, but his worried face was staring at his sister. "Lex? You sure you don't want me to—"

"Go ahead. I'm okay."

He ran to catch up with Kim Ling as Lexi kept cleaning up the mess. She watched as, little by little, Melrose's fists uncurled and her nostrils stopped flaring, until finally she crumpled into her seat with a thud.

"She didn't mean anything," Lexi assured Melrose, dabbing at what was left of the spill with wadded napkins. She could feel all eyes in the food court on them and hot embarrassment tightened her neck. "It's just her warped, in-your-face personality. And it's all the time too. But she's not a bad person." She eased into her chair, forcing a smile, which withered quickly in Melrose's steely gaze. "Really."

"Sorry about that." Melrose double-palmed her tears away across her dirty face. "It's just that—I lose it sometimes when people like her start to judge." She shoved the wet plate away. "I ain't sayin' she was totally off. My new stepfather, Frank. He's a real loser."

Lexi felt like she should say something, ask a question,

since the girl was obviously opening up—but she didn't want to cross the line and set her off again.

"My ma married him after I begged her not to," Melrose went on, "so it's kinda like she picked him over me. Whatever. I hate his freakin' guts."

"I totally understand! My dad's on his honeymoon right now with my new wicked stepmother. Can't stand the woman." A something-in-common spark had definitely ignited, but quickly fizzled into another awkward silence. At least now Lexi felt she had her complete attention. "Don't you ever get scared—if you don't mind my asking?"

"All the time. There's a lot of messed up people livin' on the streets. You don't know. Druggies, weirdos. It's brutal." She blew her nose into a napkin. Lexi handed her another one, which she began shredding into long strips. "If it gets real bad, I hide out over at this church, St. Agnes—it's about a block from here on Forty-Third just past Lexington—till things cool down."

"St. Agnes, hmm." Lexi found her fascinating, this Melrose Merritt—and talking to her alone wasn't as frightening as she had thought. "So, we're still on for tomorrow, right? Ten a.m. by the clock?" Melrose nodded, and in a strange burst of enthusiasm, Lexi dug a marker from her backpack, scrawled her cell phone number across a fresh napkin, and slid it across the table. "Call me—you know, if you're gonna be late or anything." *Giving my number to a runaway. I've officially lost my mind.*

Melrose stopped shredding and pocketed the number, thanking Lexi with a curious half smile. Lexi half-smiled back.

"So, how long has it been since—?"

"Since I left the Bronx? I dunno, a few—" Suddenly Melrose's eyes went horror-flick wide and she slid down her seat like a dead body, ending up in a heap under the table. "Don't turn around," she warned from below in a raspy whisper.

"Why?" Lexi's heart sped up. "What?"

"Cop!"

Lexi gave it a five count and nonchalantly glanced through her fingers at the policewoman ordering food at the counter. When she turned back around and peeked under the table, Melrose had vanished.

Later, as Lexi was speed-walking through the main concourse toward the Forty-Second Street exit to meet up with Kim Ling and Kevin, feeling oddly content that Melrose had told her the truth, she happened to notice the listing of Metro-North train stops posted over the ticket counter.

Manitou. Marble Hill. *Melrose. Merritt.* With two *r*'s and two *t*'s.

12

PETTY THEFT AND KILLER TOMATOES

A screaming car alarm woke Lexi with a start the next morning. Dawn's first glimmer was seeping in through the blinds of her aunt's living room and Lexi feared she would never be able to fall back asleep. The metal bar on the pullout couch felt welded onto her ribcage, and her mind was already up and doing mental aerobics. At first, thoughts of the jewel thieves were creeping through her brain; and then she couldn't stop thinking about Melrose—or whatever her real name was. *Why would she lie about it? Then again, why wouldn't she?* The last image of that poor girl crouched under the table, staring up at her with frightened eyes. Too freaky.

Lexi cemented herself into a tight fetal position and began counting sheep—the ones conveniently frolicking in the pastoral scene on Aunt Roz's toile curtains. She had only seen this done in cartoons but she would try anything to get Melrose out of her mind. She was just starting on the shepherd boys when she noticed a mysterious rainbow appear across Kevin's sleeping face. *Oh, pretty. Look at him all sprawled out on that chaise-lounge thing, dead to the world—turning colors.* The rainbow spilled over onto the fish tank that housed Romeo and Juliet, Aunt Roz's goldfish, turning them a shimmery chartreuse. It must have been the stained-glass suncatcher hanging in the window that created the colorful effect—a big pink rose surrounded by glistening borders of greens . . . yellows . . . oranges . . . reds . . .

Suddenly Lexi was eight years old again, dressed in her Sunday best and surrounded by the stained-glass windows of Our Lady of Loretto's.

"Here, cookie, drop this into the poor box while I go light a candle for Grandma Irene." Lexi's mom had handed her a dollar bill and closed her wallet with a *snap*. "Then go grab us two seats near the front of the church, okay?"

Ten o'clock mass had been their favorite because the choir sang, but it was just the two of them that Sunday. Kevin had a gross stomach thing all morning, so Lexi's dad had decided that the McGill boys had better skip church—that these were special circumstances and "God will understand."

Lexi and her mom blessed themselves with holy water from the font and headed in opposite directions—her mom toward the rack of glowing votives and Lexi for the poor box. Gabe seemed to be watching her. That was the name she had given the stained-glass angel in the vestibule window, who didn't look angelic enough to be a Gabriel. He had an especially mischievous smile on his face that day, and the sunlight shining through his amber-red robes danced across the last pew of the church where the "down-on-their-luck Delaneys" usually sat.

The poor box was so loaded, Lexi really had to cram-cram-cram the dollar deep into the slot, all the while thinking of Kaitlyn Delaney, a girl in her third-grade class who always got picked on because of her frayed, musty clothes and flat, meatless sandwiches. She didn't take free stuff from friends, either, as far as Lexi knew. At least in the form of Lunchables or seedless grapes.

A thunderous organ chord pealed from the balcony and when Lexi's fingers, still wet with holy water, slipped out of the box, so did a crisp twenty-dollar bill!

"Is a sin still a sin if it's for a good cause?" Lexi asked her mom when she scooted into the pew next to her, smelling of candle smoke. "Like—taking something that doesn't belong to you?"

"Stealing is wrong, honey. You know that."

"But would it still count as a major sin or just a minor one—you know, like a venial?"

"Where do you come up with such questions? And why're we sitting back here when there're plenty of seats up front?"

"To see the Delaneys," Lexi whispered. "I don't wanna miss the look on Kaitlyn's face when she opens her hymnal and a twenty-dollar bill drops out."

Lexi's mom clasped her hands and bowed her head in prayer. But it quickly popped up again. "Oh, Jesus, Mary, and Joseph, what did you do?"

It had been so worth it. Kaityln acted like it was some kind of miracle. An act of God. Little did she know, it was an act of Lexi.

After mass, on their way out of church, Lexi's mom had quickly shoved a handful of bills into the poor box—and with the guiltiest look on her face. But Gabe had seemed *very* pleased.

Lost in a pinwheel of stained-glass yellows, blues, and greens, Lexi found herself half awake and back in her twelve-year-old skin again, curled up on Aunt Roz's fold-out couch and staring bleary-eyed at the suncatcher. A high-pitched wail penetrated the walls of Apartment 5F and woke her up the rest of the way. *Miss Carelli, the opera singer across the hall. It has to be.* She was doing vocal exercises with musical accompaniment from a rattling drill tearing up the street. Lexi flopped onto her stomach and sandwiched her head in her pillow, which might have worked if she didn't have to breathe. *"Mah-may-mee-mo-mooo"* was attacking her in stereo now. It sounded like Aunt Roz had joined Miss Carelli for a duet—just as an ambulance was screaming by. "Okay, New York, you win! I'm up."

Lexi rolled out of bed and followed the aroma of coffee into the kitchen. Her aunt, in a terry-cloth headband with a pore-cleansing strip plastered across her nose, was leaning up against the refrigerator, holding a steaming cup of coffee.

"Morning, dear."

"Morning, dear," Lexi echoed. She tilted her aunt's cup to her lips and took a sip. "Blech! How could something that smells so fantastic taste so disgusting?"

"I prefer mine black, which is an acquired taste, I suppose—like caviar. Or reality TV. There's cream and Splenda if you like."

Lexi scrunched up her nose and yawned.

"*Nah-nay-nee-no-neeew . . .*"

"Doesn't Patrice have a marvelous instrument? I was trying not to sing along in full voice so I wouldn't wake you kids. I didn't, did I?"

"Nah, the Big Apple beat you to it. And that brother of mine can sleep through anything."

"I really shouldn't be singing along, but with an opera diva living across the hall, it's like getting free lessons." Aunt Roz opened the refrigerator and stared into it, humming. "I haven't done a musical in quite a while, so I need all the help I can get. The role of Amanda Wingfield is no small feat."

Lexi reached around her aunt and grabbed a carton of milk. "Well, they wouldn't have picked you if you weren't the best one, right?"

"Right." Aunt Roz seemed unconvinced. "A musical version of *The Glass Menagerie*. Tennessee Williams is probably turning in his grave." She scooped a bottle of syrup, a container of blueberries, and a tub of margarine into her arms and dropped them onto the counter. "Wait, he's not still alive, is he?"

Lexi shrugged.

"Well, if he was, this'd kill him."

"Ha! Good one." Lexi poured herself a glass of milk and gave it a quick freshness sniff. Her aunt wasn't the best at checking expiration dates, but it seemed okay.

"How wonderful to be born with a magnificent singing voice like Patrice," Aunt Roz said, busily making breakfast. "Not that I don't appreciate my own, but—you know what I mean. It's like God saying, 'Here's a truly incredible gift. This is what you're supposed to do for the rest of your life. Now, go do me proud.' "

Lexi didn't think her own voice was all that great, but maybe—with some training . . . She took a deep breath and in a burst of enthusiasm, joined Miss Carelli on her next "Do-mi-so-mi-*doooh*!"

"QUIET! YOU CALL THAT SINGING?!"

Lexi froze with an open mouth. The angry voice sounded as if it had come through the vent next to the stove.

"That's the grouch in Four-F," Aunt Roz whispered. "Findlay or whatever the heck his name is. What time is it anyway?"

"IT'S SIX FORTY-FIVE IN THE MORNING! I'LL CALL THE COPS!"

"Six forty-five," Lexi repeated sheepishly.

Miss Carelli had stopped singing too. There was silence except for the ticking chicken clock on the wall with its giant darting eyeballs. Lexi guzzled the rest of her milk, crossing "singing" off her mental checklist of possible talents—one she *for sure* did not possess.

"Sorry I blew your free lesson. I sound like a constipated macaw."

"Oh, that old coot's always complaining about every little thing. How about some waffles? There're fresh blueberries to top them with."

"I'm not in a very waffley mood." Lexi slid into a chair, folding one leg under the other, and plunked her glass down on the table.

"*Yeeesh!*" Aunt Roz squealed.

Had she set it right on her aunt's script? "Ooh, sorry!" Lexi moved the glass and quickly blotted the water ring with a corner of the *New York Post*. She smiled when she realized Aunt Roz hadn't reacted to the glass at all, but had just ripped off her pore strip.

"I found the perfect opening night dress, Alexandra, on sale at Macy's. A real stunner, wait till you see. Just clingy enough without making me look too hippy."

"Oh. Good."

Resting her groggy head on her palm, Lexi took in her aunt's collection of show posters and country kitsch covering the walls. There wasn't a bare spot to rest your eyes in the entire apartment, but it still somehow came across as neat. Organized clutter. And with a definite decorating motif: half theater lobby, half Vermont bed-and-breakfast.

"I'll pick it up next week." Aunt Roz loaded the toaster with frozen waffles and glanced over at Lexi. "You have to eat *something*, hon. How about my famous scrambled eggs à la Roz?"

"That's okay." Lexi slid out of her chair and lumbered over to the sink to rinse out her glass. "Not hungry." She had the odd sensation that someone was staring at her the whole time, just like with Gabe in Our Lady of Loretto—and it wasn't Aunt Roz or the chicken clock. Nothing else had eyes except a needlepoint of a goose in a bonnet hanging over the counter—and a poster from the Broadway show *Les Misérables*. Bingo! The stringy-haired, sad-eyed orphan logo was definitely the culprit. *That gastronomical feast for Melrose! Or whatever her real name was.* How could she forget?

"Oh, you know what, Aunt Roz? I changed my mind!" Now Lexi was wide awake and then some. "I'll take some waffles to go, please. And you might as well throw in those eggs, too."

"Well, of course. I thought you weren't—"

"Plastic containers? D'ya have any?"

"Um, try the cabinet next to the fridge." Her aunt looked puzzled as Lexi ran around the kitchen, buzzing like a cell phone on vibrate.

"I am so brain-dead in the morning. I totally forgot how famished I get at camp when we're off doing, you

know—camp stuff." Just like stealing to help the less for-
tunate, fibbing to loved ones was allowed under extreme
circumstances, she decided as she searched through cab-
inets and drawers, gathering plasticware, duck sauce
packets, a bag of double-stuffed Oreos . . . "Kevin does
too, so—"

"What do I do?" Kevin appeared in the doorway in
a black *Star Trek* T-shirt, rubbing sleep from his eyes.
"Something smells good."

"Waffles and eggs—come help yourself, sweetheart,"
Aunt Roz said, slaving away at the stove now, like a fry
cook at a diner. "Unless you want yours to go too."

"Huh?"

"Have some now and take some for later," Lexi said to
him with big eyes. "You know how you get. How you're
always starving to death in the middle of those long—
whatchamacallits—nature hikes." She crammed a cookie
into his questioning mouth and gave his cheeks a little slap.
"Wakey-wakey, eggs and bakey."

"There's bacon?"

He was clueless, but no matter. Aunt Roz went on to
prepare a feast worthy of a soccer team and laid it all out
on the counter. "Take it all," she said, practically fainting
into a chair with a fresh cup of coffee and a sigh. "I certainly don't want it getting back to Mark that I starved his
children."

Lexi gave her a grateful peck on the cheek and got
busy packing the food.

"I feel just awful that I haven't been able to spend much time with you kids, you know? What with the play, and camp, and the world exploding around us." Aunt Roz fluffed the *New York Post*, licked a finger, and turned the first page with it. "But tomorrow is Saturday and I promise to make it up to you. I have a music rehearsal in the morning—a costume fitting, but then I'm free the rest of the day." She crumpled down the paper. "What do you guys say we paint the town red? A Day of Family Fun! We can go to the zoo, the park, wherever you like. Are you listening or am I talking to the wall? How about the planetarium, Kevin? I'll bet you'd love that."

He was in the middle of sucking down blueberries but gave an eager nod.

"Then afterward, I'll whip up a fabulous home-cooked dinner before we head out to Radio City. An old stage manager friend of mine wrangled up four free tickets for the show that's there now—some dance troupe, I forget. We could take Kimmy!"

"Oh, joy," Lexi grumbled.

"You don't sound very excited, Alexandra."

"No, I am." *Not really.* "I'll tell her today." *Or not.*

"You may as well ask her to dinner, too, while you're at it," Aunt Roz said, and turned another page. She slowly buried her nose in the newspaper; then jutted the paper out at arm's length, blinking widely. "What in the world? 'KILLER TOMATOES THREATEN THE MIDWEST'? This has to be some kind of joke."

Lexi stopped what she was doing and zoomed over to her aunt to read the headline in question. "What? Where?" She focused in on it. "That's killer *tornadoes!*"

It took a second before they all erupted in a fit of laughter. Kevin grabbed two tomatoes off the windowsill and staggered around the kitchen, pretending they were attacking him. He accidentally knocked a huge copper kettle off the radiator, causing Mr. Findlay to yell "QUIET!" again, which made things even funnier.

"Oh, boy, that's one for the books," Aunt Roz said as the laughter died down. "I'm blind as a bat without my bifocals. Kevin, be a love and check my nightstand for them? I don't know where I possibly could've—"

Before she could finish her sentence, he did a sock-slide into the living room—then right back.

"What's bifocals?"

"Eyeglasses. I need them to see both near *and* far. Don't get old!"

Kevin disappeared again while Lexi retrieved the kettle, still giggling about the killer tomatoes. She plunked it back on the radiator and perched on the edge nearest her aunt.

"How about we get dressed to the nines for our night out on the town, Alexandra? We can do up your hair in a French twist."

Lexi gasped. Not because of the hair-don't, but because of the small headline that jumped off page two of the *Post*.

PERSON OF INTEREST NAMED IN CLEO JEWEL HEIST. MET STILL IN DE-NILE ABOUT INSIDE JOB.

"Uh, what? Sure, I'd like that," she lied, and made a mental note to rip out the article before she left. *Person of interest? We'd better get cracking.* She fingered her opal necklace, picturing the day that lay ahead. Maneuvering dark, spooky tunnels with Melrose and Kim Ling—at each others' throats, spiders in their hair, rats at their feet. She looked down at actual goose bumps sprouting on her arm and noticed something else. "Wait, aren't *those* your glasses? Hanging around your neck?"

Aunt Roz's head dropped. "Well, for heaven's sake." Sure enough, her glasses were poking out from her robe. She clucked her tongue and slid on her glasses. "Never mind, Kevin!" she called out. "Sometimes you can drive yourself crazy looking for something that's right under your nose."

Lexi's breath caught. Right under her nose, huh? *Was that another mysterious clue from the universe? Are the jewels somehow buried right under our noses?* She thought hard about it for a second and concluded that she was being supersensitive—which was normal under the circumstances.

"Look what I found on the bureau!" Kevin said, slipping and sliding back into the kitchen with a large brown package. "Can I open it, Aunt Roz? It's addressed to me and Lex."

"Oh, I completely forgot! Yes, go ahead. That arrived for you yesterday from your parents."

"*Parent,*" Lexi said with stiff curiosity, but headed in the opposite direction.

Aunt Roz went to get scissors from a kitchen drawer, but Kevin was already elbow-deep in packing popcorn before she got back. "Presents! Score!" he announced, waving a blue package tied with yellow ribbons. Seconds later, the wrappings were strewn all over the floor and he was testing out his shiny gold collapsible mini-telescope. "Awesome!" He demonstrated it for Lexi and Aunt Roz, then flew into the living room, yelling, "There's something in there for you, too, Lex!"

"Hmm." Lexi took her sweet time readying Melrose's food stash before wandering back to the table for her gift. She reluctantly dug out the beautifully wrapped box addressed to her and gave it the teeniest shake. Then a fierce rattle.

"Well?" Aunt Roz said, speed-sweeping up the popcorn as if it were nuclear waste. "Aren't you going to open it?"

"Maybe later."

"Alexandra!"

"Oh, okay." Lexi flicked open the note card and read it aloud.

Dearest Alex,

Hope you're having a lovely time in NYC.
We picked this up for you at a little antique shop
in Paris since we know how much you appreciate
pretty things. It'll last a lifetime!

Much love,
Dad & Clare

Lexi's tongue darted in and out. She hoped her aunt didn't see. It was obviously Clare's curlicue handwriting—her snooty, stuck-up words. *She's taking over already!* In one swift move Lexi tore through the paper to find a long gray velvet box. *Alex—ugh, I hate when she calls me that.* She flipped it open and her eyes went wide.

"Well, what is it?" Aunt Roz was at the garbage can, craning her neck to see. "What did you get?"

"Just a necklace." Lexi slowly pulled out the most magnificent strand of pearls she had ever seen. They shimmered against her skin in an iridescent silver-black-purple luster.

"Black pearls!" Aunt Roz practically tripped over herself to come examine them. "Oh, my goodness, and those aren't faux."

"They're gaudy."

"They're exquisite!"

"Whatever."

With purpose in her step, Lexi headed into the living room. The necklace was dragging off one hooked finger as if it were something she had dredged out of a clogged drain.

"Honey," Aunt Roz called after her, "aren't you going to try them on? For me? Alexandra?"

She strode past Kevin—who was standing on the chaise lounge, spying out the window through his telescope like the captain of a ship—directly toward Romeo and Juliet and, without even a slight hesitation, dropped the string of pearls into the scummy, smelly fish tank.

13

SUBWAY SANDWICHED

"Omigod, it's Dora the Explorer!"

"Don't make a big thing about it, Kim, I can't deal. Not today." Lexi stepped onto the front stoop of the brownstone, self-consciously fingering the short, black wig she was wearing from her aunt's collection. It had been sitting on a Styrofoam blob in the hall closet and sort of called out to her when she was leaving. "I'll just feel a lot safer being incognito today, okay?"

"*Sí*, Dora! *Te ves muy bonita como una morena.*"

"Op-dray ead-day."

Kim Ling gave her a crooked look. "Oh! Pig Latin—ha, I get it. Touché."

Lexi hooked the food-filled plastic bag on her arm and threw on Aunt Roz's movie-star sunglasses—they had called out to her too. She glanced across the street where the mysterious black Lincoln had been parked and breathed a mini sigh of relief. There was no sign of it. In fact, both Seventy-Third Street and West End Avenue were light on traffic because of some sort of street repairs.

"Oh, is that the bribe for what's-her-face?"

"Mm-hmm."

Kim Ling peeked into Lexi's bag. "Smells—interesting," she said, barely sniffing. "I hope it does the trick."

The front door of the brownstone sprang open. "Aunt Roz!" Kevin announced. He slammed the door shut and came thundering down the steps. "She's right behind me. We should scram!" He sailed down the block on his sneaker-wheels and the girls took off at a mad clip, following right behind him.

"So, why're we running from your aunt again?" Kim Ling asked Lexi over the clattering coming from her bouncing backpack.

"I just told her that your mom had volunteered to walk us to the City Camp bus every day." She grabbed a quick breath. "That it's picking us up and dropping us off, making me, like, this horrible, horrible person."

"Excellent! My mom never leaves the apartment this early, so they won't be bumping into each other in the hallway. And her Mandarin accent's so thick, even if they do cross paths later on, your aunt'll never catch wise."

That didn't make Lexi feel even the slightest bit better.

"We'll never get a cab," Kim Ling said, huffing and puffing, scanning the congested streets. "Steam pipe must've busted—happens a lot in this city—too much hot air. But we have gobs of time before we have to meet up with Cindersmella. Wanna just hop on the subway?"

Lexi's nose crinkled. "Subway?"

"Yeah, it's right on Broadway and—" Kim Ling gasped with realization and her slapping flip-flops slowed down. "Don't tell me you've never been? You must! It's the quintessential New York experience!"

"Are you kidding? If my aunt ever finds out we took a subway on our own, she'll tell my dad and he'll hang us by our thumbs from the top of the Empire State Building."

"Oh, they don't allow that."

Lexi didn't think that was funny. She was already up to lie number gazillion-and-one with Aunt Roz. And what about Kevin? It was bad enough making him go along with all the lies and rule-breaking, let alone forcing him into another dark tunnel. No, she'd use what was left of her emergency twenty dollars for a cab, if necessary, but definitely no subways. *No way. That's where I draw the line.* So how they all wound up, a few minutes later, waiting and wilting on the humid subway platform under Seventy-Second Street was anybody's guess.

"Okay, listen up," Kim Ling said in her drill sergeant voice. "You have to watch out for jerks on the subway train. Not the weirdos—well, them, too—but I mean the sudden jerks when the train stops and starts. All the clueless tourists go flying if they're not hanging on. It's hilarious."

"I'm sure," Lexi said. Yeah, she had let Kim Ling get

her way, as usual, but as it turned out, Kevin seemed happy as a clam—make that a baked clam, considering the sweltering heat. He was obviously putting on a brave front, but whatever. Lexi kept a firm grasp on him anyway, so he wouldn't accidentally roll onto the tracks with those Heelys he was wearing. After all, it was Friday the thirteenth, the unluckiest day of the year.

Lexi dug past the rabbit's foot, laminated four-leaf clover, and nine lucky pennies she had stuffed into the pocket of her cargo shorts earlier for maximum protection against bad luck, and pulled out the crumpled article from the *Post*. She waited for Kevin to pop in his iPod earbuds, then slapped it over to Kim Ling. "Here, read. The FBI thinks the jewel heist was an *inside* job."

"That's yesterday's news, my friend," Kim Ling said, and zipped through the entire article in the time it would have taken Lexi to read the first paragraph. "Hmm, the *Post*, no wonder. Yeah, according to CNN, the person of interest, Benjamin Deets, used to be director of security at the Met, but they gave him the ax because of, quote-unquote, 'suspicious behavior.' Translation: the slime bucket was caught on a security cam ripping off pricey stuff from the gift shop. The Met finally came clean this morning."

"And he'd worked in security at Grand Central before that too," Kevin said, tearing out his earbuds. "Remember? When we saw the FBI snooping around the lost and found?"

"Oh, that's right!" Kim Ling said.

"And in case you didn't know, they just searched his

apartment, his storage unit, his gym locker, *and* his mother's house in"—Kevin whipped out his cell phone and read from the screen—"B-A-Y-O-N—"

"N-E," Kim Ling finished. "Bayonne, that's in Jersey."

"And came up empty—meaning no jewels, no nothing. Total goose egg."

"Huh." Kim Ling scratched her neck. "He probably knew all the obvious places would be searched immediately, so it makes sense that he'd want to hide the booty somewhere really obscure."

"Like an abandoned train station."

"Exactly. Wait, how're you getting reception down here?"

"I'm not. My friend Billy texted me, like, five minutes ago, from space camp. He's really into this whole crime-solving thing too."

"What?" Lexi said. That was news to her. "Since when?"

"Since he blew chunks in the Multi-Axis Tumbling Trainer. It really grossed him out. He says he'd rather be solving a real live crime, like us, instead."

"Kevin, you shouldn't have blabbed!" Lexi took in a deep breath and reminded herself to lower her voice. "Why're you being so sneaky about everything all of a sudden—pretending to listening to music and eavesdropping on us just now?"

"You should talk. You're, like, the queen of eavesdropping." Kevin jammed his earbuds back into his ears. "Isn't that what started this whole thing?"

"The kid has a point," Kim Ling said to Lexi with a

crooked shrug. "Anyway, back to Deets. His life apparently fell apart after the Met canned him, and he ended up taking a job as a groundskeeper in Central Park—before vanishing off the face of the earth, that is." She slid her phone out of her back pocket and jabbed at it until a picture came up. "So?" she said, holding it in front of Lexi. "Is he one of the dudes you saw in the Whispering Gallery?"

Lexi focused in on the black-and-white photo of Benjamin Deets, a man with dark, beady eyes and big teeth. "No. Maybe. I dunno." That was when the subway train came roaring into the station like a giant, angry bullet and she found herself clamping down on Kevin's shoulders. "It was kind of shadowy in that Whispering Gallery, Kim, and one of the guys had his head turned most of the time. Plus, he was wearing a Yankees cap."

"What?" Kim Ling yelled over the noise, squinting from the gust of wind.

"I said I'm not sure!"

The subway train screeched to a stop and the doors barely rattled open before a clump of people spilled out. Kim Ling led Kevin and Lexi into the far end of the train car, where they grabbed onto a metal pole hand-over-sweaty-hand. *Slam, whoosh,* and the train took off with the threesome jostling, jerking, and staring out the grimy windows. The subway station smeared into black. Tiny lights zoomed by at dizzying speed like some life-size video game.

"Is he British?" Lexi asked Kim Ling. "This Benjamin Deets?"

"No idea. Oh, that's right, one of the guys you saw was a Brit, wasn't he?"

"Definitely. I'm guessing. Maybe not."

"She replied with her usual unmitigated conviction," Kim Ling finished.

Lexi had no idea what half those words meant, but a smirk seemed to be the right response. She couldn't concentrate on the jewel heist anyway, wondering instead how the tunnel could possibly hold up under the weight of the enormous city. And God only knew what her brother must have been thinking under that fake grin of his. "This is fun, right, Kev?" she asked him.

He was nodding along to a song on his iPod but his eyes were spinning. He was probably freaking out from the EMERGENCY EVACUATION INSTRUCTIONS posted on the door.

"Yeah, there're some seats over there, Kim. We're gonna go sit."

She waited for the train to make its first stop and rolled Kevin across the car. He grabbed on to every pole they passed like a jungle monkey until they plopped down next to a toddler in a pointy pink birthday hat, who looked relatively unthreatening. Kim Ling wedged in next to them and the entire row of people had to scoot over.

"Sorry," Lexi said to the little girl's mother. She had to be the mother—they both had the same auburn hair—just like Lexi and her mom once upon a time. Her stomach was morphing into a bag of rocks again from missing her mom when she noticed Kevin's telescope aimed right at the same mother-daughter. "Stop acting like a two-year-old," she said, pushing it down, then quickly turned to the toddler. "No offense."

The doors snapped shut and the train sped off, sending a plump lady with a Macy's shopping bag toppling onto an old man's lap. "See what I mean about clueless tourists?" Kim Ling said, cracking up.

"Happy birthday," Lexi said to the fidgety little girl, purposely ignoring Kim Ling. "How old are you today?"

"Oh, she's actually three, but it's not her birthday," the mom answered. "She's just pretending. Ariel's preschool teacher says we mustn't stifle her creativity. She's in the gifted program."

And the similarities between this kid and Lexi stopped right there.

"See, you can never take things at face value," Kim Ling said to Lexi. "Every journalist worth her salt knows that. I was digging up some dirt on Cleopatra last night—everyone always assumes she was this ravishing beauty, right? Wrong! Turns out some British academics found an old coin depicting her with this enormous schnoz and a neck like a linebacker. Never assume. Oh, and wanna know something really disgusting I found out?"

"Yeah," Kevin said, plucking out his earbuds.

"She ended up marrying her younger brother."

"No way!" Kevin shrieked.

"And how's this supposed to help us find the jewels again?" Lexi asked.

"It's not. I just thought I'd work it into my report for a little color. C'mon, we have to switch trains!"

In what seemed like a New York minute, they grabbed their things, scrambled out the doors through a tangle of commuters, and found themselves sticking to the seats of yet another subway train, the shuttle bound for Grand Central. This one was packed and felt like an oven.

"It has to be around a hundred degrees in here," Lexi said as the doors shut out the sound of a wailing saxophone.

"We got a clunker with no AC," Kim Ling told her. "Tough it out, Dora, it's just one stop. You could de-wig, you know."

Not an option. Not when we're heading into the danger zone. The smash of people lurched to one side when the train took off and Lexi almost lost her bag of food. She secured it onto her lap with one hand, slipped her NYC guidebook from her backpack pouch with the other, and began fanning herself with it.

"Oh, I almost forgot—this is huge!" Kim Ling gushed. "Fox News announced this morning that there's even more reward money up for grabs."

"Right," Kevin said. "The Mets are kicking in now, too."

"Not the Mets—that's the baseball team—but the Met, as in Museum of Art. It's up to, like, a quarter mil in U.S. dollars! Just think, red, and it's got your name all over it."

"Don't call me 'red.'" Lexi sat back, still fanning herself with a steady rhythm. She had a crazy thought. *Two hundred and fifty thousand big ones would definitely be enough to*

*support our family for a long time—and, heck, maybe even buy
a yacht. Dad could take his time getting back on his feet again—
plus, he wouldn't need Clare anymore. Quick annulment.
Everyone lives happily ever after on the S.S. Alexandra—well,
except for Clare, but that's just a plus.*

"D'you guys ever notice how those news anchors
sound all sad when they're reporting a tragedy," Kim Ling
said out of the blue, "and then instantly turn happy for a
fluff piece? 'The nation mourned the loss of one of its
heroes today when blahty-blahty-blah succumbed to a
disgustingly disfiguring disease,'" she said, all serious. "'And
on a lighter note,'" she chirped, "'Zippy the Penguin at
the Bronx Zoo just had chicks!'"

Kevin started snorting and puffing.

"C'mon, that was funny!" He gave Lexi a sharp nudge
and her guidebook flew out of her hands and landed on
the sandal of the turbaned man in front of her.

Lexi snatched it up. "Sorry," she mumbled, and focused
straight ahead on the man's shirt buttons until her embarrassment faded. A little. When she looked down at the
guidebook, she noticed something strange: messy blue ink
scrawled all over the back cover. Her first thought was
that Kevin had gotten a hold of it. But on closer examination, she realized it was her own handwriting. "Omigod!"

"What?" Kim Ling asked.

"More clues."

"Where?" Kevin asked.

"Here!" Lexi held up the book and glared at it as if it

possessed magical powers. "I'd jotted them down in the Whispering Gallery, bits and pieces I heard from the men in black. I must've been so freaked, I'd totally blocked it out!"

"Are you kidding me?" Kim Ling said. "Hold still, I can't read it with your hand all shaky." And she grabbed the guidebook from Lexi and rotated it slowly, making out the words. "*Shoot. Needle.* What is that? It's smudged. *Oval disk? Pack?*"

"*Park,*" Lexi said, swallowing hard. "Shoot, needle, oval disk, park. What the heck does that mean?"

"You tell me!"

"I wish I knew." She hugged the book to her chest, puzzling over the new clues so intensely, her brain ached. "It could all be meaningless."

Three heads with six wondering eyes slowly came together. And then Kim Ling said what they all were thinking.

"Or it could completely change everything."

14

WHAT SOPHIE SAW

By the time the train arrived at the Grand Central stop, Kim Ling and Kevin had concluded that *shoot* and *needle* were no-brainers. They most likely had something to do with guns and drugs. Lexi agreed, but decided that none of the clues should be tossed aside completely just yet—in case they had it wrong. One thing she knew for sure: she didn't want Kevin tagging along on the next leg of their jewel hunt. It was way too dangerous. He should spend the day at City Camp. Like it or not.

"On my own?"

"Look, one of us has to represent," Kim Ling told him, "or Mr. Glick and his minions might start calling to check up on us, asking questions. Think of it as a solo undercover operation. You'll get to use all of your prepubescent wiles to keep the bloodhounds at bay."

"My *what?*"

"Meaning, if anybody asks where we are, make

something up," Lexi translated. She was getting good at interpreting Kim Lingese. "Just fudge it. C'mon, Kev, we're counting on you."

"Big time," Kim Ling added.

Kevin reluctantly agreed, so the girls quickly dropped him off at the YMCA, where the green group was picking teams for Red Rover and the blue group was getting ready to leave on some field trip. According to Kim Ling, Glick was always such a complete mess on split-group days like this that he never got around to taking attendance until the very last minute, and Kevin could easily slip in under the radar.

"Shoot, needle, oval disk, park," the girls chanted non-stop on their mad rush back to the train terminal. They were maneuvering through the thick, sweaty masses on Forty-Second Street pretty well until a perky young woman appeared out of nowhere and attempted to stop them with a clipboard and a smile.

"Hi! Do you guys have a minute for global warming?"

Kim Ling warned Lexi to just keep walking and not to make eye contact. But then, half a block later, Kim Ling went out of her way to stop a weirdo with a Rip Van Winkle beard spouting Bible verses and carrying a sign that read JUDGEMENT DAY!!

"Sir? Sir? Typo! There is no *e* after the *g*. It's a very common mistake."

While Lexi stood there rolling her eyes, she made an accidental discovery. Grand Central was bordered by

Park Avenue—which was probably where the *park* clue came into play. Kim Ling thought it was a plausible possibility. But a few minutes later, leaning against the information kiosk on the main concourse, waiting for Melrose to show up, both girls still couldn't figure out a single possibility for *oval disk*.

"I'm completely confused," Kim Ling said into her fist. "That psycho runaway is about to lead us into the mouth of Hades and for all we know the jewels could be buried in some park somewhere under some oval disk. By the way, she is now officially forty—make that forty-one—minutes late!"

"Huh?" *Shoot, needle, oval disk, park* was still running through Lexi's head like bad song lyrics. She quickly checked her cell phone to see if Melrose had left a message that she somehow missed. But no. Rubbing her throbbing temples, she glanced up at the opal-faced clock. 10:42. "You know what? This is ridiculous. I'm gonna run real quick and go ask Sophie if she's seen her today."

"Ask *who*?"

"The homeless woman who sits outside—Melrose's friend. She's not in her usual spot today, but I think I saw her stroller down the block on our way back. You wait here in case Mel shows. And be nice!"

Fingering her opal necklace, Lexi exited the terminal with her spinning bag of food still in hand, and scanned through the thicket of people on sun-dappled Vanderbilt Avenue. Sure enough, the telltale baby stroller was still jutting out from behind a large red garbage trough closer to Forty-Third Street. "Sophie?" she called out, and headed toward the cup-shaking silhouette.

"Who's that?"

"Remember me?" Lexi whipped off her sunglasses to reveal her face.

Sophie squinted up at her from her blanket, shielding her eyes with her trembling brown hand. "Stand in the shade so I can see you better."

Lexi did, but the old woman's expression remained confused.

"You said I had pretty hair the other day, remember? Oh!" Lexi had forgotten she was sporting her aunt's black wig. She twisted out a bunch of her own red curls to show Sophie, then tucked them back under the netting with a pat. "I'm just trying a different look."

"It don't suit you."

Lexi smiled and made a mental note to tell that one to Kim Ling. "You haven't by any chance seen Melrose around today, have you?"

"Seen who, now?"

"Your friend—Melrose. You know, the teenage girl with the long blond hair? Purple bandanna?"

"You mean Beth?"

"Uh, probably." *That's right, Melrose was her fake name. Beth? Talk about unsuitable.*

"Not too long ago, as a matter of fact. She was in a

hurry, though," Sophie said, gesturing wildly toward Fifth Avenue. "Runnin' thataway, thataway."

Lexi looked up and down the block, chewing her lower lip. "Hmm, that's weird. She was supposed to meet us at ten. Huh." She looked down at her bag full of food and back at Sophie. "Are you hungry?" *Stupid question.* "D'ya like waffles and scrambled eggs?" She grabbed a container from the bag and set it on the blanket. "Here ya go. Still warm."

"Oh, I appreciate it, darlin', but my stomach ain't been right lately. My babies'll eat anything, though." Her gnarled fingers pried off the lid and two cat tails shot straight up out of nowhere. "Ooh, das right, you're gettin' a special treat today, aren't you?" Happy meows quickly turned into licking sounds as Sophie sank back onto her blanket, stroking the cats. "I don't think Gabby's doing too good in this heat. She's always like this with her tongue hangin' out, panting like she can't breathe right." Her demonstration sparked a sudden coughing attack. "Now I've seen dogs do dat," she said, wheezing, "but not no cats. Not no cats."

"Are you all right?" Lexi pulled a water bottle from her backpack pouch and handed it to Sophie. "Make sure your babies drink some but you have your fill first, all right? Promise?"

"Oh, don't you worry about me none."

"Okay then," Lexi said, starting to leave, "bye, Sophie.

And if you see Mel—uh, Beth, I mean—tell her Lexi is looking for her, okay? *Lexi*. And that I'll be waiting inside by the clock."

"I will if I do, but I won't. Not today."

"Why's that?"

"She won't come back. Not with them cops on her tail."

"What do you mean?"

"They really crackin' down. Raided the train station this morning and cleared out all the freeloaders 'n' runaways 'n' such. Darn near gave me a heart attack. They not messin' around this time—mm-mmm, they *not* messin' around."

15

DOWN AND DIRTY

"I don't think Mel's gonna show!" Lexi called out to Kim Ling, who was pacing in front of the information kiosk, looking as if she was about to strangle someone. "You're not gonna believe it. Sophie saw her running from the cops today after they raided Grand Central. That poor girl! Can you imagine?"

"Really?" Kim Ling blinked a few times and scratched an eyebrow. "Well, truth be told, I think we're better off without her. I swear, she's *non compos mentis*, that chick—not playin' with a full deck. On to plan B."

The word heartless sprang to Lexi's mind but she kept it to herself. "I didn't know there was a plan B."

"There's wasn't. Until now. I just don't know what it is yet."

Lexi adjusted her wig, tugging and slapping at it as if it were a too-tight football helmet, and challenged herself to come up with something before Kim Ling. She wandered around the kiosk, running her hand over the train schedule leaflets with a hopeful eye out for Melrose. But who was she kidding? She checked her phone messages again. Nothing. Coming full circle, she tossed the remaining food into a trash can with a sigh of defeat, and when she turned around—"Oh, pardon me!"—she bounced off a mound of flesh.

It was a lumpy woman in a *Phantom of the Opera* T-shirt, holding a giant street-vendor pretzel.

"Good gravy, I apologize!" the woman said in a soupy Southern drawl. "Are y'all, by any chance, here for the free walking tour of Grand Central Station?"

Kim Ling's head snapped in her direction. "Maybe."

"The fellow at the hotel desk said we should all meet up by the gilded clock."

"This is it," Lexi told her. "It's actually priceless—all four faces are genuine opal, but you'd never guess from looking at it."

"Ooh. Isn't that wonderful? Maybe *you* should be giving the tour!" The woman cackled unexpectedly and gestured to her unmistakable male counterpart in a matching *Phantom* T-shirt with a camera swinging from his neck. "Vern! Come on!"

"Ma'am," Kim Ling said in her polite voice, "what's the tour exactly?"

"We're not really sure, to be honest with you. We're just killin' time till David Letterman. Me and my husband won tickets to see a live taping of his show."

"Oh, fun," Lexi said with a polite smile.

"I know! We're real excited. We signed up for it online way back in—when was it, Vern? September! They put you in some kind of lottery and it takes—" She noticed something in the distance and her lips stopped flapping. "Oh, shh-shh-shh, this fellow looks like he might be somebody."

Through a crisscross of commuters, a nerdy little man in a rumpled blazer and glaringly white sneakers was fighting his way toward the kiosk. "If you're here for the eleven o'clock tour of the secrets of Grand Central Terminal," he said through his small bullhorn, "you've come to the right place. I'm your guide, Neil Early."

"Well, it's eleven-oh-two, Mr. Early—you're late!" Kim Ling *had* to say.

"No one thinks you're funny," Lexi whispered. "Secrets, he said. That sounds promising."

"Totally. Let's just play dumb tourists, though, okay? Ha! Look who I'm talking to."

Lexi gave her a bump with the boniest part of her hip.

"Excuse me, sir?" Kim Ling stuck out her hand as if she were hailing a cab. "Watch and learn," she whispered to Lexi.

"Is there a question?"

"If you don't mind. Yeah, I remember seeing some TV show about an old abandoned train station that's supposed to be here. Seemed pretty cool. Your tour doesn't by any chance go down there, does it, 'cause that would be awesome."

"Oh, you mean that documentary on PBS," Mr. Early said, as if he had actually heard of it. "The covert network of underground tracks and tunnels? Infamous Track Sixty-one? The hidden platform President Roosevelt used to gain secret access to the Waldorf Astoria Hotel?"

"Yes!"

"No. Strictly off-limits."

Kim Ling looked to Lexi with amazement on her face. "Well, bummer, but I didn't even know there really *was* a documentary," she whispered. "I was extemporizing."

"It's a fascinating spot to explore, though," Mr. Early mumbled. He had a telltale glint in his eye, stroking his knot of a chin. "Incredibly rich with history. And mystique."

Kim Ling leaned into Lexi. "Hello, plan B!"

"Oh, I adore FDR," the Southern lady said with a mustardy mouthful of pretzel. "Why'd he have to have secret access? To avoid the paparazzi?"

"Exactly. Plus remember, he kept the fact that he was bound to a wheelchair a big secret from the public. Everyone knew he had polio—but they didn't know he couldn't actually walk."

It was Kim Ling who rattled off that answer, which didn't make Neil Early look all too happy.

"What happened to dumb tourist?" Lexi said out of the side of her mouth.

"That may be biologically impossible for me."

"Alrighty then, folks, I'm just waiting on a group to

show—but in the meantime, let's everyone look up and appreciate this magnificent ceiling of stars, shall we?" Mr. Early raised the bullhorn to his mouth and all heads fell back in awe. "It was painted by an artist named Paul Helleu, and astute observers may notice that the signs of the zodiac are completely backward. Some thought this was a mistake, but, in all actuality, Helleu was depicting the heavens as they would have been seen from—"

"God's perspective," Kim Ling finished.

"What're you doing?" Lexi whispered. "We don't want to tick this guy off."

"If you direct your attention to the upper left-hand corner of the ceiling—*waaay* over there, you'll notice a small black rectangular swatch. See it?"

Mr. Early took a few steps away from the kiosk and pointed up to the spot. Vern snapped a picture.

"That's a smidgeon of the old ceiling. It was intentionally left during the nineteen ninety-five restoration as a stunning reminder of the vast improvement the mural had undergone. A before and after, if you will." Mr. Early motioned the group forward like a traffic cop. "The glorious spectrum of sweet summer light gleams doubly bright against wintry night," he recited in a sing-songy surge. "Forgive me. I'm afraid I'm a bit of a poet."

"Well, he ain't no Shakespeare," Kim Ling muttered.

Lexi liked his little poem. Loved it. She even repeated it to herself a few times so she wouldn't forget it. But she wasn't about to admit that to Kim Ling.

"I do have a small book of poetry available—self-published, if anyone is—" Mr. Early's voice fell from the bullhorn. "Ah, here they are now! Welcome, welcome."

Lexi and Kim Ling gasped in each others' faces. Either they were seeing things, or they were completely surrounded by a cluster of puke green—as in City Campers in their official T-shirts! Aside from their dropped jaws and astonished expressions, Lexi and Kim Ling immediately blended right in since they were wearing the same shirts.

"Let me just take a quick head count while everyone turns off your cell phones, then we'll officially begin our tour."

"Are you freakin' kidding me?" Kim Ling whispered to Lexi. She grabbed her arm and led her behind the group of gum-cracking, chattering campers, where they squatted down low to avoid Mr. Early's pecking finger.

"Is Kevin here?" Lexi asked through tight lips.

"I don't think—no, it's the green group, the older kids. I don't see Glick, either. We lucked out. Looks like pizza-face Felicia Bitterman is in charge."

"Who?" Lexi peeked around a bevy of backpacks and spotted the pimply beanpole camp counselor who had been manning one of the tables at orientation. She was so tall and skinny, she stuck out like a dehydrated giraffe.

"Alrighty then," came Mr. Early's voice through the bullhorn. "Please follow me to a very unique location in the dining concourse. But a word of warning: keep it down to a whisper."

"Uh-oh, Whispering Gallery!" Lexi said, poking Kim Ling. "How much you wanna bet?"

"No kidding, Sherlock."

The girls plotted to get through the tour as unnoticed as possible, but Lexi practically had a spaz attack watching the City Campers trying out their whispers in the exact same spot outside the Oyster Bar and Restaurant where all the craziness had begun. And when everyone insisted on taking a turn, Kim Ling stepped out of the shadows to rush things along. That was when Felicia Bitterman asked her how she even knew about the Grand Central tour in the first place, since she had obviously cut camp the day before. It went something like: "Did not." "Did so." "Did not." "Did so." *"Did not—infinity!"* And that was the end of that.

"And now, ladies and gentleman, we're heading outside to observe what is possibly the largest example of Tiffany glass in the world: the magnificent clock gracing the main entrance. Perhaps you'll recognize the gods depicted in the statues surrounding it."

"Hercules, Mercury, and Minerva," Kim Ling spouted. "With all due respect, I thought this was supposed to be a *secrets* tour. What about the abandoned train station we were talking about—in the underbelly of Grand Central?"

The group started chattering and bombarding Mr. Early with questions.

"No, no, security has really been tightened in the last twenty-four hours. There's some funny business going on.

I don't want to ruffle any feathers or I could lose my job." Mr. Early glanced around nervously, scratching his sunburned bald spot. "Then again, I suppose that really doesn't matter since I'm moving to St. Louis in two weeks," he said half to himself with a sneaky smile. "And I really *would* love to see it one last time." He checked his watch. Pursed his lips. "I'll tell you what. Let me make a quick call to my very powerful friend at Metro-North—I have a slew of favors to collect on. In the meantime, talk amongst yourselves and decide. We can either go up to the clock tower and observe this Tiffany masterpiece up close—or we can venture down to the abandoned station. It's quite spectacular, I assure you."

He whipped out his cell phone and turned his back on the group, which erupted in a babbling debate between up or down. Felicia was pro-clock tower and seemed to be convincing the majority, despite Kim Ling talking up the train station. When Mr. Early turned back around with "We're cleared" and asked for a show of hands, the vote was split down the middle.

"Go to St. Patrick's Cathedral if you want stained glass," Kim Ling scolded. "But, you guys, the secret train station is such a rare opportunity." She zeroed in on the *Phantom* clones. "Just think—it'd be not unlike exploring the caverns under the Paris Opera House where the Phantom took Christine."

Two chubby hands shot up. "Well, good gravy, Vern and me change our votes!"

"Then we have our consensus!" Mr. Early announced.

Lexi turned to Kim Ling. "You should go into politics."

The group could barely keep up with Mr. Early's brisk pace as he led them back into Grand Central, down ramps and through a roundabout maze of marbled hallways, until they reached a stand-alone elevator, where a heavy man in a dark suit was planted. They exchanged a few quick words and the man discreetly handed something to Mr. Early before disappearing. No button was ever pressed but the elevator doors immediately flew open and the whole group somehow was able to squish inside. It didn't budge at first, this stuffy, antique contraption, but then Mr. Early flashed a small plastic device in front of the button panel; there was a long beep, a red light blinked, and the elevator rumbled to life.

With her heart *pa-thumping*, Lexi counted the seconds of their rickety descent to purgatory. She was fingering the rabbit's foot, laminated four-leaf clover, and nine lucky pennies in her pocket with one hand, twisting her opal necklace with the other. At least she and Kim Ling were with other people. Sweaty people smelling of suntan lotion and B.O. maybe—but, still. *Better than going it alone.* Then it occurred to her that she and Kim had spent all their time thinking of how to get down to the abandoned station, but didn't have a plan for what to do once they got there!

Pa-thump, pa-thump, pa-thump!

"Just calm down," Kim Ling said in an intense whisper. "Follow. My. Lead."

Had she noticed the look of terror in Lexi's eyes? *Tunnels,* Lexi kept thinking as her stomach meowed like a sick cat. *Creepy, dark tunnels. I must be out of my mind.*

BAH-ROOM! Touchdown. The elevator doors rattled open and the group cautiously shuffled out of the elevator into the dank and dingy station that looked as if it had survived an explosion or something. Kim Ling grabbed Lexi's sweaty hand.

"Gross. What smells?" Felicia said, crinkling her face.

It was instantly nauseating. Like rusty, dead turtles.

"Good gravy," the Southern couple said together.

"That's history. It's positively palpable." Mr. Early actually inhaled it all in as he ventured forward in a dork-like trance. "Picture, if you will, the year is nineteen sixty-five and renowned pop artist Andy Warhol is hosting a private party on the very platform on which we're standing. There's champagne overflowing, the finest Russian caviar, anybody who's anybody is in attendance . . ."

Kim Ling pulled Lexi aside. "As soon as diarrhea-mouth points out where Track Sixty-one is, we make our move."

"No."

"We slip away quickly and quiet—wait, did you just say no?"

"It's off, I'm not doing it. We could get trapped down here and suffocate."

"The elevator's right there."

"But Mr. Early had to use his plastic thingy to get it to work."

"So, then, we just wait for someone to come along."

"That could be never!"

"Listen," Kim Ling hissed, tightening her grip on Lexi's hand, "we've come this far. All we have to do is find the spot where the jewels are buried and the rest is a breeze. We show Early our discovery—*bing, bang, boom*—the next thing you know we're telling our story on the six o'clock news."

"Sorry, but no way."

"Five o'clock news?"

Lexi pulled her hand away.

"C'mon, a quarter of a million bucks—all yours!"

"You don't understand. I can't breathe. I'm, like, totally freaking out!"

"Is there a problem back there?" Mr. Early asked over the constant hissing noise that sounded as if another steam pipe was about to burst.

"Neil, is it?" Kim Ling called out, and Lexi recoiled. "Question. Where'd you say Track Sixty-one was again?"

"I didn't. There isn't an actual 'Track Sixty-one,'" he said with accompanying air quotes. "That's simply a code word they used for this secret platform we're standing on—built for FDR so he could have private access to the Waldorf Astoria." Twitching with excitement, he cleared his throat and raised his bullhorn. "Alrighty, folks, let's venture over to that blue freight car. See it? Completely bulletproof. It was said to have secretly carried FDR's private limo. Oh, but *do* stick together and watch your step—I once saw a rat down here the size of a beaver."

"Good gravy!" Lexi blurted. The Southern couple gave her a curious look and she offered an awkward smile in return. Wringing her clammy hands, she kept in step with the rest of the group until something jerked her back. Kim Ling had a hold of her backpack strap. "Stop it. What're you doing?"

"You can cry about this later." In the span of a heartbeat, Kim Ling swung her to the edge of the platform and, without even a one-two-*three*, leaped onto the tracks, dragging a squealing Lexi with her. They landed in a dusty, twisted heap.

"You all right?"

"No!" Lexi gasped, sucking in a lungful of dirt. "You did not—*kkklugh*—you did not just do that!" A coughing fit came over her and she spit out what she could, staggering to her feet.

"Executive decision."

"He just said there is no Track Sixty-one!"

"Keep your voice down. And, no, he said it was a *secret code* for the platform." Kim Ling unzipped her backpack and began wildly rummaging through it. "And that's the platform, which means the jewels have to be buried in this general area." She whipped out two small flashlights,

switched them on, and handed one to Lexi. "I came pre-
pared. There're trowels, too. Now hustle."

"But—"

"Like you've never hustled before. You can't wimp out
after we've come this far. This is too big!"

Okay, she'd suck it up and do it. Even though her shin
was bleeding, her hands were trembling, and she didn't
have a trace of saliva left in her mouth.

"If you see anything even the slightest bit suspicious,
holler." Kim Ling shone her light on the tracks, slowly
swinging it like a pendulum. "Well, don't actually holler."

Lexi followed suit, scouring the ground in the opposite
direction, holding her breath from the floating dust bits
that never seemed to settle. "Wait!" she said, noticing
something. "Oh, never mind, false alarm. Just a cruddy old
Coke bottle." She kicked it aside.

"Keep your eyes peeled for a marker—like an X-marks-
the-spot kind of thing—or a patch of ground that was
recently dug up. Oh, and don't forget the new clues."

"Shoot, needle, oval disk, park," Lexi recited.

"Right." Kim Ling crouched down to examine a pile of
crumbling wood chips. "We already covered shoot, needle,
and park. So, be on the lookout for an *oval disk*."

Lexi switched into high gear and tried desperately to
focus on the task at hand. With a watchful eye out for
bugs, rats, and vermin of any kind, she combed the cor-
roded, crumbling train track. Steel rails, wooden ties, and

grunge. That's all she could see until something shiny caught her eye and she dove for it. "Hey, Kim, is this anything?" She held it up. "It's a disk and it's oval."

Kim Ling rushed over and shone her light on the small metal disk. "Flattened bottle cap. Probably belongs to that Coke bottle. Besides, it's not even oval. Oval means elliptical—egg-shaped. That thing's perfectly round. Keep looking."

Lexi tossed it aside and continued on. But there wasn't a thing she spied that could remotely be described as an oval disk aside from some rusty nail heads, a few flat pebbles, and a squashed Big Gulp cup. "You know, maybe I didn't hear that clue exactly right," she said, still searching. "Maybe it was something that *sounded* like oval disk. Shmoval . . . groval—nothing rhymes with oval. Tisk-frisk-bisque. Over this! Maybe they said, 'We're over this.' "

Kim Ling jolted upright and stood there thinking. "Or global risk?"

"Ooh, good one."

"Right? Unfortunately, that doesn't help us a lick. Keep looking."

But after searching the same stretch of dilapidated track for the umpteenth time and breathing in one too many lungfuls of stale, mildewy stench, Lexi had had it. "I don't see anything," she cried, slapping dirt off her hands. "The ground is rock solid and there's nothing diskish or oval. No markers, no nothing. This is nuts!"

"Keep searching and stop kvetching."

"Speak English."

Withered or not, Lexi sucked it up and carried on with her hunt until a wave of approaching chatter brought both girls to a standstill. Kim Ling immediately took cover behind a thick iron girder and Lexi followed. Standing belly to belly with panic on their faces and cobwebs tickling their necks, they switched off their flashlights and held their collective breath. It was difficult to hear clearly through the never-ending hiss of escaping steam. *TSSSSSSSSSSSSSSSSSS—*

"*—ssssso* sorry, y'all, but I'll never forgive myself if we came all this way only to miss David Letterman. Plus, I really have to use the little girl's room."

The campers were whining that they had seen enough, too, and it wasn't long before the group was back at the elevator with Mr. Early counting heads. "—eleven, twelve. That's right, isn't it? So, why does it seem like someone's missing? That rowdy Asian girl and her friend!" Mr. Early raised his bullhorn and yelled out, "Girls? Come on, we're waiting on you! *Girls!*"

"Rowdy?" Kim Ling muttered. "That little weasel."

Lexi separated her fists, which were covering her mouth. "Now what?" she asked in barely a whisper, and her fists snapped back into place like a steel trap. "Kim?"

"Ya got me. Invisibility cloak?"

16

THE BELLS OF ST. AGNES

Lexi and Kim Ling really had no choice but to give up the search for the jewels and reveal themselves—especially since they needed Mr. Early's help to hoist them off the tracks. "It was a freak accident," Kim Ling had told him on the way up in the elevator with the rest of the group. "The edge of that decrepit platform gave way. But don't worry—even though my dad's an attorney, we're not gonna sue. It's technically not your fault."

So, they were off the hook with the tour guide and wound up on Park Avenue, just outside Grand Central, with Felicia and the rest of the campers. But since they were "too shaken up to continue with the day's camp activities," and had fake-called their parents to come get them, Kim and Lexi were finally left alone, staring into a fancy window display of meats and cheeses.

"Omigod, I'm hideous!" Lexi said to her reflection. She

glanced over at Kim Ling, wondering why she didn't have a snide remark.

"That was definitely the right call," she said, lost in her own little world. "We could've been stuck down there for days."

Lexi cringed at the thought. "Weeks." She dug a can of Altoids out of her backpack and popped a mint into her mouth, then slipped off her mangy wig. Her gross, flattened hair made her look even worse—not to mention the battered shins and filthy clothes. It was official: less than a week in New York City and she had been beaten down to a bloody stump. "I still can't believe you just yanked me onto the tracks like that. I could've broken something."

"That ground was untouched," Kim Ling said, still reviewing the situation. "And the perps would've had to have left a marker or something, otherwise, how could they possibly return to the exact spot—in those ruins? No, the more I think about it, the more I'm convinced that Cleopatra's jewels aren't buried down there at all—which means at least part of what you heard in the Whispering Gallery was bogus—which means we have to reassess, regroup, and start again from square one." She snapped her fingers in Lexi's face. "Hello? Is anyone there?"

Lexi was lost in her reflection again. "I guess this is what destitute looks like."

"At least your vocabulary is improving. Did you hear a word I said just now?"

"I heard."

Kim Ling was studying Lexi, her mouth in a twist. "How did you end up getting so much grodier than me? You could give Melrose Merritt a run for her money." She brushed a splotch of soot off Lexi's shoulder. "Ugh, speaking of the devil, I'm glad she never showed up today, aren't you? At least we don't have to deal with that nut job anymore."

"Mmm." Lexi was rubbing her right eye, which was suddenly stinging and watery.

"Oh, turdballs, you're not crying, are you?"

"No. I've got a lump of coal or something in my eye."

In a flash, Kim Ling had the corner of a tissue rolled into a point and ready to come to the rescue. "Look to the left," she said, prying open Lexi's quivering eyelid. "Look to the right." Lexi's eyeballs did as they were told. "Stand up, sit down, fight, fight, *fight!*"

A burst of laughter sent the mint shooting from Lexi's mouth right onto Kim Ling's cheek. Lexi tried to flick it off, but Kim Ling was flailing and swatted at her face as if she were being attacked by killer bees. Finally, the mint went flying and they both laughed themselves teary-eyed.

"Hey, it worked," Lexi said, blinking wide blinks. "That crud in my eye got totally washed away!"

"Along with my last shred of dignity." Kim Ling wiped the slobber off her cheek with her sleeve. "You know," she said, still cracking up, "I'm suddenly famished. C'mon, I'll treat you to a bagel with a schmear while we come up with our next plan of attack."

Lexi shot her a curious look.

"Cream cheese."

They took off down the street with Lexi hoping that no one would stare and point at her, unsightly wreck that she was. Nobody did. That was the thing about New York— even if you looked like the biggest oddball ever, there were always at least ten odder balls on any given block. Even so, she was still trying to fluff up her hair as they stopped at a little deli on Vanderbilt Avenue that Kim Ling insisted on going to. The line was long, so Lexi lingered outside, killing time counting lit-up OFF DUTY signs on passing taxicabs and thinking about how *this* was a side of Kim Ling she really sort of liked—the funny-helpful-generous side.

A banging and clattering interrupted her thoughts. It just so happened to come from way down the block, where Sophie, the homeless woman, usually sat—and before Lexi could stop herself, she was rushing toward the racket.

"What's going on?" she called out to a policeman with a squawking walkie-talkie. "Excuse me, officer—no! You can't throw that stuff away. It belongs to someone I know."

Apparently, he had just heaved Sophie's broken stroller into the giant Dumpster. He flung the blanket in next, along with the container of food Lexi had dropped off earlier. Pigeons took off flying through an explosion of scrambled eggs.

"Please, stop!" Lexi cried, tugging at his arm, her heart racing.

"You wanna be arrested for obstructing justice? Then I suggest you unhand me."

She quickly let him go. "Destroying an old woman's private property is justice?"

"Take it easy, kid. I'm just clearing Sophie's junk off the public street, that's all."

"But you can't just—wait, you know Sophie?"

"Everybody knew her."

Knew? Just then a black cat zoomed across Lexi's feet with a pitiful *maaow*. She lurched forward to grab it but the cat was slippery fast. It had to be Gabby, one of Sophie's babies. *A black cat crossing your path on Friday the thirteenth. Bad luck times two.*

"I tell ya, the homeless don't stand a chance in this city. They can drop just like that." The cop snapped his fingers. "The ambulance got here as fast as it could but . . ."

Lexi twisted to her feet and started speed-walking away, not needing nor *wanting* to hear the rest of the officer's explanation. It was only too obvious.

"And where do you think you're going, girly? Hey, I'm talkin' to you!"

Without thinking, Lexi took off running as fast as she could up the street and around the corner to the front of the train terminal, where she was swallowed up by a swarm of pedestrians. Overcome by a bout of dizziness, she collapsed onto a fire hydrant behind a newsstand, panting and sweating, looking for any sign of the policeman. Thankfully, there were none. Her insides felt battered. Fluttery. Like a suffocating butterfly was trying to escape. She tried pushing what had just happened out of her head, but somehow her mother's death began playing out instead, and she had to bite her lip to keep from bawling.

Through a splotch of sunlight, Lexi noticed a pair of gray high heels scrape to a halt in front of her. Something floated onto her lap. *A ten-dollar bill?* Lexi immediately snatched it up. "Miss?" she called out, waving the money. "I think you dropped this."

"Don't do anything foolish with it, okay?" The woman flashed Lexi a weak smile and kept going. "Call your parents. They must be worried sick."

"What?" And then it sunk in. "No, wait. I'm not a runaway!"

It cut like a sword, that look of pity in the woman's eyes. It was soul damaging. Something Lexi would never forget. *Had the cop thought she was a runaway too? Is this all really happening?*

In a burst of panic, she dug her phone out of her backpack to call Kim Ling and tell her where to meet up with her, but just as she was about to dial, it rang.

"Kim? Hello?"

"No. It's me—Melrose. I'm, uh—sorry for standing you guys up but—"

"Melrose? I can barely hear you. What's that clanging?"

"It just started. I'm at a pay phone outside of—"

"What? Outside of where?"

"Ugh! I can't hear a freakin' thing! You know what? Bad timing—forget it!"

"No, wait—are you all right? Hello? Oh, no . . ."

Lexi tried calling back but there was no answer. Suddenly the city seemed harsh and horrible and closing in on her. She stared up past the silvery art deco topper of the Chrysler building, past the wispy clouds, desperately wondering what to do. Horns were still honking and sirens screaming and yet the most glorious sound was bleeding through. Church bells? Clanging in the distance? *Melrose had mentioned there was a church near Grand Central when they were at the pizza place—St. Agnes, was it?—where she hid out sometimes. Whenever things got really bad.* She scrambled to her feet with a sudden purpose.

"Excuse me, ma'am?" Lexi called out to a ruddy-faced woman selling flowers from plastic buckets on the corner. "Do you happen to know where St. Agnes is?"

"I dunno—a few blocks east, I think," the woman croaked, barely looking up from her tulips. "Just follow your ears."

Lexi did just that, texting Kim Ling along the way.

MEET UP @3 IN FRNT OF Y 2 PICK UP KEV . . .
XPLAIN L8R.

Sure enough, she found Melrose slouched in the back pew of the church, watching a poorly attended funeral. She was eating a stash of broken Oreos, her face streaked with tears. After having had just a taste of what it felt like to be a runaway herself, Lexi knew right there and then that she had to help this poor girl—or at least try. And before the priest had finished his eulogy, she had come up with a brilliant plan.

17

FRETTING AT THE MET

"Up and at 'em, kids!" Aunt Roz sang, parading through the living room first thing Saturday morning. "You don't want to sleep away our Day of Family Fun!"

At least Friday was over. It had been the second most horrible day of Lexi's life. Between the terrifying experience in the bowels of Grand Central, Sophie's death, and then being mistaken for a runaway, Lexi couldn't decide which was worse. Thank goodness she had heard those church bells—a definite sign from the universe. And even though the plan she had come up with at St. Agnes was risky and broke so many rules you could never keep count, Lexi knew deep inside she was doing the right thing. Now she would have to skillfully maneuver her way through Aunt Roz's DOFF, which wouldn't be easy. Part one, as it turned out, was a breakfast of hot dogs and smoothies at the neighborhood Papaya King. And part two? Lexi's choice: the Metropolitan Museum of Art.

You could spot it from blocks away, the museum—
right on Fifth Avenue, flanked by enormous pillars and
big, colorful banners rippling in the breeze. It was almost
like some classy white palace, if the king and queen
allowed dozens of tourists to sit on their endless front
steps, gawking, snacking, and taking pictures. Aunt Roz
insisted they go straight up to the European paintings section, so they could soak in the masterpieces of the French
Impressionists, like Renoir, Monet, and Degas. Kevin was
busy texting Space Camp Billy but Lexi really absorbed
all the art. She liked the colorful flower paintings mostly
and the misty landscapes, but what really drew her attention was a bronze ballerina statue wearing a real cotton
skirt and a faded satin hair ribbon called *The Little
Fourteen-Year-Old Dancer*, by Edgar Degas.

"Whoa, the model for this was a real live girl who
danced with the Paris Opera," Lexi told Aunt Roz, reading
the plaque at the base. She studied the rigid ballerina up
close. "Way to go, mademoiselle."

Lexi had to remind herself not to get too caught up in
her surroundings, though, and focus on business. She
needed to keep her eye on the clock if she was to carry
out her plan on time. Plus, this was the museum where
Cleopatra's jewels were headed when they got ripped off,
which was why she chose it in the first place. There was
potential sniffing around to do.

"I always get so emotional, drinking in these wonderful works of art," Aunt Roz said dreamily. "The

first time I saw *Woman with Chrysanthemums*, I actually cried."

"Oh, that's so sweet," Lexi said.

"So, all they have here," Kevin asked, "is just, like— art?"

"No. There's ice-fishing on the lower level," Lexi said sarcastically. "Kevin, it's called the Metropolitan Museum of—"

"I know, I know."

Lexi unfolded her museum map in Kevin's face and zeroed in on it. "The Temple of Dendur sounds interesting. It's an Egyptian monument from fifteen BCE—in the Sackler Wing, downstairs, part of the giant Egyptian Art section. I'm sure they have a ton of mummified stuff even a ten-year-old boy with the attention span of a gnat might like." Her head popped up over the map and she glanced down at Kevin. "And probably info on *Cleopatra*."

"Oh, okay," he said, obviously catching her drift. "Let's go!"

What Lexi was hoping to find there, she wasn't quite sure. Slivers of clues maybe? Mystical vibes? Something.

"Well, the Met was your pick, Alexandra, so lead the way," Aunt Roz said. "Kevin can be in charge when we get to the planetarium."

They started through the maze of art-filled rooms with Lexi in front wrestling with the map; Kevin a few steps behind, snapping photos; and Aunt Roz pulling up the rear, unwrapping a hard candy she had dug out of her straw tote. "It's terrible, isn't it?" she said, and popped the candy into her mouth. "That Cleopatra jewel heist—well, they probably weren't *really* her jewels but that's what they're calling them in the press even though there was no actual proof."

Lexi came to a standstill. Suddenly she was stiffer than *The Little Fourteen-Year-Old Dancer*.

"You kids must've heard about it, right? There's so much hoopla. It was supposed to be opening here next week, the Queen of the Nile exhibit."

Kevin and Lexi gave each other blank looks—with a layer of knowing-all-too-well-what-she-was-talking-about underneath.

"They charge extra for those special exhibits," Aunt Roz went on, "which is absolutely ludicrous. Or am I thinking of the Museum of Natural History? Hard candy?"

"The ones with the fruity centers?" Kevin asked, scrunching up his nose. "Pass."

"No? Alexandra?"

"No, thanks. Oh, look," she said, pointing down the hall, "stairs!" They had conveniently come into view so she grabbed Kevin and took off in a power-walk toward the top of the staircase.

"I suppose that doesn't matter a fig at this point anyway," Aunt Roz said, trotting to catch up with them and sucking on her candy, "since the doggone jewels vanished into thin air. Kiss that exhibit good-bye. Such a shame. I was really looking forward to it."

In the Egyptian Art section on the main level, Lexi did her best to change the sticky subject of Cleopatra's jewels, but how could she? They were knee-deep in creepy sarcophagi, relics, and pharaoh statues. At least Kevin was being cooperative. Letting him in on her secret plan before leaving the house was definitely the right decision—but the whole "pulling yet another one over on Aunt Roz" thing was tearing up her insides like a paper shredder.

"There was supposed to be a fabulous emerald necklace too," Aunt Roz said, studying a stone relief of Cleopatra's head from the Ptolemaic period. "Emeralds were her favorite, so they say."

Would she *ever* let up about the jewel heist and the special exhibit? By the time they had reached the wing where the Temple of Dendur stood, Lexi was about to spontaneously combust from nervousness. "I need to sit," she said, perching at the end of a large black pool peppered with coins.

Aunt Roz politely nodded at two security guards strolling by. "Maybe we should all take a little break."

"No, you guys go ahead. Seriously. I'll be here by this reflecting pool . . . reflecting."

The room was sunny and open with a big wall of tilted windows overlooking Central Park. Lexi watched as Kevin and Aunt Roz disappeared between the pillars of one of the ancient sandstone temples on display, and hugged the map to her chest. *Hmm, maybe if I really concentrate, I can pick up something from the spirit of Cleopatra herself. Or is that too crazy? I mean, if anyone's going to know* *where her missing jewels are* . . . She mentally hit "select-all-delete" to erase her thoughts and make room for incoming messages. Nothing at first. Then, slowly but surely, a caravan of camels began floating through her mind—and sand. Lots of sand. *Think jewels—not deserts.* She tried for a few more minutes, but all she ended up with was a dry mouth, a throbbing headache, and a case of the heebie-jeebies.

"Yeah, he was just a normal, friendly guy—smart as a whip, had everything going for him. Next thing you know, he's an international fugitive. Every time I click on the news now, it's 'Benjamin Deets this and Benjamin Deets that.' Crazy world."

Lexi's eyes popped open. And if her ears could have perked up any more, they would have sprung from her head. The two security guards who had been reminding people to turn off their flashes were standing next to the reflecting pool having a loudish conversation about the perp.

"You know, I saw him right out that window one time after he got the boot," the man went on, "trimming hedges in the park. Not that there's anything wrong with that—lots of folks enjoy that line of work, but to go from director of security . . . you know what I mean?"

"Yeah," the female security guard agreed.

"I heard he even used to have a cushy side job at some television network as a—whaddya call it?—you know, like, when they call in professionals on shows to make sure everything looks genuine."

"Consultant?"

"A consultant, that's it. He was at the top of his game and he flushed it all down the toilet—and for what? Revenge? Crazy world."

"Crazy world."

Lexi couldn't believe she was eavesdropping again. *Revenge,* she repeated in her mind so she wouldn't forget. *Consultant. Trimming hedges in the park.* She followed the guards as they wandered through the Sackler Wing in starts and stops, hoping to pick up more revealing tidbits of conversation about Benjamin Deets. Unfortunately, she never heard another word—except for "Miss, miss? You with the red curly hair. Please don't lean on the exhibit."

"Oh. Sorry."

She had almost bolted, but the words "From Cleopatra's Needle" caught her eye. They were on the plaque next to the glass case she had illegally been leaning on. *Shoot, needle, oval disk, park* flashed in her brain in neon as she studied the deformed-looking bronze crab that was on display inside the case. According to the plaque, it was from 13 BCE, Roman period, a gift of Henry H. Gorringe, 1881, and had originally been part of an ancient Egyptian monument that still stood in Central Park. *Needle and park!* Her heartbeat quickened. She and Kim Ling had originally thought *needle* had something to do with drugs and *park* was Park Avenue—but since they had ruled out Grand

Central as the spot where the jewels were buried, all the clues were up for grabs again. Until now. *That's two clues in one—a doubleheader. Major score! I have to tell Kim Ling!*

Aunt Roz and Kevin caught up with her seconds later, so it wasn't until their taxicab ride on the way to the Rose Center for Earth and Science that Lexi had the chance to text her news to Kim Ling. And then it was 2:45. Time for her own plan to go into full swing. Juggling two undercover operations at the same time might drive her off the deep end, but she had to do what she had to do. So she faked a bad headache and told Aunt Roz she had better drop her off at the apartment first, that she needed some Tylenol plus a nice, long nap for fear of missing their big night out.

Talk about guilt—now her lies had become even more complicated, involving cheap theatrics and over-the-counter drugs.

18

LIBRARY OF LIPS

"Were you kids rolling around in the mud at City Camp yesterday?" Aunt Roz asked Lexi a few hours later. She was at the white vanity table in her bedroom brushing her hair in the mirror, prepping for Part Two of their DOFF: homemade dinner and a show. "There's a ring around the tub that'll need to be sandblasted off."

"Yeah, we did get pretty filthy playing soccer," Lexi answered in a mousy voice, as if the softer the lie, the less it counted against you. "Sorry." Dressed and ready, she was sitting on the window seat, fiddling with the drapes and clicking her pink kitten-heel pumps. Even though her heart was rattling underneath, it still felt nice being all dressed up and girly—especially after being covered in grunge and smelling like a sweaty goat only twenty-four hours earlier.

"Feeling better, sweetheart?"

"Much."

"Too bad you missed that planetarium show, 'Journey to the Stars.' It was awe-inspiring."

"I know—Kevin keeps going on and on about it. I did have a really good time at the museum, though." *And picked up some really good clues!*

"Good." Aunt Roz gave her a look over her shoulder that lingered. "Don't have a conniption fit, but do you know what would look absolutely fabulous with your outfit?"

Of course she knew. Those hateful black pearls that Clare had sent. They would go perfectly with the pink-and-gray dress Lexi was wearing. It was her most sophisticated outfit, even though it was straight off the clearance rack at Target.

"My opal necklace goes with everything." Plus, she believed if she ever took it off, that disaster would strike— but that part she kept to herself.

"Yes, dear," Aunt Roz said, her mascara wand coming to a standstill, "that looks lovely too." She sent Lexi a knowing smile via the mirror, then went back to applying gobs of mascara over the gobs that were already there. "We really should give Mark and Clare a call to thank them for your gifts, don't you think? And tomorrow is Father's Day. That'll be perfect." She moved on to her lips, outlining them in a brownish pencil and coloring them in with a deep cranberry-red lipstick, then carefully blotted her mouth on a tissue and tossed it into a wicker waste-basket. "Oh, and in case you're wondering, I took the pearls out of the fish tank and put them in the lacquer box on the coffee table. I was afraid the clasp might rust."

Lexi felt she should speak just to fill up the dead air but nothing came out.

"Well, I'd better go check on the chicken. Our guest will be arriving soon." Aunt Roz spritzed the air with two blasts of perfume and lingered in the cloud for a second before sweeping into the living room.

"This is the proper way to apply it, cookie. Spray, stay, and walk away. So the scent isn't too overpowering."

Her mom's voice played in Lexi's head as she breathed in the flowery scent and watched the mist disintegrate into nothingness. Her gaze fell onto the crumpled tissue with the lipstick smear and her heart went numb. Lexi had watched her mom do it a thousand times: after putting on her lipstick, she would carefully blot her lips on a folded tissue, then add it to a neat stack in the little top drawer of her antique dresser. A library of lips.

"Mom, why do you save your lip prints?" she had asked her one day, just after she had turned eight.

Her mother had stopped what she was doing, like she was caught off guard.

"For posterity?" she said with an awkward shrug. "Force of habit? It's just a silly little game." She studied the tissue in her hand as if she were thinking even further back in time. "Let's see. The first one I ever saved—I think it was because the lip print came out so plump and perfect. I thought it was pretty, like a little work of art. Then before you know it . . ." Her fingers started digging their way through the thick stack. "You know, it must still be in here, the good one. Way at the—oh, here it is!" And she slipped the original tissue out of the drawer and gently laid it onto Lexi's palm.

"Cool," Lexi said, and examined the lip print from all angles. "It really is perfect. Can I have it?"

"Really? I can't imagine what for."

"Just 'cause."

"All right. But—let's just keep this between you and me, though, hon. I don't want people thinking I've gone off the deep end."

Over the years, that tiny drawer got filled to the brim. And after her mom had passed away, Lexi knew those tissues were way too precious to throw out in the trash. So without telling a soul, she had stored the entire library of lips in a silk-lined hatbox under her bed. A lifetime of kisses at her fingertips.

The doorbell rang five times in a row and Lexi flew out of her trance and shot to her feet, clutching her opal necklace.

"That must be Kim Ling!" Aunt Roz called out from the kitchen.

"It's showtime," Lexi muttered to herself. She wasn't at all convinced she could pull off the whopper of a stunt she had planned—but she was definitely about to find out.

19

ANGEL OF SILENCE

Lexi beat her aunt to the door, took a second to breathe, then pulled it open as if it were the ripcord on a parachute. "Last minute change of plans. Kim Ling couldn't make it tonight, Aunt Roz, so I invited my new friend—"

"Melrose!" The runaway teen thrust out her arm and pumped Aunt Roz's hand furiously. "How ya doin'?"

"A pleasure," Aunt Roz said through a quivering smile.

"She's my new BFF from City Camp," Lexi squeaked out.

Her lies were lingering in the air like a bad smell. And Melrose was lingering in the doorway chewing her newly polished fingernail stubs and smelling like gardenias. Except for the ever-present purple bandanna, which she wore as a sort of headband, the girl was hardly recognizable with her clean blond hair flowing over the crisp white blouse Lexi had lent her. They were both skinny-minnies, so size wasn't too much of an issue except for shoes—Melrose had canoes. But Lexi's stretchy ballet flats did the trick.

She had transformed this street urchin into someone presentable and all under an hour and a half. It had been quite a feat convincing Melrose to come in the first place, but the promise of a bubble bath and a home-cooked meal had sealed the deal. Sneaking her into the apartment past Kim Ling's radar was feat number two; and choosing an outfit that didn't make her gag was big fat feat number three.

"Do come in and make yourself at home." Aunt Roz welcomed Melrose into the living room as if she were hosting some fancy soiree. "I'm thrilled that Alexandra met a new companion." She bunched up her apron and ditched it in a closet on her way back to the kitchen, whispering to Lexi, "You might've given me fair warning, dear."

As soon as Aunt Roz was out of earshot, Lexi pulled Melrose aside. "I forgot to tell you how sorry I am about Sophie. I know she was your friend."

Melrose shot her a curious look, as if she was wondering how she had found out the homeless woman had died, but didn't ask. "What kills me is the cops trashed all her stuff. Just a buncha worthless junk, but still—it's like she never existed."

For some reason the library of lips popped into Lexi's mind. She was about to give Melrose a comforting hug but Aunt Roz announced dinner and they both made a bee-line for the kitchen. Kevin and Aunt Roz were already seated at the tiny kitchen table, so Lexi and Melrose had to sort of jam themselves in, ending up right in front of the air conditioner, which blew frigid air directly in their faces. Other than that, Lexi thought the meal started normally enough. She had previously warned both Kevin and Melrose about what topics to avoid, so the conversation revolved mostly around made-up camp stories, which Melrose was surprisingly good at inventing. And then Aunt Roz served the entrée.

"Chicken McNuggets?" Melrose lunged for the platter and helped herself to way too many pieces. "I thought you said this was gonna be home-cooked," she said to Lexi out of the side of her mouth.

"It *is*."

"These are homemade chicken croquettes," Aunt Roz said, obviously overhearing, and slid the vegetable medley onto the trivet. "Baked instead of deep-fried. So much healthier."

Melrose popped one into each cheek like a squirrel would do with acorns or something. "Okay, I know my McNuggets and these are McNuggets—but whatever. You got any of those little dipping sauces they come with? The honey mustard?"

"No, but there's low-fat yogurt to top them with, if you like. These aren't the ones from McDonald's, sweetheart."

"Uh-huh."

"Honestly. Chicken croquettes."

"Ain't croquette that game?" Melrose asked.

Lexi cringed inwardly and hurriedly passed her the hot bowl of parsley potatoes, hoping she would drop the subject. But like a dog with a bone, she wouldn't let go.

"You know, that game they play in England or Britain or somewhere? You know! Where they knock around giant pool balls on the grass with, like, those big wooden sticks?"

"That's polo, I think," Kevin offered.

"Polo's on horses," Lexi said.

Aunt Roz grabbed the bottle of light ranch dressing and spanked the bottom until a giant blob spewed onto her salad. "I'm sure she means *croquet*," she said, emphasizing the *ay* sound.

"I don't think so," Melrose sang, licking her fingers.

"Yes." Aunt Roz plunked the bottle down. "Croquet."

The conversation couldn't have been stupider or the mood more uncomfortable. Lexi was avoiding looking directly at Aunt Roz, who was daintily nibbling on a lettuce leaf while Melrose was sucking up the meal like a DustBuster. Kevin, on the other hand, had stopped eating altogether and was forming his initials out of baby carrots plucked from his salad. The only sound filling the room was the clatter of forks on plates and the faint jingling of Aunt Roz's charm bracelets.

" 'An angel of silence is flying over our heads,' " she said softly, stroking her neck. "That's a quote from Chekhov— you know, the famous Russian playwright? The man was a genius."

Melrose was about to say something, but instead of words, out came the loudest, nastiest belch ever belched in the tristate area. It probably registered a five on the Richter scale. " 'Better an empty house than a bad tenant,' " she said, laughing. "And that ain't Chekhov."

Everyone else sat stone-faced. For Lexi, the sheer rudeness of it all outweighed the humor, and she was beginning to regret her good deed.

More clatter and jingling.

"Yeah, so my aunt's a professional actress," Lexi said into her hand. She hadn't realized it had flown up to cover her mouth and quickly let it drop. "She's opening in a play next week at the Minetta Lane in the Village—a musical called *Shattered Glass*. Melrose is into acting, too, aren't you?"

Melrose garbled something that sounded like "Yes" or "I guess" and smacked her lips. She was gazing across the collection of show posters covering the walls and her eyes settled on a faded silkscreen of *The Sound of Music*. "Were you in that, Roz?" she asked, pointing to the poster with a forked cherry tomato.

Aunt Roz delicately wiped the corners of her mouth with her napkin before turning to look. "Mm-hmm, back in college," she said, nodding. "I had the role of Maria."

"The Julie Andrews part? No way, that's the lead!" Melrose's mouth hung open as if it was the greatest thing ever. She should have swallowed first. "I played the youngest Von Trapp brat in a church production in the Bronx when I was, like, seven. I forget the name of my character. What the heck was it? Greta . . . or Gretl, or—Grumpy, Sneezy, Dopey."

This time Kevin cracked up along with her. The mood was definitely ten times lighter since the subject turned to theater. Safe territory. Lexi knew for a fact that her aunt could happily reminisce on the subject for hours.

"The boys never noticed me until I'd won that role, and then everything changed just like that." Aunt Roz snapped her fingers and her face lit up as if she had just cued the spotlight. "From day one of rehearsals the young man playing the Captain tried desperately to win my heart."

"So, did he?" Kevin asked, leaning in with a wicked grin.

"Wouldn't you like to know?" Aunt Roz grinned right back. "There was someone else—Louie, was it? A senior who played Uncle Max. Not so much in the looks department but he used to make me laugh. Ooh, but the one I really had my eye on was the stage manager, Joe Molinaro."

"Omigod!" Melrose said, slamming down her fork. "All those guys? You were, like, Maria Von *Man*-Trap!"

The angel of silence was suddenly back with a vengeance. Thank goodness for the timely knock on the door, or so Lexi thought until she ran to answer it. Kim Ling's beady eyeball was staring back at her through the peephole. For a split second Lexi considered pretending no one was home—but maybe she had some important news.

"I can see your tiny pointed shoes under the door, Lexington Avenue. Open up!"

Lexi slipped into the hall and quietly closed the door behind her.

"What's going on?" Kim Ling asked. "Why're you dressed like a Barbie doll? I've been leaving endless voice mails but you won't answer."

"Oh, my phone's off."

"I smell food," she said sniffing. "Why won't you let me in?"

"Geez, enough with the tenth degree. My aunt's busy cooking and she needs her space. Why? What?"

"Major development! Observe." Kim Ling held up a messy legal pad covered in scribbles and diagrams. "I researched that info you discovered at the Met—you know, Cleopatra's Needle. It turns out it's this thirty-five-hundred-year-old Egyptian obelisk—isn't that fantastic?" She pointed to a drawing of a long, fat, pencil-looking thing. "An *obelisk*. Get it?"

"Not even a little."

"Think about the clues: shoot, needle—"

"—oval disk, park." Then it dawned on Lexi. "Oh! *O-val disk* is really *o-bel-isk!*"

"Ding-ding-ding! Which, according to Wikipedia, is a four-sided monument with a pyramidal top, which I already sort of knew. But for some strange reason, I'd never even heard of Cleopatra's Needle." She drummed her pen on a puffed-out cheek and her eyes darted back and forth like the chicken clock. "There're a bunch of bronze crabs sort of holding it up—the one you saw at the Met was one of the originals that fell off or something. Anyway, the obelisk is completely covered in hieroglyphics and sits in Central Park—just opposite the Met."

"Oh, wow. So, that's where Cleopatra's jewels are buried?"

"Exactamundo! Those other clues that had us digging through Grand Central—the perps must've been spitballin' ideas when you heard them, and that one probably got tossed out. Just an educated guess." She thought for a second. "So, we never should've even tried to bribe that crazy Melrose chick at all. Man, was she ever messed up."

"Alexandra!" Aunt Roz's faraway voice penetrated the door.

Lexi swallowed hard as a single bead of sweat dripped off the tip of her nose. "We still don't know how the word *shoot* plays into it, though," she whispered to Kim Ling, rushing along the conversation.

"Hopefully, not the obvious—but *needle*, *obelisk*, and *park* are more than enough to go on. We have to check it out ASA-humanly-P. Like, tonight!"

"Uh—I have reservations."

"About what?"

"No, no, I mean, *we* do. At a nice restaurant—it's a family thing."

"Dude, this is major! And I thought you said your aunt was cooking."

"She is. We're—going out for a fancy dessert."

There were what sounded like running footsteps coming from inside the apartment, and Aunt Roz could be heard shouting distant questions about who was at the door.

"No one important!"

"Thanks a lot." Kim Ling parked her pen behind her ear and pointed a pistol finger at Lexi. "Okay, then tomorrow night for sure. It'll give me time to round up more excavating equipment." And she turned and clomped down the stairs in her chartreuse cowboy boots. "Just don't wimp out on me. Time is of the essence."

Excavating equipment? No need to start freaking out about tomorrow night's misadventure until she made it through tonight's—and she had already left Melrose's mouth in the apartment with her aunt for way too long. She rushed back inside just as Melrose was barging in on Kevin in the bathroom.

"Don't you knock?"

"Don't you lock?"

Do it now, Lexi said to herself, *before you change your mind!* She grabbed Melrose, who looked like she didn't know what hit her but still managed to grab a fistful of lemon squares off the coffee table as they flew through the living room. "We'll be right back, Aunt Roz!" Lexi called out from the doorway and checked to make sure the coast was clear of Kim Ling. "Miss Carelli just came home and Mel's mom is a huge opera fan, so she wants to get her an autograph!" And the lies kept on coming.

Melrose must've known it was a ploy because she followed Lexi out into the hall without asking questions. She tiptoed up the stairs behind her and shadowed her maneuver as Lexi ducked under the burglar alarm sensor—the same exact routine Lexi had gone through on the first day with Kim Ling, only without that nasty alarm going off.

"Okay, what's the deal?" Melrose croaked when they finally stepped onto the rooftop, shoving the last of her lemon squares into her mouth. "You gonna push me off the roof for callin' your aunt a mantrap?" A powdered-sugar puff exploded from her lips.

"Don't tempt me." Lexi carefully wedged a small two-by-four between the doorframe and the door to keep it from closing. "No. Look around." She twisted to her feet and started toward Melrose, brushing dirt off her hem. "That deck chair opens all the way like a bed, there's even pillows, and, look, a ginormous table umbrella in case it rains. Plus, it's safe up here. That's the main thing." Lexi dug into her pocket before she lost her nerve, pulled out a key that she had attached to a long pink ribbon, and pressed it into Melrose's sticky hand. "This unlocks the two front doors of the brownstone. Whatever you do, don't lose it."

Confusion gradually lifted from Melrose's sugar-dusted face like storm clouds on a sunny day. She stood silently fingering the key.

"But you have to swear you'll only come up here in emergency situations—alone. I'm talking life or death stuff. Oh! And you cannot tell a soul about this or I'm dead meat. Promise?"

A wailing siren came and went on West End Avenue below and Melrose still hadn't answered. The proverbial limb Lexi had crawled out on was bending in the wind.

"You don't even know me. Why you tryin' to help?"

Lexi shrugged. "Temporary insanity?" She folded her goose-pimply arms and stared deep into Melrose's squint. You would think the girl would have been jumping for joy, but she didn't even crack a smile. "I'm taking a huge risk here, okay? This'd better not come back to bite me on the butt."

Who was she kidding? She could picture the teeth marks already.

Melrose gathered her blond mane up behind her neck and let it cascade behind her shoulders, rolling her lips like she was struggling to come up with the right words to say. "You really are somethin' else, you know that?"

"Yeah, I know," Lexi answered with a questioning look. "And you're welcome."

20

RADIO CITY

The big finale of Aunt Roz's Day of Family Fun was a show at Radio City Music Hall. Lexi had never been there before and her first impression was—*holy cow!*—totally overwhelming. Entering the lobby was like stepping into a giant Donald Trump living room, provided Donald Trump liked lots of plush red and gold—and crowds. Long, shimmering chandeliers; a winding staircase just made for grand entrances; a gigantic Art Deco mural painted on the wall, which Aunt Roz said was a style that was all the rage in the 1930s. And the jaw-dropping grandiosity continued inside the theater itself. Lexi had never seen so many seats. They extended clear into the heavens, tier after tier, like a humongous wedding cake.

"Can you believe they were actually going to tear this down?" Aunt Roz said as the usher led them toward the stage, which was a glowing orange sunburst that was practically as big as the sun. "I haven't been inside since the renovation. Melrose, have you ever been?"

"I saw the Christmas Spectacular once, back when I was, like, a fetus. Alls I remember is one of the camels in the livin' nativity scene takin' a dump onstage."

That angel-of-silence thing was happening again—the fifth time that night, if you were counting, and Lexi was. Something was definitely strange with Melrose—well, stranger than usual. She had started off the evening glowing and now she was glowering, and Lexi couldn't figure out why. "Hey, Mel, my aunt used to be one of the kickline dancers here."

"A Rocket!" Kevin said. "Right, Aunt Roz?"

"Rockette. But that was a hundred years ago." Aunt Roz took four programs from the usher and led the way down their row distributing them among the kids. "Oh, these are choice," she said, meaning the seats her old friend Henry had gotten them. "It pays to know people in high places. Literally! Henry operates the spotlight from way up there." She waved at the highest balcony as if the guy could see her pinprick of a head ten miles away.

Lexi settled into her seat, reminding herself that the hard part was over. They had already made it through half the evening without Melrose blowing her cover and now they would just have to sit through a few hours of watching the Celtic Breeze Steppers, an Irish dance troupe. In a single day she had treated Melrose to a luxurious bubble bath and a fresh change of clothes while Aunt Roz and Kevin were at the planetarium, a delicious home-cooked meal, access to the brownstone roof in case of emergency, and now a fun night out at a New York landmark. Mission accomplished and then some! After being mistaken for homeless herself, how could Lexi *not* do a few good deeds for someone in need? She should feel fantastic. So why, instead, was she squirming in her seat and anxiously rubbing her opal?

"Oh, check out the bling." Melrose zeroed in on Lexi's opal necklace. "That stone real?"

"Yeah. My mom gave me this a few years before she died."

"Well, that really sucks. I mean, the dyin' part. Gum?" she said, offering a limp stick. "It's Cinnamint." She blew her minty breath right into Lexi's face as a sample.

Lexi winced. "Nuh-uh. Where'd you get gum?" As soon as she said it, she wondered if it came off as an insult, like a runaway couldn't afford such a luxury.

"Your pants pocket. Or your *capris*, as you called them," Melrose said mockingly. She crossed her legs, foot over knee like a man, and waggled her ankle fiercely. "Listen, I know there's somethin' you ain't tellin' me." Now she was staring Lexi up and down. "Why'd you really wanna hook up in Grand Central? C'mon, the truth?"

Whoa. That one came out of left field. "Um—my friend wanted some info for her story, like we said. And please keep your voice down."

"And now—I mean, what's in all this for you? Why're you bendin' over backward for me?"

"Just 'cause."

Nobody wants to hear that you feel incredibly sorry for them and you're afraid for their lives. Lexi turned away to check out the audience, wondering what had gotten into Melrose—and what had she found out?

Over the stadium of chattering heads, Lexi spotted a sea of green flooding into the rear seats. *A busload of Celtic Breeze fans maybe? But why're they all so short? Leprechauns?* She could make out the faint outline of trees on their T-shirts. Their *puke-green* T-shirts! *No way! Not again!* Her nails dug hard into the armrest, which actually turned out to be Kevin's arm.

"Ow!"

"Don't look now but this place is crawling with City Campers!" she whispered to him. "What're they doing out at night? Do not turn around."

Lexi had to think of something fast. If her aunt found out that she had been ditching camp, it would get back to her dad and she would be grounded until she was forty.

"Switch seats with me, Kev, switch seats!"

They scrambled over each other and Lexi slid into the seat next to Aunt Roz. Of course Kevin couldn't resist turning around, and when he saw all the campers he gasped. Luckily, Aunt Roz was too busy powdering her nose to notice.

Lexi sat desperately fingering her curls, not knowing

what to do until she spotted the glint of a single blue rhinestone. It was coming from her aunt's glasses, which were jutting out of her program on her lap. The lights dimmed and—*Oh, God, please forgive me for what I'm about to do!*—Lexi faked a sneeze and snatched the glasses.

"Bless you," Aunt Roz said. "It is a little chilly in here." She wrapped half of her silvery ribbon-shawl around Lexi's shoulders. "Better?"

"Much," Lexi said and slipped the glasses into her dress pocket. The first note of the overture rattled her and her guilt swelled along with the music. The enormous orchestra rose from the pit, just like Aunt Roz had said it might, and floated to the back of the stage as if by magic. Kevin was lured to his feet in wonder and Lexi tugged him back down. In her peripheral vision, Lexi could see her aunt feeling around her seat.

"For the love of . . . I could've sworn . . . where the heck . . . ?" Aunt Roz finally leaned into Lexi. "Do you see my glasses anywhere?" she whispered. "I seem to have misplaced the darn things again."

Lexi escaped the shawl and pretended to check. "Nope. Did you try your purse?"

"Not there."

"Hmm, that's funny."

No, it wasn't. She was going to fry. Good deed or not, on her day of reckoning, she was definitely going to fry.

An army of clogging feet hit the stage like an explosion of fireworks, and Lexi allowed herself to get instantly swept away from all the drama surrounding her. Propeller legs on rigid bodies moving in perfect unison—amazing! If her great-grandmother had never emigrated from Kilcarney to New York, would Lexi be expected to learn such a wacky dance, living as an Irish lassie? She smiled at the thought of herself struggling to get through it—her corkscrew curls bouncing wildly.

It wasn't humanly possible for feet to move so fast for a solid hour, but there they were. And faster still for the big finish—the Celtic Breeze Steppers were working themselves into a gale-force wind! When the orchestra struck a final chord and the lights came up, Kevin was pie-eyed, Aunt Roz was squinting, and Melrose was rubbing her head with her palm as if she had gotten bonked by a renegade tap shoe.

"Thank God that's over," Melrose said, hoisting herself to her feet.

"It's only intermission," Lexi yelled to her over the wild applause. She popped up and scooted past Kevin. "There's a whole 'nother part."

"Oh, no way! I mean, I gotta get outta here. This just ain't my thing."

"But—"

"No, really. Somethin's come up."

"What could possibly—?"

Before Lexi could finish her sentence, Melrose gave her a rough hug and bolted. "Later," she said, barreling down the aisle. "Thanks for the McNuggets, Aunt Roz!"

Why she would be in such a big hurry to get back to life on the gritty streets was beyond Lexi.

"Apparently, not a big fan of ethnic dance," Aunt Roz said, straining to see over her shoulder. "Will she make it home okay?"

"That's the million-dollar question."

Lexi didn't have time to worry about Melrose now. She couldn't risk Aunt Roz bumping into any telltale campers up close in the lobby, so she started in about how horribly long the line at the ladies' room must be, managing to keep her in her seat throughout the intermission. And as soon as the steppers began stomping through Act Two, she got to work plotting her detailed after-show plan.

"Kev. Kev." Lexi crumpled down to align her mouth with Kevin's ear. "Listen carefully to what I'm about to say," she whispered. "Aunt Roz is gonna want us to meet her friend afterward and he'll probably want to show us around the theater and stuff. This is good. We'll go, but I'm gonna make up an excuse early on—say I'm freezing from the AC and want to warm up outside or something, which is true, but really I'll be spying on the City Campers to make sure they leave without running into us. Your job is to stall, stall, stall. Take lots of pictures; ask annoying questions. Shouldn't be hard, just act like you usually do. Then when the campers are gone, I'll meet up with you guys outside the bathrooms by the big naked-lady statue and we'll be home free. Got it?" She nudged him. "Kevin, got it?"

"What?"

"What do you mean, 'what'? What didn't you get?"

"I can't hear you! The music's too loud! And now my ear's all wet."

Nevertheless, by the time the curtain fell, Lexi made certain her message had gotten through. Everything was going according to plan with slow-talking Henry giving them a backstage tour, from which she excused herself almost immediately. She tore up the steps and through the lobby, where the audience was emptying quickly, considering its size, and wound up outside hiding behind a thick marble pillar, watching the last of the rowdy City Campers pile into a bus. Her eyes fluttered shut with relief. When she opened them again, she nearly jumped out of her skin.

"You are a born nurturer."

"Excuse me?" Lexi said to the caramel-colored woman standing right in front of her. With her skunk-striped hair and threadbare tunic, she looked as if she had just stepped out of another time and place.

"Yes, I am correct. I could see it right there." The strange woman pointed to the middle of Lexi's forehead. "Don't be frightened. I am a *yogini*—a female yogi. A yogi or yogini is someone who has achieved a state of unshakable peace and oneness with the universe. We can see all things."

"Oh. Good," was all Lexi heard herself say, planning

her escape route back into the theater. The woman's ratty-looking cloak smelled of exotic incense, and as she moved even closer, Lexi tried not to stare at her milky left eye—or scream for the two cops, who were chatting on the corner, a stone's throw away.

"Yes, yes, very good, very good," the woman said with her deep, foreign accent. "What is your name?"

"Alexandra" slipped right out before she could stop it.

The yogini smiled. "It means mankind's helper."

"Mankind's helper." Lexi instantly liked the sound of that.

"You are stubborn, it's true, but you have a kind, generous heart."

Which happened to be beating like jungle tom-toms at the moment. "Well, gotta go. My aunt is meeting—"

"But it is broken, your heart. You have suffered a great loss."

How did she know?

"I see you are always searching, searching. For what do you search? Your self-worth, perhaps?"

Okay, getting spooky. But it was enough to keep Lexi glued to her spot. So with Avenue of the Americas as a murky backdrop, she watched the woman tear a blank page from the ragged leather-bound book she was carrying, scribble something on it with a miniature-golf-sized pencil, and fold the paper into the size of an illegal classroom note.

"Hold this in your left hand and give me your right," the yogini said, drawing Lexi in with her haunting gaze. "I can read your palm."

Then, as if "Don't speak to strangers" had not been drummed into her head since birth, and as if she had never seen countless television shows about the unthinkable things that happen to kidnapping victims, Lexi did exactly as the woman had instructed.

"Ah, a very long lifeline." Her steady brown finger traced a crease on Lexi's palm. "You will have three children, two boys, one girl. And there is wealth!"

A twinge of excitement tickled her insides. Okay, she was risking her life a little, but she needed to know more.

"Now, concentrate on the paper in your grasp," the yogini whispered, "and think of a number between one and twenty-five. Close your eyes and see it clearly in your mind's eye."

Part of Lexi's brain was yelling at her to stop this game right now—just say, "No, thank you, I'm not interested," the way her dad did with telemarketers. *Be polite, but firm, 'cause these people won't take no for an answer.* Still, Lexi followed the yogini's instructions. She closed her eyes and visualized a murky number nine, outlining it with her eyeballs.

"Now, look at the paper."

Lexi quickly unfolded it. Her jaw dropped. There it was—a giant nine!

"Your lucky number, no?" the woman said simply, seeming pleased with herself.

Unbelievable! "How'd you do that?"

"Nine is a celestial and angelic number, symbolic of compassion, completion, the beginning and the end. There is a reason you—" Suddenly her forehead wrinkled with concern as if she had just noticed something she had almost missed. Her cloudy eye twitched. "You must avoid ill-fated entanglements," she warned, staring directly at Lexi with laser-beam intensity. "Ill-fated entanglements for which you will pay dearly."

Is she kidding? My entire New York visit has been nothing but ill-fated entanglements! Lexi wondered whether she was allowed to ask for details. Like, was all this written in stone or was there still some wiggle room?

"You can see it is true then, that I am a yogi—a yogini. Now, place five dollars in the book and you will have good luck." She flipped it open and thrust it toward Lexi.

Uh-oh! Lexi's face went hot. *Since when does luck come with a price tag?*

"Just five dollars," the woman insisted, keeping a steady gaze.

"Uh, sorry." Lexi quickly handed her back the paper with the nine. "I really don't have—" She was about to lie, make up an excuse, yell for the cops—when she heard the *clip-clop* of high heels. It was Aunt Roz, with Kevin leading her like a guide dog.

"There she is," Kevin called out.

"Alexandra!"

In the instant it took for Lexi to glance toward them and back again, the yogini had disappeared. Lexi shuddered. Her hand flew up to clutch her opal touchstone for comfort and froze into an empty fist. "Omigod!"

Her necklace wasn't there.

21

BOOK OF ANSWERS

"Happy Father's Day, Dad!"

Kevin's cheerful voice first thing Sunday morning was as comforting as a chorus of kazoos.

Lexi had more than willingly let him go first on their surprise phone call to Dad on his "special day." *Puke.* Now he and the wicked step-demon were in Santorini, some Greek island, which meant a huge time difference, which meant Aunt Roz woke them up at the crack of dawn. Again. Lexi thought she had better monitor Kevin's conversation to be ready with an explanation in case he let anything questionable slip, but she was twisted in her sheets, too weak to bust free.

"Beware of ill-fated entanglements." If only the yogini had been referring to bed linens. Her warning had haunted Lexi through her dreams, and she wondered if the "for which you will pay dearly" part had anything to do with her missing opal. It must. That necklace meant the world to her and she felt naked and hollow without it. *First, Cleopatra's jewels go missing—and now my own. What're the chances?* Lexi's first instinct was that the money-grubbing yogini herself was the ill-fated entanglement. She could have snapped off the necklace while she was performing her number trick—right before Lexi's very closed eyes. But if she was the culprit, did that mean she was a complete phony? A faux yogi—a fogi? Or fogini? What about Lexi being a born nurturer, destined for motherhood and wealth? Were all her words of wisdom just a load of poo?

Then again, Lexi could have lost the necklace. Or Melrose could have stolen it when they were in the dark theater. Was she awful for thinking that? Just because Melrose was a runaway didn't mean she was a thief. But why had she been acting so odd after dinner? And then raced out of Radio City like her seat was on fire?

"Yeah, I will." Kevin was buzzing around the living room, winding down his portion of the conversation. " 'Kay, bye, Dad! Love you too."

Before Lexi was ready, the receiver hit her bed. She stared at it like a brick through a broken window and gave herself a steady five count before lifting it to her ear. *"Haargh—"* Phlegm. Clear throat, start again. "Hello?"

"Lexi?"

"Yeah, it's me, hi." Her stomach gurgled like a drowning cat. "Happy Father's Day" eked out.

Okay, not very convincing, but it was all that was

needed to spark a one-sided conversation about language barriers, snorkeling mishaps, and lost luggage. The main purpose of the call was to thank Dad for the gift, but Lexi decided she could keep things upbeat only if they steered clear of two ugly topics: the pearls and Clare.

"Hey, your aunt says you just about flipped over the string of pearls we sent. Clare spent hours picking them out."

She punched her pillow in disbelief.

"I hear you stored them in a very special place," her dad finished.

Ha! The fish tank. "Yep. That'd be true."

Clever Aunt Roz. If only the stupid pearls were missing instead of her opal. If only her father was in Greece with her mother instead of Cruella. She could "if only" till the cows came home, but it wasn't going to change a thing. Lexi challenged herself to keep things upbeat anyway.

"So, Dad, is Europe everything it's cracked up to be?"

"For the most part. How's New York treating you? How's City Camp? Are you whittling little Statues of Liberty out of tree branches?"

"Nah, just little Empire State Buildings. And guess who's getting them all for Christmas?"

He let one of his belly-laugh chortles rip. Something Lexi hadn't heard in a long time. "I should've seen that one coming. Seriously, though, how are you handling things? Are you okay? Is your brother driving you up the wall?"

"No more than usual. I'm fine."

"You're sure now? Clare and I can cut our honeymoon short if there's a problem and—"

"No, no, everything's cool—great. Fantastic." Lie, lie, lie. "Hey, Dad, can I ask a stupid question?"

"Go ahead."

"Say a miracle happened—just suppose—and I suddenly came into a whole bunch of money. Like, a ridiculous amount. I want you to know I'd share it with the family—definitely—I mean, you and Kevin."

"Um, okay, but that's not a question." Breathy pause. "What's going on? Did you discover a buried treasure in Central Park or something?"

Oh. My. God. Lexi was speechless for a second. "Not quite."

"Your aunt wasn't talking about her will again, was she? You know how she can get carried away."

"No, no, nothing like that. It's just—" Lexi was suddenly tongue-tied after sounding like a complete goofball. "Never mind."

"Alrighty then. Well, we miss you two knuckleheads a lot, but it won't be long—we're flying to New York a week from Saturday, on the twenty-eighth. The plan is to meet up with you guys in Grand Central Station so we can all take the train home together. Won't that be fun?"

"Uh-huh."

"It was great hearing your voice. You take care now, okay? Love ya, cookie."

Lexi recoiled and her insides instantly crumbled into sawdust. "Don't call me that. *Mom* called me that."

It was as if their candy-coated conversation hit a cavity with an exposed nerve. *Ugh!* Couldn't she simply have said "Love ya" back and let him hang up with a smile on his face? *Rewind—rewind!*

"Well, I should go, Lex, checkout time was a half hour ago. See you kids soon."

The *click* came fast, as if he didn't want to chance hearing another harsh word. Hot tears were forming but Lexi willed them away. How could she get through the day, let alone the stressful night that lay ahead, digging for the jewels in Central Park, if she allowed herself to be a crybaby weakling? No. She would be strong. She had to.

A perfumed breeze rushed by. It was Aunt Roz on her way to the front door. "There. Don't you feel better after speaking with your father?" She hoisted her giant straw tote over her shoulder and grabbed her keys off the wall hook. "Well, I'm off. The fridge is fully stocked, emergency numbers are by the phone. I hope you guys won't be too bored stuck around the apartment all day long. I'm sure Kimmy will keep you entertained."

To say the least, Lexi thought, collecting herself.

"I shouldn't be too, too late, but for goodness' sake, don't wait up!"

Even though it was Sunday, Aunt Roz had to work. *Shattered Glass* was in tech rehearsals, which meant a very long day at the theater—plus, she was doing what she called "extra-work" after that. Kevin would happily spend the entire day fused to the massage chair, texting Space Camp Billy and messing with the laptop—so why shouldn't Lexi lounge around in bed? Where it was safe. At least until Kim Ling, the most ill-fated entanglement of them all, dragged her off to the park. The timing couldn't be worse. With Lexi's opal necklace gone, disaster was sure to strike. If phone calls counted, it was striking already!

"This photo I took of Aunt Roz in the Whispering Gallery," Kevin said, staring into the computer screen, "with the mystery perp's inky fingers holding a cup in the background. I still think it might be a clue as to who he is. Waiter . . . novelist . . ."

"We went over that, Kev, forever ago. Anyone could have inky fingers."

"But—" He peered over his shoulder at Lexi. "Are you ever getting out of bed?"

"Eventually."

"When?"

As it turned out, not until 2:48 p.m., when Kim Ling came pounding at the door. Lexi had barely opened it when she burst into the room, sending a basket of pinecones flying off a small antique cabinet—and the chunky black book that served as a makeshift cabinet leg spun to the middle of the floor.

"Geez, did you booby-trap this place or something?" Kim Ling said, kicking away a pinecone. "Your aunt told me you weren't feeling well when I called earlier, Tex-Lex, so I brought you some of my mom's soup. You can't buy this stuff." She handed Lexi a sloshing plastic tub with doughy lumps bobbing inside. "Hot and sour matzo-ball. It's Chinese *and* Jewish—Chi-new-ish. If I were food, this would be me."

"Thanks," Lexi said, setting it on the coffee table. "It looks yummy but I'm fine."

"Good. I need you in peak form for tonight."

Without even stretching first, Kim Ling slid into half-splits on the floor and started tossing the scattered pinecones one by one back into their basket. With her blue-streaked hair and multicolored toe socks, she looked like something out of Cirque du Soleil.

"Slight change of plans," she said. "My mom freakin' booked us on a freakin' Father's Day dinner cruise tonight, unbeknownst to me. It's the early bird one so we can still make it to the park by around twenty-one hundred hours."

"What's that in human time?" Lexi asked, plopping down next to her.

"Nine."

"Are we sure we want to do this? I'm not even supposed to leave the brownstone, let alone venture into the park at night. The more I think about it, the stupider the whole thing seems. I mean, who in their right mind buries a bunch of jewels in Central Park?"

"Who in their right mind thinks criminals are in their right minds? Didn't you hear the latest on Benjamin Deets? Apparently, he pulled some pretty outrageous pranks during his college days at NYU—like hacking into the school's computer system and changing grades. That's just for starters."

"I saw that too!" Kevin shot across the room carrying his open laptop and sat between the girls. "Billy says a lot of criminally minded youth go into law enforcement. Looks like Deets did a full three-sixty right back into a life of crime."

"He actually talks like that?" Kim Ling asked Kevin. " 'Criminally minded youth'? Sounds pretentious."

"Maybe you two are related," Lexi said with a smirk. "Oh, Kim, I meant to tell you. When we were at the Met, I was eavesdropping on some security guards . . ."

"You do that a lot, don't you? And?"

"They were talking about Deets. How he'd had everything in life, and now he had nothing and wanted revenge."

"Against the Met for firing him," Kim Ling said, thinking about it. "Makes sense. And revenge, like that scab on your shin, can get really, really ugly."

Lexi stretched her nightgown over her knees as far as it would go and stuck out her tongue as far as *it* would go.

"So," Kevin said, scratching his chin as a Saturn screensaver spun onto his laptop, "Deets winds up with a job as a Central Park groundskeeper, right?" His eyebrows jumped. "That means he could be digging around Cleopatra's Needle all he wants and never be suspected of foul play."

"Exactly!" Kim Ling rose to her knees with a victory

grunt worthy of a football jock. "Nice work, you guys. How stoked am I that this is all beginning to make sense!"

Lexi was still wallowing in doubt, but Kim Ling seemed unstoppable. Her enthusiasm was a lot like quicksand— bubbly but deadly.

"Okay, let's get real here." Lexi hugged her knees tightly and spun to face Kim Ling. "How dangerous do you think this whole mission's gonna be tonight? Honestly. On a risk- your-life scale from one to ten—ten being you're-crazy-for- even-attempting-this?"

"Oh, about a fifty."

"*What?*"

"Well, think about it," Kim Ling said, sitting back on her heels. "These are thieves we're dealing with, so any- thing could happen. Then again, it might all turn out to be just a stroll in the park. Ha! No pun intended." She snorted, glancing at the McGills' blank expressions. "And apparently none noticed."

"A fifty?" Kevin said. "For real?"

"You don't have to tag along, sprout. Nobody's holding a gun to your—I mean, if you want, you could spend the evening with the Family Levine, which is an adventure unto itself." Kim Ling tousled his hair and sprang to her feet. "You guys work it out, but I've got to jet." Then she made a mad dash to the door and did an about-face. "So, Lex, we'll rendezvous on the front stoop at twenty-thirty hours with or without the sib."

"Speak English."

"Sib-ling. Eight thir-ty," she said, spelling the words out in sign language. "Just come carbo-loaded for energy, and wear dark clothes and sensible shoes. Oh, and pray, pray, pray it doesn't rain. I'll have the rest covered." A burst of excitement had her drum-rolling on the door-frame. "I'm totally psyched, aren't you?"

Quicksand.

As soon as she left, Kevin slammed the laptop shut and popped up like a done piece of toast. "I'm definitely going with you!" he announced.

"Are not. You could stay with Kim's parents, like she said."

"Listen, Billy got to experience weightlessness in an actual Space Shot simulator. Me? I get dumped at City Camp for a lame game of Red Rover while you and Kim Ling go off and have all the fun—so you've gotta give me something. I'm going!"

"I'm still not a hundred percent sure *I'm* even going. This is idiotic and dangerous—and you're only ten, Kev, seriously."

He fell face-first onto the chaise lounge. "I'm not a baby. Why're you always acting like I'm afraid of every little thing?"

Because he *was* afraid of every little thing—they just never talked about it. "You know why." Lexi rolled him over and glared down at him over folded arms. "Two words: Kingsley Park."

Kevin just lay there, gritting his teeth. "Okay, maybe

I freak out once in a while on amusement rides—or in tunnels," he said, sitting up, his cheeks turning bloodred, "but other than that, I'm fine! I've been fine for a really long time."

"Oh, really? I think not."

"Yuh-huh." He shot to his feet. *"You're* the one who still has to see Dr. Lucy every Saturday, Lexi—not me!"

Ouch. That was something else Lexi had never talked about. And definitely tried not to think about between therapist appointments. Ever.

"Admit it, Kevin. The only reason you wanna come with is 'cause I don't want you to, which is tough 'cause I'm in charge and what I say goes. Case closed."

Kevin flapped his arms like a frustrated penguin and zoomed out the front door.

"Hey," Lexi said, chasing him, "you're not allowed to go outside alone."

"I'm just gonna sit on the front steps, Mother!"

He did not *just say that!* "Don't talk to strangers. Under any circumstances. I don't care how brave you think you are all of a sudden."

Lexi slammed the door, then rushed to the window and peeked through bended blinds, waiting for Kevin to appear on the porch below. Geez, she really was acting like a smothering mother. What was happening to her? She slowly slunk away and—*"Ow!"*—stepped on a corner of that chunky black book—the one Kim Ling had knocked out of place. She was about to give it a good kick but the title caught her eye: *The Book of Answers* by Carol Bolt. "Sounds promising," she muttered, and snatched it up. There were instructions on the back cover, so she hopped into bed and sat cross-legged reading them while she massaged her throbbing big toe. Apparently, the book worked like a Magic 8 Ball, answering life's burning questions. Exactly what she needed.

Following the instructions, she held the book between both palms, stroking the edge of the pages back to front, while asking her question out loud. "Should I go to Central Park tonight with Kim Ling to dig up Cleopatra's stolen jewels or is that as nutty an idea as I think?" Too complicated. She streamlined it to "Should I go to Central Park tonight?" Lexi repeated her question over and over again, feeling a bit idiotic, but stroking the pages anyway and visualizing the scene in the park. When she felt an inner *ding*, she cracked open the book. A feather fell out! White. Perfect. *Whoa.* Was it an odd coincidence? Or had she left one of her feathers lying around the apartment that Aunt Roz had used as a quick bookmark? Either way, it certainly added weight to the answer on the page. Lexi's heartbeat sped up as she slowly lowered her gaze.

You will find out everything you'll need to know.

22

THE PARK AFTER DARK

At 2030 hours, the sky was stuck somewhere between daytime and night, as if the sun was too stubborn to set and make way for the moon. The air was so breezeless and sticky even birds refused to take wing, but somehow Lexi remained cool and strangely calm on the way to their adventure in Central Park. She knew her guardian-angel mom was watching over her—that last white feather was a definite sign. So, of course she added it to her pocket of good luck charms: the rabbit's foot keychain, laminated four-leaf clover, and nine shiny pennies. She would never reveal her superstitious quirks to anyone, not even Kevin, who she had decided could tag along just to end his whining—and avoid World War III.

The cab pulled up at Seventy-Ninth and Fifth, and Lexi's hand flew out the door before she did, checking the weather. "Not a drop of rain. So far, so good."

"Shhh!" Kim Ling hissed. She dragged Kevin and a deflated duffel out of the back seat and slammed the cab door. "Now you put a *kenahara* on it."

Lexi's face scrunched up. "A what?"

"A Yiddish jinx. You can't brag about things going right or they'll fail. *Pu-pu-pu!*" she puffed, doing a ritualistic kind of fake spitting on her fingers as she led the way into Central Park. "Not that I believe in that drivel, you understand, but why risk it?"

"No, I totally get it." Lexi had never seen Kim Ling's superstitious side before. She was starting to think they had more in common than either of them was willing to admit. "So, what's with the empty bag?"

"It's not empty. There're flashlights and gardening trowels inside. Besides, how else're we supposed to haul off the jewels—in your pink clutch?"

"I don't have a pink clutch. Well, I do, but not with me."

"Okay, we're entering the park now," Kevin reported into his cell phone to Space Camp Billy. He had been gabbing away during the entire cab ride, much to the annoyance of Kim Ling. "What? No. I'll call you later—I've really gotta go. Yes, I'm serious—over and out."

Lexi grabbed his hand. She had already warned him that due to the extreme circumstances, the mothering thing would be in full swing and he had better not even think about complaining. "I can't believe we're actually doing this. I'm a little bit freaking out." She automatically reached for her opal necklace, which was missing of course, and grasped the safety whistle hanging in its place. Kim Ling had supplied one for each of them.

"If the authorities stop us in the middle of everything," Kim Ling said quietly over the clink-clink-clinking of her bag, "we tell them we're digging up night crawlers to go fishing, okay? And, worst case scenario, if we actually run into the thieves face-to-face, we hightail it the heck out of here—no questions asked. Try not to split up, but if we do, we'll meet on the corner where the cab just let us out— Seventy-Ninth and Fifth. Got it?"

"Roger that," Kevin said.

Lexi took a deep breath. She chipped away at her thumbnail polish as they followed the road alongside the Metropolitan Museum's giant sloping wall of windows that were glowing orange in the hot, sluggish sunset. When they stopped at a 3-D map sprouting up from the ground to check their route, Lexi was already dripping in sweat. "How could you wear a black turtleneck in this heat?" she asked Kim Ling. "It's not like we're robbing a bank."

"Who cares what I'm wearing? How is that helping?"

Strangely enough, Lexi's conversation with the yogini popped into her head. "You know, Alexandra actually means *mankind's helper*," she said matter-of-factly, gathering her hair off her neck. "Isn't that cool? You know how names have meanings?"

Kim Ling's finger went from the map to her own face. "Chinese, remember? We practically invented that stuff. Kim Ling, roughly translated, means tinkling jade."

"Pretty."

A desperate moan came out of Kevin. *"Tinkling?* Oh, great—now I have to pee!"

Kim Ling muttered something about sucking it up and, seeming assured of their direction, she took off with purpose in her step, leading Kevin and Lexi past some shadowy joggers and speeding bicyclists until they came to the underpass of a fancy stone bridge she called the Greywacke Arch. She dug two flashlights out of her duffel, switched them on, and did a quick safety scan of the dark tunnel before handing one flashlight to Kevin and venturing inside.

"I'm not a big fan of tunnels," he grumbled, and they all started running at breakneck speed.

It was eye-wateringly smelly but short, thank goodness. And when they emerged from the tunnel, gulping heaps of fresh air, night was finally taking hold, thick and starless.

"Look!" Kevin swung his light beam to the pointy top of Cleopatra's Needle, the huge stone obelisk, which was jutting out from the trees not too far away. "That's it, right, Kim? It's awesome."

"Ānjìng!" she said. "Quiet! We're trying to keep a low profile."

"Sorry."

She looked around to make sure no one was watching, and shined her light on the obelisk too. "Did you know that sucker weighs two hundred and forty tons?" she said quietly. "It has a twin in London and there's another one in Paris—and get this: they're all called Cleopatra's Needle, yet they're not even connected to Queen Cleopatra. Strange but true. They were already over a thousand years old in her lifetime."

"Well, someone's been doing her homework," Lexi whispered, craning her neck to get a better view. "It kinda looks like the Washington Monument, huh?"

"The Washington Monument isn't covered in hieroglyphics."

"I said *kinda!*"

Side by sweaty side, the threesome scurried down the dirt path and around the bend, where a small crowd was gathered at the foot of the steps leading to the courtyard where the obelisk stood. It was magnificent, seeing it even closer—like an enormous dagger awash in light, piercing the ebony sky. Kim Ling mumbled that something strange was definitely going on—but it was hard to tell exactly what that was with trees blocking their full view. They slipped past a bunch of people holding panting pugs and bent down to peek through a curtain of droopy junipers. The entire courtyard was buzzing with activity. It was outlined in bright yellow CRIME SCENE DO NOT CROSS tape, and glowing brighter than Times Square.

"What's happening?" Lexi said, her heart sputtering in her chest. "You don't think—"

Kevin gasped, and Kim Ling's eyes went round as the full moon.

"I *knew* we should've come last night!" she said. "We're too freakin' late!"

No! After everything they had gone through, had the authorities beaten them to the buried treasure by a matter of hours—or minutes?

Kim Ling was slumped over like a slain gladiator, cursing in angry Chinese. So it was Lexi who dared approach a Frankensteinish policeman who was guarding the steps.

"What's happening, officer?"

"This area is closed off to the general public," he told her.

"Why?" Kim Ling asked, springing to life. "Did they find the jewels?"

"I don't know what you're talking about. C'mon, people, break it up—you're blocking the pathway."

"Bullcrackers!" Kim Ling said, and took off in a huff.

Lexi was right behind her with Kevin in tow, her stomach turning sour and sick.

They hurried up a patchy hill to the only other entrance to the glowing courtyard, but there was another small crowd gathered behind a lineup of metal, fence-like police barriers. Glimpses of cops, cameras, and cables could be seen through spiky tree branches, but that was about it.

"It's useless, Kim," Lexi said, looking around and chewing her thumbnail. "Maybe we should just go home and find out what happened on TV."

"No way, José. We've come this far. I'm not leaving till I get firsthand info."

It was probably wise to let Kim Ling be her usual bossy
self and call all the shots, Lexi figured, since Central Park
at night was no place for one of their ugly spats. And so
once again, she and Kevin followed her clomping combat
boots, this time over a carpet of thick ivy, until they settled behind a tangle of skinny, curvy trees where they
could spy on the crime scene just a few yards away.

A tall brute of a woman in a Foo Fighters T-shirt seemed
to be running the show. Either an undercover cop or news
crew techie—they couldn't decide which. She was holding a walkie-talkie and having a heated conversation with
some man sitting on a bench in the courtyard. Nothing
too strange about that.

"Hey, what's this?" Kevin said, and the girls immediately shushed him. He was aiming his flashlight beam on
a splotch of purple material dangling from the lowest tree
branch. "Someone's T-shirt?" he whispered. "No—looks
like a bandanna."

"Don't touch it," Lexi warned. "You don't know where
it's been."

His curious eyes examined it up close. "It looks kinda
like the one Melrose wore. Same color and everything.
Don't you think that's weird?"

Lexi's mind was instantly racing, wondering how it
could possibly have wound up there. "Yes," she said. "Very
weird."

Kim Ling shined her light on it, sending an astonished-
looking squirrel scampering straight up the tree. "Definitely

curious, but—there must be hundreds of purple bandan-
nas lying around New York City." She thought about it
for a second. "Well, at least a few. No big deal."

Just as Kevin plucked it off the branch anyway, the
argument between the Foo Fighter lady and the man on
the bench reached fever pitch. The kids all turned their
heads to listen.

"This is absolutely ridiculous," the man yelled in a
thick British accent. "How long am I to remain captive
on this *bloody* bench, in this godforsaken heat and this
bloody, bloody humidity?"

Lexi grabbed on to Kim Ling's arm in a sudden panic.
"Omigod."

"What is it?"

Her lips were forming words but no sound was coming, since her heart was lodged in her throat.

"What?" Kevin asked.

"I think that's—him," she finally muttered.

"Him?" Kim Ling repeated.

"One of the guys I saw in the Whispering Gallery. You
know, the thief, the thug, the perp!"

An eruption of rolling thunder could not have been
more perfectly timed. It shook the earth. Shook Lexi to
the core.

"Okay, red, calm down. Are you sure that's the guy?"

"Yes—maybe. Well, look, he's bald, right? And I know
for sure that one of the guys I saw in Grand Central was

bald. And remember I told you he said 'bloody' a lot? So—oh, gosh—I'm *pretty* sure. Like, ninety-nine-point-nine-nine-nine—"

"I almost forgot," Kevin blurted, "I brought my new telescope!" He slipped it out of the back pocket of his shorts, extended it to its full length, and handed it to Lexi.

With one eye shut and the other eye spying through the glass piece, she could see the entire crime scene at least three times its original size. She focused on the man in question—at the back of his bald, shiny head. Suddenly he turned with his hand on his chin, revealing strange orange glasses, a funky soul patch, and *inky fingers!*

"One hundred percent!" Lexi exclaimed. "It's *him!*"

Luckily, the thud that followed came from Kevin's flashlight hitting the ground and not Lexi. Without even bothering to retrieve it, all three escaped the tangle of trees, dodged a flurry of pigeons, and raced over to the clump of people at the entrance of the crime scene. Ignoring complaints, they butted their way to the very front of the sweaty crowd. They were still yards away from the action, though, with the fence-like barriers keeping everyone at bay.

"Frig! I wish those loudmouthed crickets would clam up so we could hear better." Kim Ling was on her tiptoes, struggling to pick up whatever she could. "This place is crawling with cops. So, if that *is* him," she said, mulling over her words as she spoke, "he must've just gotten arrested, right? They must've caught him in the act."

A look of realization splashed across all three faces. Kevin turned to Lexi, and Lexi turned to Kim Ling, who grunted like a wild boar and threw up her hands in defeat.

"So, I guess that's it then—it's over!" she ranted. "Crime solved but not by us. Serves us right for being a day late and a dollar short. No—make that two hundred and twenty-five *thousand* dollars short!"

Lexi bit her lip. "You said you didn't even want the money anyway." A small part of her was relieved, she had to admit—if it was humanly possible to be relieved and extremely disappointed at the same time. Kevin seemed desperately defeated, so she put a comforting hand on his shoulder as she thought about the facts. "Geez, it sure took him long enough to get around to burying the jewels, didn't it?" she said as it was dawning on her. "And where's Benjamin Deets?"

"Maybe he ran away," Kevin said, "or got wounded—or bowed out at the last minute. Or all of the above."

"How could it be all of the above?" Lexi went back to watching the scene through the telescope, trying to hold it steady with jittery, sweaty hands. Some of the actual jewels were in full view now, resting on velvet pillows in an open crate spilling packing straw. A dazzling green necklace with emeralds for days, a rainbow of sparkling rings, the thickest jewel-encrusted bracelets, and a pair of twisty armbands—golden snakes with ruby red eyes.

She zeroed in on the perp again. *How could he do such a heinous act? That's a real word, right? Heinous?* And then she noticed something was off. "Wait. Why is he still sitting there all la-di-da? Shouldn't he be wearing handcuffs?"

Kevin grabbed the telescope from Lexi and took a look. "Yeah. Or crammed in the back of a squad car by now—instead of eating a prune Danish?"

"How can you tell it's prune?" Kim Ling snatched the telescope to take her turn, which lasted forever. "You guys're absolutely right. What's wrong with this picture?" She collapsed the telescope with a clack and handed it back to Kevin. Her eyes were darting back and forth as if she was trying to answer a *Jeopardy!* question before the buzzer sounded. "I'm gonna go find out!"

"How?" Lexi and Kevin asked at the same time.

Kim Ling's answer came in the form of a laminated photo ID that she whipped out of her back pocket. "Meet the new cub reporter for the Associated Press."

Kevin's jaw dropped. "Is this thing for real?"

"It's real in the sense that it exists, but if you're asking if it's authentic, then no. I made it in Photoshop. Here, hold this." She handed Lexi the duffel, unzipped it, pulled out a small pad and pencil, then zipped it back up. "Now wish me luck—I'm going in."

"Are you crazy?" Lexi said, latching on to her arm. "You

can't just barge in and start asking questions. You'll be arrested or something."

Kim Ling tore her arm away with such force it snapped around her torso like a whip. A bolt of lightning ripped through the night sky, and by the time the crack of thunder followed, Kim Ling had cleared the barrier and was straining up against the yellow CRIME SCENE tape, waving her notepad to get someone's attention.

23

EVERYTHING YOU'LL NEED TO KNOW

"Excuse me!" Kim Ling called out, flashing her fake ID to the leathery-faced lady in the Foo Fighters T-shirt. "Kim Ling Levine, reporter for the AP."

"And I'm Angelina Jolie."

"I just need a few quick quotes from—"

"Uh, nice try, kid, but it's not gonna happen," the woman said over her squawking walkie-talkie. "Yeah, Josh, go ahead." She scratched her head, listening to the distorted voice. "Uh-huh, I understand, but we really have to step it up. It's gonna pour any minute."

"Miss?" Kim Ling insisted. "I'd really appreciate it if—"

"Hang on," the woman said. She gave Kim Ling the look of death. "Okay, I'm really gonna need you to clear the area."

"But—"

"Now!" she barked, and went back to the walkie-talkie. "Some kid wanting quotes for her school paper or something. Listen, they've already had their break so get 'em back. No—*no!*" And lost in her conversation, she wandered off to the side.

Lexi and Kevin were crouched in the overgrown bushes alongside the courtyard, as close to the action as possible without being noticed. Lexi was fingering the good luck charms in her pocket, trying to activate them somehow; Kevin was taking deep breaths. Together they watched as Kim Ling breezed right past the female watchdog and went skipping over cables and wires in an awkward game of hopscotch, making her way directly to the perp on the bench.

"Sir, good evening. Kim Ling Levine, AP reporter."

Lexi cringed when she saw Kim Ling actually shake the criminal's hand! *The girl is gutsy, that's for sure.* Thank goodness there were two thick-armed cops the size of tanks within spitting distance.

"I realize this is a difficult time for you," Kim Ling said, "but I wonder if I can bother you for a few quick quotes?"

"Well, this is a bit unusual, isn't it?" the perp said in his thick British accent. "But, sure, why not? Off you go."

"He's polite for a convict," Kevin whispered to Lexi.

"Shhh!"

"Appreciate it," Kim Ling said, and cleared her throat. "Let's see—can I have your name, just for the record?"

"Nigel Humphries. H-U-M-P-H-R-I-E-S."

"And can you describe what you're feeling right now, Mr. Humphries? Remorse? Regret? Humiliation?"

"What I'm feeling?" His face twitched. "Is this some sort of joke?"

"I assure you, it's legit," Kim Ling replied without missing a beat.

Lexi's heart did, though. In fact, she was having wild palpitations. *Now, why is there a perfectly good pair of handcuffs lying next to the perp on the bench? And—is that a Taser?*

"Let's just skip ahead to the nitty-gritty then, shall we?" Kim Ling flipped through her pad, searching through imaginary notes. "All right. So—sir—what led you to such an unlikely location to carry out your plot?"

"Fair question. Well, originally we were leaning toward another spot entirely, but after a stroke of brilliance we decided to rework things a bit and shoot at Cleopatra's Needle—this fantastic obelisk in the midst of the park."

Shoot, needle, obelisk, park. Lexi checked off the clues in her head as he spoke, but was more confused than ever.

"Excuse me?" Kim Ling said. "I don't understand."

"We really wanted to push the envelope for our last go-round," Nigel told her as rolling thunder rattled the ground. "Really sort of leave our mark."

"What?"

"Nigel! *Niiigel!*" someone called out. It turned out to be a bearded little man in a headset, making a beeline to the bench. "Andy needs the new pages pronto." He turned to the two policemen. "And he wants all background personnel back to position one!"

Lexi could see the perp hand the bearded man a bunch of papers as the two cops grabbed the handcuffs and Taser off the bench and vanished into a wash of white light. She wasn't sure what was happening exactly—her brain had gone numb.

"I'm not following," Kim Ling muttered, her eyebrows furling into knots.

"Yes, of course," Nigel went on, "they haven't announced it to the press yet—so, I suppose I'm giving you a scoop then, aren't I? No more Primetime Crime-Time Wednesday nights," he said, rubbing his soul patch like he was trying to erase it, "and after personally winning the network a bloody Emmy for writing the subway-slasher episode last season. Thanks a lot and out with the bathwater—ungrateful sods! Don't quote me." He ripped off his glasses and crossed his arms and legs in a tangle. "You see, young lady, I'm afraid our show is being canceled."

"Your—*show?*"

"Yes. This is the final curtain for *The Streets of New York.*"

That was when the downpour came. Dense, furious, and stinging. Everyone immediately spilled in different directions like a broken strand of pearls, except for Lexi, Kevin, and Kim Ling, who stood motionless. Dumbfounded. Drowning in gallons of realization—and rain.

Lexi tried piecing everything together in her head, but her thoughts were spinning at tornado speed and all she could do was cry out, "Argh! A stupid TV show! *That's* what this was all about? No freakin' way!" She practically fell out of the bushes but Kevin acted quickly enough to prevent her from landing facedown in the mud. Suddenly she felt as if she had been sucker-punched and kicked in the shins at the same time. And idiotic. Incredibly idiotic. "Omigod. How off in left field could we possibly be?"

She and Kevin watched grimly as the crew splashed around the courtyard, scrambling to collect cables and covering cameras in large plastic sheets. Kim Ling was still planted right in the middle of the chaos—probably in shock.

"Whoa," Kevin muttered, shaking leaves off his head. "Whoa . . ."

"Is that all you can say?"

He looked up at Lexi through a hard squint. "Okay, so, let me get this straight. That angry British guy—Nigel— he really *isn't* the thief, right? He's really a—?"

"Scriptwriter."

"Huh. And everything you heard in the Whispering Gallery was just a bunch of—?"

"Hooey."

"So, all this time we've been risking our lives for—?"

"Nothing."

They stared into each others' stunned, wet faces, riddled with disbelief.

"I'm totally sick to my—"

"Stomach," Lexi finished. "I *knew* this whole thing didn't make sense!"

All of a sudden, Lexi saw Kim Ling bolt like a frightened deer, so she shouldered the duffel, grabbed Kevin's hand, and together they took off after her, shouting, "Kim, wait up!"

"We're officially wrapped, people!" blared through a passing bullhorn. *"Extras, do not take off before seeing an AD or you will not get paid!"*

Lexi and Kevin busted through the yellow crime tape, blowing their whistles to get Kim Ling to stop, but she didn't even slow down. They kept up the chase around the perimeter of the courtyard, slipping through mud, leaping over puddles—wincing at a fierce flash of lightning that split the sky in two.

"I still don't get it," Kevin said, panting. "The jewels really were stolen, right? It was in all the news."

"Yeah, but the show does stories ripped from today's headlines—and they make up their own crazy endings." Lexi took a quick gulp of air. "We must've been following clues for the made-for-TV version."

When they finally caught up with Kim Ling, under a lamppost just beyond the opposite end of the courtyard, she was sopping wet and gasping for breath. Lexi handed her the duffel, which she promptly flung across the grass.

"Talk about remorse, regret, and humiliation! I mean, I really didn't see that one coming."

"I guess we screwed up big time, huh?" Kevin said.

"Understatement of the year!" Kim Ling gave the lamppost a swift kick—*"Ooow!"*—then recoiled from the pain.

"Well, I hope you're happy, red," she growled. "I wasted a butt-load of time and energy, not to mention a substantial part of my summer, thanks to you."

"Thanks to—don't even!" Lexi bit her tongue. *Where does she get off? It was her brilliant idea to go searching for the jewels in the first place.* "And it's only been, like, a week."

"Check your freakin' sources. That's, like, journalism rule number one." Kim Ling slapped at her temples as if to brand it onto her brain. "What a colossal boondoggle!"

"Well, at least we didn't get shot in the head," Lexi said.

"Now, that would've been a kick-butt story. As it stands, I've got *bubkes*—you understand? *Bubkes!*"

Lexi didn't understand. It was probably more Yiddish or Chinese. Kim Ling stomped away but before Lexi could follow her, she got swallowed up in a flurry of pinks and purples. "Hey!" Female joggers? They just kept on coming. A whole troop of them wearing waterlogged pastel sweat suits. They had appeared out of nowhere, and Lexi couldn't seem to break free from all the wet fleece. "Kevin, where'd you go?" *Can tonight possibly get any worse?*

"Alexandra? Is that you?"

"Aunt Roz!"

And we have an answer.

Lexi's heart fossilized in her chest.

"What on earth are you doing here, young lady?"

Okay, this is NOT actually happening. Life couldn't be that cruel.

"I—was about to ask you the same question."

"Background work. For *The Streets of New York.* You knew that! I even told you specifically I'd be playing a jogger, remember?" With a frustrated groan, Aunt Roz threw off her lavender hood and glared at Lexi through a mask of runny mascara. If she was expecting a response, it wasn't coming. "My God, I can't believe it. Where's your brother?"

Kevin peeked around the last of the soggy joggers, holding up a meek finger. "Right here."

"Is that Kimmy over there? Are her parents here?"

Lexi shook her head, her bottom lip trembling.

"Then what's going on? What could possibly have possessed you kids to come to the park at this hour? Alone?" Aunt Roz's mouth tightened as she waited for an answer that never came. "Oh, Alexandra, I'm so angry I could shake you!"

Lexi could hardly breathe as the sharp rain beat at her face. Had her aunt really told her about the jogger thing being tonight? In Central Park? Had she not been paying close enough attention? She tried stitching together snippets of past conversations—but it was no use. Her brain had turned to fudge.

"This was totally my idea, Ms. M.," Kim Ling said, sloshing into the glow of the lamppost. "There was this concert earlier—at the Naumburg Bandshell. I thought it'd be fun."

Taking one for the team? Well, that's kind of a shocker.

"Fun? I'm—I can't even respond to that right now.

Let's just get everyone home and dry and we'll discuss this in the morning. Thank God you didn't get lost, or hurt, or worse!"

The cab ride home was soggy and silent except for the harsh pelting of rain against the windows. When they arrived at the brownstone, a shadowy figure was tripping down the steps carrying two giant plastic bins—another one of Mr. Carney's weird relatives, Lexi guessed. Or maybe their apartment had just gotten ripped off—who knew? She would never assume anything ever again.

As soon as she got upstairs, she dumped all her good-luck charms in the trash, except for the white feather—*that* she couldn't let go of—took a fast shower, and climbed into bed, hoping to escape quickly into sleep.

But the bone-rattling alarm that went off when her head hit the pillow wasn't about to let that happen.

24

HITTING THE ROOF

Please, please, please let it be a burglar and not who I think it is! At least give me that. With goose bumps in full bloom, Lexi jumped out of bed, flew past the chaise—where her headphone-wearing brother was already fast asleep—and dashed into the hallway. She covered her ears and peeked over the banister to see tenants gathering on the various floors below. Mr. Carney, clutching a squirmy cat; Miss Carelli in a Japanese kimono; Mr. Findlay bickering with Mrs. Rivera, who was rocking her wailing baby—but even little Julio was no match for the brutal alarm.

Lexi swallowed a lump of fear at the sound of climbing footsteps, which she could just barely hear over the nonstop *RIIIING*. It turned out to be Kim Ling in her cowboy boots with a baseball bat in hand.

"Was it you, red?" she shouted over the noise. "Did you accidentally set the thing off again?"

"Nuh-uh." Technically it was Kevin who had set it off before, but this was no time for petty details.

Kim Ling reached up on tiptoes and switched off the alarm in less than a millisecond. A groan of relief came from the tenants below as she clomped over to the metal door that led to the rooftop and pounded it with her fist. "Who goes there?" she yelled.

"Kim!" A lanky man in a cranberry robe and slippers came whooshing up the steps right past Lexi. "You never listen! I specifically told you *not* to go upstairs!"

"Well, how else was I supposed to dismantle the alarm, Dad? I'm not defenseless—I've got a bat. And four-and-a-half years of tae kwon do. "

Lexi had only seen Kim Ling's father in passing once before. Tonight he was barely recognizable with extreme bed-head, beard stubble, and an angry distorted face.

"All clear down here!" someone shouted from below. "No sign of any intruders inside the building."

Mr. Levine looked instantly relieved. "The alarm must've scared them off." With a rattling exhale, he turned to the gaggle of tenants peppered on the steps. "It's all over, folks," he announced. "Nothing to be afraid of. Just double-lock your doors and go back to bed."

"But just in case . . ." Kim Ling leaned into the door again and yelled, "The cops'll be here any minute, sicko! So, if anyone's still out there, FYI, you're gonna fry!" She turned back, seeming pleased with herself. "That ought to do the—"

Suddenly the door burst open and something came charging in like a wild bull escaping its chute. Shrieks from the tenants. Lexi squealed too and went tripping down the stairs. Through a blur of railing spindles above her she could see flailing limbs and flying hair. There was a furious tussle. A high-pitched scream and then *bang!*

"You!" Kim Ling shouted.

"Stop—don't!" Lexi cried out, thinking she had heard a gunshot. She turned to realize Kim Ling's bat had slammed down onto the banister to trap the intruder. "Melrose Merritt!" Exactly as she had feared.

"You know this girl?" Mr. Levine turned to ask Lexi.

That was when Melrose ducked under the bat to make a run for it. Mr. Levine caught her by the arm and she struggled and squawked—squirming to break free like a wet fish on a hook.

"Yes, let her go! She's a friend."

With a confused look on his face, he unhanded Melrose and everything came to a standstill. They slowly backed away from each other, panting heavily and examining scratches on their arms and wrists.

"Friend," Kim Ling scoffed, "yeah, right." She cautiously moved in on Melrose like a lioness stalking her soaking-wet prey. "You've got some nerve. What the heck are you doing here?"

"I—was invited," Melrose answered, catching her breath.

"*What?* Invited by whom, may I ask?"

"The queen of freakin' England. Who d'ya think?"

Kim Ling followed Melrose's glare down to Lexi, who was crouched on the fifth floor stairwell, hand over mouth. "Well? Do you have something to say, your majesty?"

A sour panic rose inside Lexi so fast she could taste it. She boosted herself up to her feet and reluctantly started to climb, chewing her bottom lip and thinking she had better fess up.

"*Kim Ling!*" Mrs. Levine's piercing voice came echoing through the stairwell. "*What's happening? You get your butt downstairs right now!*"

"Don't worry, Mom," Kim Ling called out. "It's all over."

"False alarm," Mr. Levine said.

"*Come down, come down. You give me coronary!*"

"Mom, really—just go back to bed. That goes for everyone!"

"Easy for you to say," Mr. Findlay yelled up from the fourth floor. "This whole building's going to pot!"

"That's not fair, Arthur!" Mr. Levine yelled back. He went tripping down the steps to the sound of doors slamming, locks clicking, and chain bolts sliding into place.

With an argument grumbling up from the floor below, Lexi slowly approached Melrose. "Life and death emergencies *only*," she reminded her in barely a whisper. "So was it?" Melrose's non-response was answer enough. "Great. And after I risked my neck to help you out."

"If by help you mean *use.*"

"What?"

"Never mind."

"What're you talking about?" Kim Ling asked, tuning in to the conversation.

"Nothing," Melrose spat.

"Spill your guts right now or I call nine-one-one and you're doing five to ten for breaking and entering."

Melrose palmed the rain off her face, her cagey eyes darting from Kim Ling to Lexi and back again. "You guys were just usin' me," she said, crossing her goose-pimply arms. "The both of you, and you know it. Bribin' me to take you through the tunnels in Grand Central—on some *lame* treasure hunt for Cleopatra's jewels."

Lexi gasped.

"Oh, don't look so surprised. I heard you guys talkin' all about it through the door when I was here for dinner the other night. I'm not as dumb as *you* look."

There was the slapping sound of bare feet on concrete and all heads turned as Kevin came barreling up the steps. "Well, if the treasure hunt was so lame," he said, moving in on Melrose, "then why'd you go searching for the jewels yourself in Central Park? Huh? Trying to beat us to the punch?"

"I don't know what you're talkin' about."

"We found proof!" He produced the purple bandanna from behind his back and waved it in her face like a flag of victory.

"Hey, gimme!" she said, swiping it. "I've been lookin' all over for that!"

"Ahha!" Kevin exclaimed. "I rest my case."

Melrose had the guiltiest look on her face but she shrugged it off. "So, I double-crossed a buncha double-crossers—big whoop. I'd have to be brain-dead not to at least check it out." And she tied the filthy bandanna on her upper arm like some princess warrior. "The reward money's supposed to be a freakin' fortune—and in case you ain't noticed, I could really use the cash."

"See!" Kim Ling said, turning to Lexi, "I told you we never should've trusted—" She stopped midsentence. Her eyes narrowed. "Wait, back up. What did she say before about *dinner?*"

Lexi's insides instantly crumbled into dust. "Oh, crud."

"Uh, excuse me, blondie—and I use the term loosely—exactly *when* were you here for dinner?"

"Saturday night," Melrose answered without hesitation. She plunged her hand into the top of her borrowed blouse, which was now a wet, see-through, dirty mess, and pulled out the long pink ribbon holding the key to the brownstone. "That's when Lexi gave me this—which was how I got in tonight, if you must know."

I cannot believe I'm being stabbed in the back right in front of my face!

Kim Ling's cheeks went red with rage. "Uh-uh, no way," she said, turning to Lexi. *"Please* tell me you did not give the key to our brownstone to a psycho runaway."

"Just a copy."

"Just a—*ugh!* Have you lost what's left of your so-called mind?" She ripped the key off of Melrose's neck and fisted it.

"Hey! Don't call me a psycho or I'll rearrange your face!"

"Bring it on—psycho!"

Just as they were about to go at it big time, Aunt Roz came rushing up the steps, crying, "Girls, for heaven's sake!" and flew right in between them, shielding her face like an awkward referee. She quickly managed to separate the two—Melrose against the banister and Kim Ling against the wall—and planted herself in the middle with her hands on her hips, breathing heavily. "Kevin, honey, go downstairs before you get hurt."

"But—"

"No buts. Go!" She had switched to her no-nonsense voice, so Kevin took off immediately. "What's going on, girls?" she said, plucking out her earplugs one by one. "Really. Why is Melrose here at this hour—and why are you behaving like wild animals? I thought she was your friend from City Camp."

"Oh, please," Kim Ling said with a scowl. "More like runaway street trash we met in Grand Central—not City Camp, Ms. M. There is no City Camp. Well, there is, obviously, but we've been ditching it this whole time." She gave Lexi a poisonous glare. "Your precious niece has

been hiding things from you since the day she arrived—
and apparently she's pulled a few over on me, too."

Her surge of hateful words knocked the air right out
of Lexi.

"What is she talking about, Alexandra?"

"Wait a second," Melrose snarled, getting into Kim
Ling's face. "Now you're callin' me street trash?"

"Well, *hobo* is so dated."

"Kim, that's enough!" Mr. Levine was standing on the
top step—his neck pulsing so fiercely, it looked like a
jugular was about to blow. "And did I just hear you say
you ditched camp? If you think you're getting away with
that, young lady, you've got another think—"

Kim Ling started making excuses but a violent crack
of thunder shut her up—and sent Lexi's heart racing even
faster than it already had been. She hugged herself tightly,
wondering if she was still asleep and this was all one big,
horrible nightmare. Had a single good intention ever gone
so wrong?

"I want that *trash* off our property right now, Dad.
And I want *her* out, too!"

It took a second for Lexi to realize that Kim Ling was
pointing directly at her—the wave of hot anger radiating
out of the girl felt like heat from an oven. Lexi had never
seen her so vicious. Pushy and obnoxious, yes, but not
vicious. Lexi just stood there, rubbing the hollow of her
neck where her opal necklace should have been hanging,

comforting her. She was struggling for something to say—anything that would make the situation even a tiny bit better, when a loud crash came from the roof deck.

Everyone froze.

"Okay, that was not thunder." Mr. Levine gestured for the group to stand back. He tightened his rope belt, scooped up the bat, and cautiously approached the metal door. "Who's out there?" he yelled. "Hello?"

"Melrose, did you come alone?" Aunt Roz whispered.

"Yes!"

"We obviously can't believe a word she says," Kim Ling blurted.

Mr. Levine positioned the bat like a battering ram, then, to shouts of "Dad, be careful!" and "Joel, don't!" he barged through the door with a resounding *boom!* The rain was hammering the ground in a thick, crooked sheet, the fierce, howling wind blowing pink petals across the roof deck. Broken pots of hydrangeas could be seen along the roofline just beyond the inside-out patio umbrella. Kim Ling warily joined her father on the rooftop while Lexi and Aunt Roz huddled against the doorjamb watching. No one was out there. It was clear that the wind was the culprit and the noise had come from the crashing pots.

Mr. Levine dashed back inside, dripping wet, and trudged down the steps with the bat still in hand. Kim Ling followed him in but came to an abrupt stop. "Where's— what happened to Melrose?"

Lexi and Aunt Roz whipped their heads around. The runaway had disappeared.

"Snaggit!" Kim Ling shrieked. "I apologize in advance, Ms. M., for what you're about to hear." And with that, she thundered down the stairs, letting real curse words fly for all six flights; then she slammed her apartment door so hard the banisters shook.

A sudden thrash of cold rain had Lexi and Aunt Roz struggling to close the rooftop door against the merciless wind. "I can't believe Melrose just took off like that," Lexi said. "Again." *Beware of ill-fated entanglements* ran across her mind like a smirking screen saver. *And—shoot—why didn't I confront her about stealing my necklace while I had the chance?*

Without even thinking about it, Lexi wound up sitting with her aunt on the top step. Damp and stupefied.

"That scared the bejesus out of me." Aunt Roz brushed a clump of hair off Lexi's forehead, looking beyond flustered. "What you kids have put me through tonight must've taken ten years off my life. First the park and now this. Honestly." She clutched the top of her robe and sighed. "And I still don't have a grasp of what's going on. Why was Melrose here? And what was Kimmy saying during that hissy fit of hers—about runaways—and trash?"

It was almost funny but not quite. With what had just played out, Lexi figured it was time to come 100 percent clean to her aunt about the whole situation. She owed her that—at least. So, she took her aunt's hand and a shaky breath, then confessed it all. Cutting City Camp to hunt for Cleopatra's jewels, taking the subway, sneaking Melrose into the apartment for a bath and a change of clothes, hiding the eyeglasses at Radio City. Everything. It felt freeing. And yet . . . horrible. She ended with a sincere apology for all the secrets she had been keeping.

"Secrets?" Aunt Roz slipped her hand away from Lexi's. "You mean lies."

A wave of ferocious rain hit the metal door, sounding like a round of machine-gun fire. The expression on her aunt's face was even worse than earlier in the park. Too much for Lexi to bear. "I'm sorry. *Really* sorry." She waited for "That's okay, sweetheart" or "All's well that ends well"— the usual upbeat Aunt Roz response. Cold silence. Enough to send an icy shiver up Lexi's spine.

"I think your dad and Clare should end their trip early to come get you and your brother. I'll phone them first thing in the morning."

Lexi couldn't object. Or speak even. She wiped the rain off her face, or tears—she couldn't tell which—and stared into her aunt's tired, wounded eyes.

"And of course you're completely grounded. Is that what they still call it? Oh, Alexandra. I'm so disappointed in you."

25

RED DRESSES

The stillness that filled the apartment Monday morning should have been a welcome thing, considering the insanity of the last few days. But it definitely wasn't I-feel-like-cracking-open-a-book stillness; more like funeral-parlor stillness. Or waiting for an algebra exam. As promised, before leaving for rehearsal, Aunt Roz had made the dreaded phone call to Lexi's dad, who was somewhere in Greece. He and Clare would arrange to be in New York on Wednesday to pick up Lexi and Kevin—and no, he didn't need to speak to them. It wasn't going to be pretty. Aunt Roz had been giving Lexi the silent treatment, complete with looks of deep disappointment every time she breezed by. *Every single time!* She only spoke once to lay down the law: "Until you're packed and leaving for Cold Spring, you are absolutely not to step foot off the front stoop of this brownstone. Understood?"

So that's where Lexi sat, on the concrete steps, which

were still damp and gritty from last night's storm, testing the limits of her house arrest. This was all wrong. She was a good girl—before New York City at least. She had always been a good girl, and good girls don't get punished.

Lexi did a slow head roll and her neck crackled like a bowl of Rice Krispies—probably from all the stress. On her second roll to the right, she noticed a splotch of yellow at her feet. A legal pad? "BOONDOGGLE SUMMER" was scrawled across the first page in bold, aggressive caps. Kim Ling's handwriting—it had to be. That essay for her journalism contest, no doubt. With a cautionary glance at the front door, Lexi grabbed the pad and began reading a random paragraph.

Imagine the look of shock and dismay on this reporter's face when I discovered the lives and limbs of myself and my cantankerous cohorts had been risked for naught. The cryptic clues we were following on our quest to uncover Cleopatra's stolen jewels were actually the far-fetched fantasies of some overpaid crime-drama writers. Color me crimson with embarrassment, not to mention black and blue.

"Still trespassing I see."

Lexi flinched. She turned to see Kim Ling posed at the top of the stoop in a paint-splattered tank, holding a steaming mug.

"Not exactly the killer story I was hoping for but . . .

keep reading." Kim Ling took a careful sip of her drink. "Out loud."

" 'So I guess' "—Lexi cleared her throat, surprised that Kim Ling hadn't jumped down it—" 'I guess it all comes down to the basics,' " she read aloud, flipping the page. " 'Check your sources. Do your research. Case in point: if your mother tells you she loves you, find proof.' "

"I might hate that line."

" 'If Rabbi Martin swears that the smoked whitefish at Katz's Deli is fresh, second-guess him. If the crazy cat-man in Apartment one-R insists he's not pirating illegal DVDs, even as he's being arrested—' " Lexi gasped and turned to Kim Ling. "What? Mr. Carney?"

"Yeah, last night when the cops showed up."

"The cops came?"

"Didn't you hear the sirens?"

"When *don't* I hear sirens?"

"I thought they showed up 'cause of the burglar alarm fiasco, but no, they came to arrest Carney. Turns out he had this whole bootleg operation going on. You should've seen the setup in his apartment. Un-freakin'-believable. I'll bet that's why that black Lincoln was always parked out front. FBI."

Lexi took a moment to digest the information. "Wow. Huh. That's totally insane."

"Tell me about it."

She turned back to read the essay, but a bell went off in her head. "So wait. You mean a *real* crime was happening under our own roof while we were out on that wild goose chase?"

"Ironic, isn't it? I should probably take that out of my essay. I don't want to appear—what's the word?"

"Obtuse? Oblivious? Inept?"

"I taught you well, grasshopper." Kim Ling's near smile disappeared behind her mug and she took another noisy sip, studying Lexi. "Some investigative reporter I am— that's what you're thinking, right, Lexicon?"

"No, I wasn't gonna—"

"Some journalist I'll make. You can say it."

"Well—you have to admit—" Lexi snorted, harnessing a laugh. "I mean, come on, it *is* pretty funny. Doesn't he live right across the hall from you?" And then she let her laughter fly.

The glint in Kim Ling's eyes disappeared instantly, as if someone had blown out the candle in a jack-o'-lantern. "Yeah? Well, I really don't care what you think." She flip-flopped down the stairs, ripped the legal pad out of Lexi's hand, and started up again. "Stop being so condescending, okay?"

"Um, okay—and ouch. You just gave me, like, seventeen paper cuts."

"Too bad, so sad."

"I was obviously kidding," Lexi said, twisting to her feet. "Listen, I'm sorry about the whole Melrose thing— for giving her that key, if that's what you're really getting all cranky about. But I was worried about her safety, okay?

You should've seen her on Friday after the cops raided Grand Central. She had nowhere to go." Lexi waited for a reaction. "Kim? C'mon, I thought we were making up."

"Wrong." Kim Ling turned abruptly, spilling hot liquid on her hand. "*Ow!* Just because we had a polite exchange doesn't mean everything's copacetic. You lied to my face, remember? I still despise you with the white-hot intensity of a thousand suns!"

"Got it."

Lexi was out of there faster than her paper cuts could bleed. She willed herself not to cry as she stomped past Kim Ling, up a zillion steps, and into her aunt's apartment. *You will not shed a single tear over that girl!* she warned herself. *Don't you dare.*

Kevin was at the desk on the laptop and she stormed right past him, sucking her stinging finger and heading for the bathroom. Maybe a bubble bath would make her feel better—she could scrub Kim Ling and New York City out of her pores forever. But passing Aunt Roz's bedroom, something caught her eye. Draped across the bed was the opening-night dress from Macy's that Aunt Roz had gone on and on about. Lexi couldn't resist taking a peek. It was gorgeous. Sooo elegant. *And that color,* she thought on her way into the bathroom. *In-your-face red.*

The gushing bathwater couldn't fill the tub fast enough for Lexi, and couldn't be hot enough—even on such a miserable summer day. Only her big toe could stand it at first, but little by little she submerged her entire body.

Lexi soup. Her brain went as limp as her body, too foggy to complete another thought. Fine by her. And if the smell of jasmine bath salts transported her to somewhere far-away and exotic, so much the better.

With the scented bubbles at nose level, she turned off the spigot with her foot and waited for the sloshing water to settle. Her arms floated to the top and her eyelids fluttered as she watched the steam rise in ghostly swirls. The hypnotic *drip, drip, drip* from the faucet transforming into a distant *chug, chug, chug* . . . and all at once she was ten years old, sitting next to her mother on a train traveling along the Hudson.

"I'm not sleeping, cookie," her mom had insisted. "I'm just resting my eyes."

"Well, Mom, we don't want to miss our stop. What's the name of it again?"

"Tarrytown. We're almost there." Lexi's mom folded her hands on her lap, admiring her new French tips. "Oh, for heaven's sake—"

"What is it?"

"I forgot to wear my lucky charm bracelet—we were in such a hurry."

"You don't need it. You've got me."

"I know, but of all days . . ." She took a deep breath, hooking her arm through Lexi's. "Thanks for coming with me on the train again, sweetie. I was just too rattled to drive. I love you to pieces for holding my hand through this whole thing."

"Well, I'm proud of you. And I don't mind taking trains—they're so retro. You look awesome, by the way."

"I really splurged on this dress, so don't tell your father when he gets back from his business trip or he'll flip his lid. But I needed a red one for today, so I figured what the heck? It's not every day I get to do something so— extraordinary."

Her mother had never looked so chic in her life. She was a newly appointed ambassador for the "Go Red" campaign—something about promoting awareness of heart disease in women, which she herself had survived. She had hardly ever worn dresses, let alone one from Saks Fifth Avenue! The saleslady had said it was made for her, that she looked simply stunning in red. It was cut kind of low, though. Not sexy low, but low enough that her scar showed a little. But Lexi had convinced her she could camouflage it with makeup and no one would notice. It worked.

"Mom, do you want to go over your speech one more time before we get there?"

"No, thanks," she said, closing her eyes. "I think I'll just go over it in my head."

Lexi closed her eyes, too, but chewed on a stick of gum so she wouldn't accidentally nod off—the rocking of the train was way too risky. Before the flavor had even left her Carefree Sugarless, several stops had whizzed by and the conductor called out, "Ossining! This is Ossining. Tarrytown is next."

"Mom, wake up, that's us," Lexi said, nudging her mother gently. "C'mon, Sleeping Beauty, your audience awaits." She shook her arm. Nothing. *One-one-thousand, two-one-thousand . . .* "Mooom?" Again. Harder. "We're gonna miss our—" Her words got stuck in her throat. "Do you need me to get our bag down from the overhead rack? Okay, I can do that—I'll get our—" Lexi jolted to her feet and reached for the suitcase with trembling fingers. She had to jump for the strap and the thing came crashing to the floor. Her mother didn't even budge. "Oh, God, this can't be happening."

Just breathe, Lexi told herself, kicking the bag out of the aisle. Kicking, kicking. *She's a heavy sleeper just like Kevin, and you're overreacting. You always overreact, freak! Just stop it.*

"Tarrytown!"

"*Mom?*"

There was the hiss of the train pulling into the station. Doors were rattling. Slamming shut. A haze of people rushed by, knocking Lexi back into her seat. She took her mother's hand and began gently rubbing it. "C'mon, c'mon, Mom," she whispered, "please, wake up. You have to—"

"Tarrytown! This is Tarrytown."

Hot blood pulsing in her temples. Silent screams in her head.

"Yonkers is next!"

"Omigod, help me," she had heard herself cry out. "I

don't know what to—stop the train! Somebody, *please* help!"

The bathroom door flew open and she was shockingly back in her twelve-year-old body again as Kevin came barging in.

"Lexi!"

"Get out!" she screeched, pulling a towel down over herself. "I'm in the tub!"

"I didn't see anything." He turned his back. "Are you okay?"

"Of course I'm okay. Why wouldn't I be okay?"

"You were screaming for help, Lex—at the top of your lungs."

26

CRACKS

Lexi had never revisited that horrible morning on the Metro-North quite so vividly before. You would think all those sessions with Dr. Lucy would have helped it feel less scary by now. She threw on her aunt's chenille robe that was hanging on the bathroom door, thinking it might comfort her. It did not. Withered and still a bit shaky, she decided to focus her energy into packing. At least she would be that much closer to getting out of Crazy Town, USA. *Stuff socks into shoes to save room . . .* She could hear her mom's packing instructions in her head. *Don't fold pants, but roll them up to prevent wrinkling; double-check pockets for anything you might need.* When she grabbed her khaki shorts, they were stiff and crinkly. A newspaper article was sticking out of the back pocket, with the head-line that had started it all:

CLEOPATRA'S JEWELS VANISH!

It still packed a wallop. She skimmed the article on her way into the living room and tossed it onto the faux-leather massage chair. "If only I knew then what I know now." *Another Momism.* Collapsing into the chair, she grabbed the remote and switched on the TV. A DVD of *The Streets of New York: Season One* was playing, which made her shudder and immediately switch it off. *I wonder if Aunt Roz got a deal on it from Mr. Carney.* "Hey, Kev, toss me my cell, will you?" she said in her business-as-usual voice. "It's next to the paper-clip thingy. In case Aunt Roz calls."

Kevin was at the desk, hypnotized by the laptop screen. "Guess what hippopotomonstrosesquipedaliophobia means? Fear of long words. Isn't that the coolest? And fear of your stepmother is novercaphobia. That's what you have, Lex. Nover—"

"Easy for you to say."

"Get this," he said over his shoulder. "I googled Nigel Humphries—you know, the head writer of *The Streets of New York*, and he went to NYU at the exact same time as Benjamin Deets—the film school. Isn't that weird?"

"I don't really care anymore. It's over, as far as I'm concerned. The fat lady has sung."

"Don't talk about Miss Carelli that way."

"Kevin!"

He closed the laptop with a snort and delivered the phone personally, flopping down onto the chair next to Lexi. It was so not like him.

"Thanks." With a curious smile, Lexi turned on her phone and slipped it into one of her droopy pockets. "Oh, Kev, how could everything go so incredibly wrong?" she said more to herself than to her brother. "I just don't get it." She strummed her fingers on the armrest and studied the control-box massage options as if there would be a pop quiz afterward: neck and shoulders; upper back; middle; lumbar; legs; gentle massage; deep tissue . . .

"So, Lex? Don't bite my head off—"

"Don't *make* me have to bite your head off."

"—but are we supposed to just pretend like it never happened?"

"The jewel hunt? For the thousandth time, I said drop it."

"That's not what I—I mean, before. In the tub. You kinda scared me. Were you having that dream about Mom?"

Lexi gathered her damp curls on the top of her head and settled into a tight fetal position facing away from Kevin. "You'd have to be asleep to be dreaming, and I doubt I was sleeping in a scalding hot tub." Conversation over. She lay motionless, focusing on the hum of the air conditioner and visually dissecting the wreath of dried flowers, ribbons, and bluebirds hanging next to the mirror over the bureau.

"I miss her a lot," Kevin said. "Don't you?"

"Don't ask stupid questions."

"Well, you never talk about her."

"I don't need to."

"Yes, you do! Dr. Lucy said—"

"Save it. I know all about what Dr. Lucy says. Believe me."

Kevin sprang up to leave, but Lexi yanked him back onto the chair. She wriggled over to give him room and they lay side by side in silence, leg over leg, staring up at the ceiling.

"All those cracks." Lexi tilted her head. "It's like studying cloud formations. If you look long enough, you can see pictures. Like, see, there's a crooked sailboat." She pointed it out. "And a funky butterfly."

Kevin was right. Dr. Lucy was always telling her to share her feelings, share her thoughts, share her fears; and her dad kept accusing her of keeping everything bottled up inside, which really irked her. But did she tell him how she felt about it? Never.

"Remember how she used to save all kinds of strange stuff," Lexi said, "like lipstick blots and pigeon feathers?"

"Just the white ones. Dad said she had enough for an Indian headdress."

"Native American. No one says Indian anymore."

"Dad does." A smile spread over Kevin's face and his eyes lit up. " 'Member how she sewed matching covers for everything in the house?"

"Cozies."

"The can opener, the toaster, the toilet paper . . ."

"Dad's circular saw."

They laughed a little but it soon faded into solemn stillness. Kevin reached over Lexi to grab the control box and fiddled with the switch. "Houston, do you read me? All systems go. Prepare for liftoff!" He clicked the knob to Full-Body Massage, making sloppy launch sounds with his mouth.

"Take it down a notch, captain."

Kevin turned the dial until the chair purred softly.

"Remember when Mom spent all day making you that smiley-face pizza for your birthday?" Lexi said with an elbow jab. She did seem to feel a little lighter or something just talking about these things. "Pepperoni eyes. Pepper smile. Then totally dropped it on the way out of the oven."

"Facedown, too! *Puh-lop!*"

"You ended up eating it anyway. Dork."

"Five-second rule."

Kevin seemed determined to test out the entire menu of massage options during their stroll down memory lane. Mechanical knuckles were kneading their shoulders one minute; then thumping down their backs the next. Suddenly their butts were being pummeled like punching bags.

"Okay, this thing's getting way too personal." Lexi snatched the controls away from Kevin and switched it to Gentle Vibrate.

The quiet hum was relaxing. Their eyes seemed to close automatically.

"You think she can see us, Lex? Mom, I mean."

"Definitely."

"Me, too. You think she's mad at Dad for getting married again?"

Both pairs of eyes popped open.

"Enough with the questions already."

"Do you?"

"How am I supposed to know?" Lexi turned her back to Kevin and rearranged herself, tucking the bulky robe around her feet. "*I* am."

"Mad? Is that why you hate Clare so much? Is it?"

"I don't hate her. I just—despise her with the white-hot intensity of a thousand suns." She was still burnt from that line, but she had to admit it was a good one.

"Why? She's so nice. All she does is give us presents to try to get us to like her."

"It's called bribery and it's not working. Some nerve giving me those old-lady pearls. Could she be more obvious?" The heat rising through her neck had Lexi scooching up as far as she could. "She wants to replace the opal necklace Mom gave me, just like *she* wants to replace Mom. Doesn't take a genius to figure that out. Probably conjured up some wicked spell, 'cause now my opal's gone for good. Way to go, woman, but you still have me to deal with." She took a deep, cleansing breath to release her inner sizzle— one of Dr. Lucy's exercises. *Inhale pink; exhale blue.*

Kevin's nose crinkled. "Ew, did you eat hummus?"

Lexi gave him a face-load of bad breath; he pigged her nose with his thumb, which led to a full-on tickle attack. When the giggles faded, they relaxed back into deciphering ceiling cracks again.

"Boot," Kevin muttered.

"What?"

"To the left of the light thingy. A giant boot."

"Or Italy, depending on what you want to see."

"It's not Clare's fault, though, right?" His rag-doll arm flopped over Lexi's. "I mean, if you really think about it. She can't help it if she loves Dad and Dad loves her."

Love? Hardly. "I just don't trust that woman. Did you know she signed us up for City Camp before even asking if we wanted to go? Dad let it slip. Talk about putting the cart before the horse." Another momism. *Inhale pink . . . Exhale blue . . .*

The next thing Lexi knew, she was awakening from a deep sleep with Kevin still conked out on the massage chair next to her. "Geez, how long was I asleep?" She staggered to her feet, catching a glimpse of herself in the mirror over the bureau. Her hair had dried into a lopsided tumbleweed and the newspaper article was stuck to her face. She peeled it off on her way into the kitchen and for some odd reason the date jumped out at her and she couldn't let it go. June tenth, June tenth, June tenth. But what was so weird about that? She tossed the article onto the kitchen table with a *"Hmmph"* and started socking life back into her butt, which seemed to have morphed into two tingly pincushions. That's when it hit her.

Wait. We arrived early on June ninth—nine, my lucky number. The robbery happened late that night. So how could those TV writers have been whispering about a story they'd ripped from the headlines when the headlines didn't even appear till the next day? She gasped. *Cart before the horse!*

"Omigod, this is huge!" She grabbed the newspaper article, raced back into the living room, and shook Kevin into consciousness. "Nigel what's-his-puss must've been in on the whole thing!" she blurted, shoving the article in front of him.

"Huh? What time is it?"

"Kevin! I need you to focus." She tossed the article aside and recounted her discovery to him, exactly as she had just gone over it in her own mind. "So, maybe the guy I saw him with in the Whispering Gallery really *was* Benjamin Deets!"

Kevin's eyes went wide. "Yeah? Yeah! Well, they did go to school together."

"That's right, that's right. And Benjamin Deets was a consultant too—for *The Streets of New York*—the guards at the museum were chatting all about it." Her hands flew to cover her mouth. "It makes total sense, then, right? Deets and Humphries were probably in cahoots!" She started chewing on a jagged cuticle, her head aching from the racing thoughts. "So, now what?"

"You have to tell Kim Ling—she'll know what to do."

"Yes. Oh, wait!" Lexi said, remembering their quarrel. *"No,* not an option! Shoot, shoot, shoot!"

Lexi flew around the entire apartment like a deflating balloon and wound up flat on her back on the massage chair again, staring at cracks. She shot up with a jolt. Phone in hand. Heart in mouth. "I'll do it myself. I can do this." And after three deep breaths and a sign of the cross, she turned on her phone. "I—I don't even know what I'm supposed to dial."

Kevin ran over to the laptop on the desk, mumbling something about looking it up, but Lexi was already dialing 411 and reminding herself not to sound like a frightened little girl this time.

"For service in English, press one, or stay on the line. En Español, para información—" BEEP!

"Ugh!" After answering too many automated questions, she was directed to dial 311. Finally, there was a live human voice on the line from the NYPD Manhattan headquarters.

"Yes, hello. My name is Alexandra McGill and I have some very important information regarding the Cleopatra jewel heist. Okay, I'll start from the beginning . . ."

27

CHANGE OF HEART

Whether anything would come of Lexi's reporting her theory to the police didn't seem to matter to her much as the hours passed—although getting her hands on that hefty reward would certainly be sweet. The best part was that she had figured it out herself and actually felt, for the first time in her life, kind of smart. That was what she was thinking outside the Minetta Lane Theatre in Greenwich Village the next night, waiting with Kevin for their aunt to come out of the stage door after the opening night performance of *Shattered Glass*. Aunt Roz had caved at the last minute and decided to release them both from brownstone jail to attend. "A promise is a promise" was her excuse, even though Lexi didn't recall her ever promising anything of the kind. She chalked it up to the fact that kindhearted people were bad at holding grudges—unlike certain Chi-new-ish journalist wannabes who shall remain nameless.

Lexi decided to be semi-forgiving, too, so she explained all the latest developments of the jewel heist to her "frenemy" in a long e-mail, even wishing her well at the end. It was what adults called closure or something. She consulted *The Book of Answers* before she went through with sending it, though—after all, it had been spot-on about their misadventure in Central Park. **Startling events may occur as a result,** it warned this time. But she simply crossed her fingers for luck and clicked SEND anyway.

"Brava, brava!" a small crowd of theatergoers cheered as the actress who played Laura Wingfield exited the stage door, carrying a bouquet of long-stemmed roses.

"Oh, look, they're blue!" Lexi said, pointing them out to Kevin. " 'Cause she sang that 'Blue Roses' song, remember?"

"Yeah, I didn't get that part."

"Her character had some ancient disease called pleurosis, right? Which is why she kept limping around the stage. When her high school crush asked what was wrong with her, he thought she said blue roses—instead of pleurosis—"

"Yeah, so?"

Kevin obviously couldn't have cared less. With no special effects, rocket ships, or mutant aliens in the play, he must've been bored out of his mind. Lexi, on the other hand, had gotten completely sucked in. It was about an overbearing mother, Amanda Wingfield, aka Aunt Roz, forcing her shy, crippled daughter to come out of her shell or die trying.

Another burst of applause as the actor who played the gentleman caller burst through the stage door followed by Aunt Roz, who looked very much the star in her silver ribbon wrap. Lexi and Kevin were hooting and hollering, and she threw them a little wave and started weaving her way toward them through the eager crowd. When she stopped to autograph a program, her shawl fell to her shoulders and Lexi's eyes widened. Her aunt wasn't wearing that gorgeous red dress after all, the one that had been draped across her bed—but an eggplant-colored one instead.

"That's bizarre," Lexi said, turning to Kevin. "You didn't tell her about the thing I told you *not* to tell her about, did you? You know, the whole red-dress-bathtub situation?"

"I refuse to answer on the grounds I might be intimidated."

"Incriminated, and that's a yes." She swatted him. "Kevin! Is that why she let us come tonight? Out of pity?"

Aunt Roz was closer now, giving them an "I'm trying to get to you!" look, but two shiny-faced men were clinging to her and gushing.

"We'll see you at Palma, my dear, after you've dealt with all your stage-door Johnnies—You are coming to the party, right?—You must!—We can gorge ourselves on jumbo shrimp, wait for the reviews—and toast to how *fabulous* you were!"

"I wouldn't miss it for the world!" Aunt Roz blew them a kiss, then collected Lexi and Kevin in a giant hug. "Lord," she said with a sigh, "I can't smile anymore or my face'll fall off."

Lexi gave her a peck on her heavily powdered cheek. "Thanks again for letting us come. I really appreciate it—I mean, after everything that I—well, you know."

"Yes. I know. Well, I've never been much of a disciplinarian. I figure Mark and Clare ending their honeymoon early to come pick you kids up will probably result in punishment enough."

No doubt. "Anyway, you were awesome tonight."

"No, you were *fabulous, my dear!*" Kevin mocked.

"Why, thank you, kind sir," Aunt Roz said using her Southern drawl from the play. "I hope you're not just saying that." She batted her false eyelashes a few times and turned to a handful of people to sign more autographs.

"Nah, they ain't lyin', Mrs. McGill. You rocked."

"Well, I apprec—" Aunt Roz looked up from the program she was signing and gasped, fumbling her pen. "Melrose?"

Lexi did a double take that could have given her whiplash. There Melrose stood in the dappled shadows of the streetlight, flipping her stringy blond hair—still wearing the outfit Lexi had lent her—but it looked as if it had been dragged through the Lincoln Tunnel.

"What're you doing here?" Lexi said, her guts suddenly in a knot. "Just your usual stalking? Or did you come for the dagger you left stuck in my back?" *Okay, that was mean, but . . .*

"I was in the neighborhood, so I snuck into the theater and caught, like, the last fifteen minutes of the play. Your aunt was the best thing in it."

"Oh"—Aunt Roz cleared her throat—"well, I'm flattered."

"That ain't the only reason I came."

Lexi, Kevin, and Aunt Roz stared her down. Waiting. Wondering. That angel-of-silence thing was happening again, just like at the dinner party of doom.

"Well, what is it already?" Kevin asked. "We're not getting any younger."

"Lemme guess," Lexi said. "You've decided to come clean and return my opal necklace that you *stole*."

"What necklace? No. But you're close." And in one smooth move, Melrose whipped something pink out of her back pocket and slapped it into Lexi's hands.

Her eyes nearly sprang out of her skull. "My *wallet?* Where'd you find my wallet? How'd you even know it was—?"

"I didn't exactly find it. 'Member, like, a week and a half ago? Someone slammin' into you in Grand Central?"

Lexi thought back to the day she had arrived. A bull-dozer of a girl had crashed right into her without apologizing. The black-and-blue mark on her arm was just fading. "That was *you?*"

"You were such an easy mark—standin' there with your bag hangin' open. You were practically beggin'—"

"Okay, okay!" The rush of confused emotions vibrating through Lexi had her either wanting to hug the girl or slug her. *Is it still there?* she wondered and immediately flipped to the last plastic insert in her wallet. The only copy of her absolute favorite photo of all time—her mom on the boardwalk in Atlantic City holding up that gnarled shoe? *Yes!* And right next to it, tucked in a separate sleeve, was the tissue from the library of lips, the one with the perfect lipstick print. Before she knew it, hot tears were stinging her eyes.

"Sorry about the missing cash if that's what you're bawlin' about, but it's long gone." Melrose turned to leave. "Sorry about—everything."

"Wait, don't go!" Lexi choked out. "You're always running off."

"Well, I *am* a runaway. It's what we do."

Aunt Roz insisted they carry on their conversation at Niko's down the block—that the cast party could wait, and when she added that they could order whatever they wanted, Melrose was all gung ho. Minutes later, it seemed, they were all piling into a taped-up vinyl booth at the little coffee shop, giving their orders to a sleepy-looking waiter. He brought the drinks right away, and while the fry cook was grilling their tuna melts, Lexi grilled Melrose.

"So, where'd you end up going after that night on the roof? You're not still living in tunnels, I hope?"

"Nah, the cops're all over the place these days. Even St. Agnes. I can't hack it out there on my own no more. So, I finally bit the bullet and—long story short—"

"You moved back home?" Lexi asked.

"Lemme finish. I checked into Covenant House—this teen shelter in midtown. Didn't have much of a choice— and they don't turn anyone away, so . . ." She started fingering her army of ear studs. "Anyway, I'm there, unpacking my stuff, right? That's when I come across your wallet. For some reason I *had* to return it. Too much freakin' guilt."

"Yay, guilt!"

Kevin's hand shot up. "High five!"

"Nah," Melrose groaned, "I don't do that."

Aunt Roz seemed deep in thought, staring into her tea. She took a careful sip, and as her cup hit the saucer, she looked up with a splash of excitement on her face. "Melrose, were you serious before when you said you wanted to become an actress?"

"Dead."

"You'd be a great one too," Kevin said, shoving a handful of fries into his face. "I don't know how I know, I just do."

"I was thinking," Aunt Roz went on, "our theater has an apprentice program for teens. They offer workshops and classes in exchange for doing odd jobs. Would you be interested in such a thing?"

"Are you kidding? That'd be awesome!"

Unfortunately, that enthusiastic response came from Kevin, not Melrose, who was suddenly absorbed in the U.S. Presidents quiz on her paper placemat. She scratched an armpit, twisted her hair. Finally she asked, "Like what kinda odd jobs?"

"Does it matter? Building sets, answering phones." Aunt Roz ripped off a false eyelash and smooshed it onto the table like a dead centipede. "Nothing glamorous."

Lexi waited for Melrose to speak. Why wasn't she jumping at the chance?

"You have to audition to get accepted," Aunt Roz went on, removing eyelash number two, "but I suppose I can help in that department."

"She can help," Lexi echoed.

That was when the mountains of food came. Melrose never gave Aunt Roz a definite answer through the entire meal but from the glint in her eye and the hint of a smile on her greasy face, Lexi knew it was a done deal. "I bring the check," the waiter said when they had finished, which he did very quickly, and they all began gathering their things.

"Here, don't forget your shawl," Lexi said to Aunt Roz. "It fell on the floor." She handed it across the table and her aunt flung it around her shoulders with a movie-star flourish. *Ping!* Something had landed on Lexi's plate. She brushed aside a few abandoned fries and plucked off a long, golden strand of—"Omigod, look!"

Dangling from her fingertips, spinning and winking in the fluorescent light, was her opal necklace. "Oooh!" The sparkling stone was white-white and a thousand different colors all at the same time. And not a hint of damage. Well, except for the pickle juice, which she immediately wiped off on her napkin. She kissed the opal, draped the cool, delicate chain around her neck where it belonged, and secured the clasp. *Snap.* There. She felt complete again.

"That's the same shawl you wrapped around me in Radio City, isn't it?" Lexi asked Aunt Roz, putting two and two together—which she was getting pretty darn good at, she had to admit. "My necklace must've gotten tangled. I just can't believe it! Oh, this is a good, good night."

"And to think," Aunt Roz said, "I was planning on going with my black pashmina, had I worn that new red dress. It just goes to show . . ."

In the taxi, on their way to dropping off Melrose, Lexi had the funniest thought: *Ill-fated entanglements! Ha! The yogini was right.* Mini-mystery solved. She still couldn't help wondering about the biggie, though—the Cleo jewel heist—and if the police had even paid attention to her phone call at all, or just dismissed it like they did the first time around.

The LCD screen in the seatback of the taxi flashed from the weather forecast to local news and Lexi zeroed in. Something about the stock market plunging to an all-time low and unemployment rising to an all-time high, but not a single mention of "the crime of the century." She slumped back in her seat, defeated. That's what she got for sticking her nose where no twelve-year-old nose ought to be.

28

EXTRAORDINARY

Lexi's last night in New York City was another sleepless one. Too many questions swirling around in her head; too few concrete answers. And she had wanted to look especially rested and refreshed when she met up with Dad and Cruella. *Oh, well.*

"Why the sour puss?" Aunt Roz asked her Wednesday morning, setting a glass of orange juice in front of her on the bathroom sink. "Sweetie, you'll be fine."

Lexi kept the blow-dryer diffuser, looking like the miniature spaceship Kevin had once mistaken it for, hovering over her wet curls and managed a sip of juice. "I know. Eventually."

"Chug it, Lex!" Kevin rolled by the bathroom on his sneaker-wheels. "We don't want to be late meeting Dad and Clare."

"Well, you're half right. And no Heelys in the house!"

"We have oodles of time, Kevin," Aunt Roz called out.

"We're going for a farewell breakfast first, don't forget!" She opened the cabinet to grab her calcium pills and leaned into the mirror, cleaning the gunk from the corners of her eyes. "We deserve at least that after all the hoopla we've been through."

Lexi kept her focus on her own reflection, grasping at bunches of her hair so it would dry in a fuller curl. "Think Melrose'll take you up on your offer?"

"Well, it'll be up to her if she turns the corner—but she'll certainly have you to thank if she does." Aunt Roz shook a pill onto her hand and washed it down with a swig of juice. "When I think of the lengths you went to in order to help that girl, well, it's far more than most people would've dreamed of going—although I didn't necessarily agree with your entire process." She swatted Lexi's rear end. "You're quite an amazing girl—destined for extraordinary things."

There was that word again. *Extraordinary.* Even though her aunt sounded as if she were still doing a monologue from a play instead of just talking, it sounded sincere.

"I mean it," Aunt Roz insisted. "Your mother would be so proud of the strong young lady you're becoming."

Lexi closed her eyes for a second so the words would sink in good and tight and she could take them back to Cold Spring. "I wish *she* was meeting us at the station today instead of—"

"Of course you do, dear, but try and give Clare a fighting chance. It can't be too easy for her, either."

"You know what I'm gonna do when we get back to Cold Spring?" Kevin said, dragging a duffel past the door like it was a limp carcass. "Ask Dad to drive us out to Kingsley Park—I want to try the Haunted Mansion ride again. I figure after risking my life trying to solve a big New York crime, it'll be a cinch." He sat on the bag and started scooting it backward down the hall. "What'd you stuff in this thing, Lex—anvils?"

Lexi switched off the dryer. "*Whoa,*" she muttered to Aunt Roz. "Can't wait to tell Dr. Lucy about that." They locked eyes and shared a hopeful smile via the mirror.

"You want to know what I think?" Aunt Roz grabbed a brush off the counter and began brushing her silvery hair. "I think it's time to stop playing mother to your little brother. That's Clare's job now. You just enjoy being a girl."

It sounded easy. It sounded impossible.

"Which reminds me of a song from *South Pacific,* but I'll spare you my Nellie Forbush. Now, c'mon, it's time to bid the Big Apple adieu," she said, floating out of the bathroom, still brushing. "And don't forget your pearls!"

Oh, those. Lexi had planned on forgetting them accidentally on purpose. "I won't."

The restaurant was too noisy to have a decent conversation and the cab ride to Grand Central was another quiet one, except for Aunt Roz fawning over the driver's African dashiki shirt. "Is that tie-dye?" Lexi stared out the window, doing that adieu-bidding thing her aunt had mentioned—saying good-bye to the city. Another taxicab stopped at the red light next to them and she did a double-take. A beaming little girl in a navy beret was in the back seat pressing a long white feather against the window. Huh. Lexi could actually feel goose bumps sprouting on her arm. No, even bigger. Ostrich bumps. Major sign—if she still believed in such things.

"This is good, Muchungwa!" Aunt Roz told the driver. "You can let us out right here."

The cab stopped about half a block away from Grand Central, so Lexi, Kevin, and Aunt Roz had to maneuver their way through the Wednesday morning masses swarming Forty-Second Street. As they approached the entrance of the train terminal, Lexi's right arm felt pinched and heavy—not just from the weight of her bag. She had decided to wear the hateful pearls as a goodwill gesture, but wrapped around her wrist as a funky bracelet. No way was that thing going around her neck, competing with her opal.

Through the doors of Grand Central they trudged, lugging their duffels and backpacks. Up the ramp. Around the corner and into the main concourse with its whirlwind of business suits and briefcases Lexi had come to know so well.

"There she is!" someone shouted.

Lexi looked over her shoulder to see who they were talking about.

A swarm of cameras, lights, and reporters worthy of a rock star came rushing right at her. Microphones in Lexi's face. Blinding flashes. Questions, questions, questions. Too many being fired all at once.

"What the—?" Lexi's first instinct was to make a run for it, but she was instantly surrounded. Trapped. She dropped her duffel, her heartbeat sputtering. "What's going on? This must be a mistake."

"You *are* Alexandra McGill, correct?" a blue-suited reporter asked.

Lexi didn't even know the answer to the question. Her head was spinning like a carousel gone haywire.

"Yes, that's her, that's her!" It was Kim Ling, shoving her way to the front of the pack. "She's obviously clueless about what happened."

"Kim—what're you doing here? Are you in your pajamas?"

Again, Lexi was bombarded with a hundred questions.

"Okay, this is ridiculous, being accosted like this," Aunt Roz said, stepping forward. "Could someone please explain what's going on? One at a time."

"An arrest was made in the Cleopatra jewel heist case, ma'am," a tight-lipped female reporter declared, "thanks to a tip-off from—your daughter?"

"Niece."

The reporter glanced at her notepad. "Nigel Humphries, head writer for the TV show *The Streets of New York*, confessed everything last night when the cops showed up at his house in Astoria."

"No way," Lexi muttered.

"Way!" Kim Ling said, stepping forward. "And when they reported his arrest without even mentioning your name, I thought, 'Oh, heck to the no!' I mean, I knew it had to be because of your epiphany, Lex, after spelling it all out for me in that e-mail. So, I took it upon myself to alert the media that a shy little Amish girl from Cold Spring had actually solved the crime of the century single-handedly and *voilà*—they're all over the story like, if you'll excuse the cliché, white on rice. They showed up at the brownstone en masse this morning but you guys had already left, so"—she hunched over suddenly, gasping for breath—"that's when I steered them—here."

"Omigod, Billy," Kevin said into his cell phone, "are you getting all this? My sister's, like, some hero! What? No, we're not Amish."

"Apparently, Benjamin Deets, the main suspect, and Nigel Humphries were in an alliance," the female reporter said. "They had an ongoing—well, here, let me play you the lead-in I just taped. It'll explain."

She gestured to the NBC cameraman, and Lexi, Kevin, Kim Ling, and Aunt Roz quickly gathered around the front of his camera and focused on the LCD screen. Snowy haze. Beeps. Numbers. Then the reporter's image appeared.

"This is Yolanda Sanchez reporting from Grand Central Terminal where I await the arrival of Alexandra McGill, the twelve-year-old from Cold Spring who single-handedly—"

"Fast-forward, fast-forward," the live Yolanda said, gesturing to the cameraman.

BLEEET-BLEEEEEEEEEEEEET . . .

"—exhibit at the Metropolitan Museum of— *BLEEEET*—former college roommates. Nigel Humphries had hired Deets as a crime consultant on his Emmy Award–winning drama, *The Streets of New York*. Despite its accolades, the show, famous for exaggerating real-life stories ripped from today's headlines, had been slipping in the ratings recently and was on the network's chopping block.

"According to Humphries, it was Deets's diabolical plan to steal the jewels headed for an exhibit at the Met as an act of revenge against his former employer, then recreate the entire scenario in an episode of *Streets*, incorporating a totally outrageous ending—burying the jewels next to Cleopatra's Needle in Central Park. Humphries, having his own personal vendetta against the network, had agreed. They were reportedly relying on the theory that real life couldn't possibly imitate art—that no one would ever suspect the actual jewels to be buried in the exact same area."

"But they were?" Lexi asked through her trembling hand.

"Keep watching," the reporter said.

"As a fitting conclusion to this truly bizarre case, Cleopatra's jewels, as they're being called, have indeed been unearthed from Central Park completely intact, and will undergo a thorough examination before being returned to the Cairo Museum. Nigel Humphries has been arrested and is currently being held at the Metropolitan Correctional Center in lower Manhattan while Benjamin Deets remains at large."

"Apparently these jokers planned on retrieving the jewels after the story died down," Yolanda said as the screen went black. "Stripping them down to sell overseas and splitting the profits. But they were recovered, thanks to you, Miss McGill."

"I'm—uh, I don't know what to say."

Without warning, Aunt Roz smothered Lexi in one of her trademark rocking hugs. "Oh, Alexandra," she whispered, "I didn't expect extraordinary to happen so soon! Your mother would be absolutely thrilled." She kissed her cheek. Stroked her hair. Then suddenly she was gazing at her through worried eyes. "My goodness, you're white as a ghost. This must be so overwhelming for you. Do you need anything—are you okay?"

"Why wouldn't she be okay?" the blue-suited reporter said, coming at them with a microphone. "She's about to receive a staggering amount of reward money."

"Omigod, that's right," Kevin gushed. "Score! We're rich!" He launched into his happy dance and was about to knock into a camera when Aunt Roz grabbed him by the wrist.

"Come on," she said, "let's run and get your sister a bottled water real quick—before she passes out." And she pulled him toward the main concourse, calling out to Lexi, "Talk to the reporters, dear—and, for heaven's sake, breathe, *breathe*! We'll be back in two shakes!"

"Can we get a statement, sweetheart?" the same reporter asked.

Five more microphones instantly came at Lexi—fifty more questions.

"Tell us the whole story in your own words," Yolanda said, and signaled to her cameraman. "How did you piece it all together? Roll camera, roll camera! In three . . . two . . ."

What came out of Lexi's mouth at that point was a mystery to her. An out-of-body experience. Did it even make sense? Who knows? She would have to wait to find out on the five o'clock news like everyone else—provided she returned to earth by then. "Okay, are we through?" she asked over her thundering heartbeat. "My dad's meeting us over by the clock and I really don't want to miss him."

"What are your plans for the money? Do you have your top picks for college yet? Anything else you'd like to say?" the reporters shouted over each other.

"Give her a break, guys," Kim Ling told them. "Can't you see she's had enough?"

The never-ending rush of questions had almost knocked Lexi over. She was shaking her head, about to walk away—but—"No, wait." She summoned her courage and leaned into the microphones. "There *is* something else. I didn't exactly do this alone. First off, my little brother helped.

A lot. And the truth is, I wouldn't have done it at all if it weren't for this awesome girl right over here." Lexi reached past the reporters and pulled a stunned-looking Kim Ling on camera. "She's the brains behind everything—Kim Ling Levine. Remember that name, 'cause she's gonna be a hotshot journalist someday."

"Oh, wow," Kim Ling said, tapping on one of the microphones, "I'm making my television debut in my ducky pajamas. How surreal is this?" She cleared her throat. "Sibilant, sibilant. Hello, America—members of the press, ladies and gentlemen . . ."

Kim Ling's voice became a distant hum as Lexi shouldered her backpack and grabbed her duffel. Thoughts of the abandoned railway station, Mr. Gibbs and the lost and found, Melrose Merritt, and the Whispering Gallery played out in her head like a movie montage. She floated across the concourse toward the big opal clock— that priceless treasure that hardly anyone recognized as being priceless or a treasure. Suddenly the world was treating *her* like a priceless treasure. Could she ever live up to it all?

She glanced up at the magnificent ceiling of zodiac symbols and spotted the small patch of black the tour guide, Mr. Early, had pointed out. How did his little poem go that she liked so much? "The wondrous—" no, "The glorious *something* of sweet summer light gleams doubly bright next to wintry night." Lexi took it to mean that good things seem even better when you've got a little bit of bad to compare them with, which was true. Memories of her mom were sweeter, more precious somehow because of the heartache. And even though New York had been a giant quilt of dark patches, right now it was the best place on the planet.

"That was amazing—brief but amazing! Um, hello? Mankind's helper? Let me know if you're, like, having a stroke or something, 'cause I know CPR."

"Kim. No, I'm—just spacing out. So, how'd it go?"

"Are you kidding? I'm totally *plotzing!*"

"So, I guess you don't despise me anymore with the white-hot intensity of a thousand suns, huh?"

Kim Ling rolled her eyes. "Not my finest hour. That's Shakespeare, by the way. I like to give credit where credit is due. And speaking of which—way to go, Lex!" She did a little idol-worship bow. "I mean, how could you not be jumping up and down right now?"

"Well, my insides are. I'm still in shock, I guess. It's just all too unbelieva—"

"*YOO-HOO, ALEX!*"

"—bull."

The voice of doom. It was her. Clare. Waving from across the terminal. Lexi immediately snapped back into reality and her stomach tumbled down a cliff, dragging her intestines with it. Facing the TV cameras was easier than facing—"Dad and Bridezilla. Here they come."

"Well, I should split." Kim Ling scratched her neck, backing away.

"*What?* You don't want to meet them?"

"Rain check. But thanks for everything—and don't forget to say good-bye to the kid for me, okay?" And with that she did a sharp one-eighty and started speed-walking through the crowd.

"So, that's it?" Lexi called out. "Really? After all we've been through—shouldn't we at least shake hands or something?"

Kim Ling's hand shot up in a stiff "so long" and she kept going. "I don't do sloppy farewell scenes."

Lexi's eyes were instantly overflowing. "Typical." Funny how she hadn't cried for years, since her mother had passed, and lately she was a crying freak! She composed herself as best she could and zeroed in on her father and his wife, who were gaining ground from the opposite direction. Her poor dad looked like a beast of burden, struggling to carry a village's worth of luggage through the crowd. Lexi decided to lend him a hand, but before she could take one step—"Argh!"—something rammed into her!

"And you *are* the best friend *I've* ever had, dude, so deal with it!" It was Kim Ling and she was hugging the life out of her. "God, I loathe myself right now." She backed away and took off even faster than before.

Lexi tried desperately to think of something meaningful to say, but all that came out was "Text me!"

She watched Kim Ling fly by the straggling reporters and stop for a street person carrying a sign: GIVE TO THE NEW YORK WILDLIFE PIZZA FUND. *Isn't that the same guy I saw on day one?* Kim Ling actually reached into her pocket and dropped coins into his basket! Now, that sight alone was worth the entire trip.

"ALEX!"

The sight of her stepmother, however, clip-clopping toward her in noisy high heels, had Lexi bracing herself against the kiosk. *Inhale pink . . . exhale blue.* She palmed her tears away and gripped her opal pendant for all it was worth. All of a sudden it didn't matter that she was being touted as some kind of hero. The dreaded moment had arrived. The official beginning of life in Clare's lair.

Did she have to face her alone? Where had Aunt Roz and Kevin gone for that bottled water? Poland Springs?

Clare was up to a full canter when her ankle wobbled and she lurched forward. Lexi's father dropped a suitcase to save her from plummeting.

"Klutz," Lexi muttered to herself. "Walk much?"

He scooped her up in a loving embrace.

Yelch. Bleah. Please.

But the instant Clare stepped into the silver light beams streaming from the enormous arched windows, something changed in Lexi. Suddenly she wasn't cringing. She was grinning uncontrollably instead. Not because Clare had almost taken a nosedive in the middle of Grand Central. Not because her hairdo was smooshed. Not even because of her completely ridiculous pigeon-toed limp.

It was what she was wearing that told Lexi, without a doubt, that everything was going to be all right. Just a dress, but with a heavenly print—a thousand *feathers*—white, fluffy, glorious feathers swirling this way and that.

Lexi glanced up again at the vast celestial ceiling. "Thanks, Mom," she whispered. "I read you loud and clear."

She heard running footsteps coming from behind.

"C'mon, Kevin—what took you guys so long?" And with happy tears suddenly spilling down her face, Lexi eagerly reached out to greet her two parents.

ACKNOWLEDGMENTS

THANK YOU to Chris Woodworth and Lisa Williams Kline, my loyal critique group buddies, for their invaluable input; Steven Chudney, my superb agent, for his unflagging support; Mary Kate Castellani, my brilliant editor, for her ingenious ideas; Erwin Madrid, my gifted cover illustrator, for his fantastic work of art; Mary-Ann Trippet, my self-proclaimed sounding board, for her willingness to listen; and, last but not least, New York, New York, my incomparable city, for its endless inspiration—and twenty-four-hour food delivery.